WELCOME TO THE LEGEND OF THE FIVE RINGS!

You are about to enter Rokugan, a land of honorable samurai, mighty dragons, powerful magics, arcane monks, cunning ninja, and twisted demons from the Shadowlands. Based on the mythic tales of Japan, China, and Korea, Rokugan is a vast empire, a unique world of fantastic adventure.

Enjoy your stay in Rokugan, a place where heroes walk with gods, where a daimyo's mighty army can be thwarted by a simple word whispered into the right ear, and where honor truly is more powerful than steel.

Legend of the Five Rings™

BOOKS

THE SCORPION
Stephen D. Sullivan

THE UNICORN
A. L. Lassieur

THE CRANE
Ree Soesbee

Available November 2000

THE PHOENIX
Stephen D. Sullivan

Available March 2001

Legend of the Five Rings™

THE UNICORN

A.L. LASSIEUR

CLAN WAR
Second Scroll

Cover art by Brom
First Printing: September 2000
Library of Congress Catalog Card Number: 00-101631

9 8 7 6 5 4 3 2 1

ISBN: 0-7869-1658-3
620-T21658

U.S., CANADA, ASIA,   EUROPEAN HEADQUARTERS
PACIFIC, & LATIN AMERICA   Wizards of the Coast, Belgium
Wizards of the Coast, Inc   P.B. 2031
P.O. Box 707   2600 Berchem
Renton, WA 98057-0707   Belgium
+1-800-324-6496   +32-70-23-32-77

Visit our web site at **www.wizards.com/fiverings**

To Chuck

Acknowledgments

I'd like to thank Eric and Jen Munson for their encouragement and for the use of their extensive personal library of Japanese history, gardening, textiles, and society. Also, I wish to thank Rob King, who gave me my first fiction-writing break.

1   BREATH OF THE SHADOW

A thunderstorm had left the woods soggy. In the gray-black shadows of the nighttime forest, a steamy, oppressive heat rose. Moonlight sifted through the darkened canopy and made watery pools of light on the forest path.

Tetsuko felt sweat trickle down the back of her neck as she pressed against a tree. The rough bark dug into her back. She concentrated on taking shallow breaths and letting them out silently so that whatever was on the path would not hear her.

Slowly, she brought her hand to rest on her katana and felt the familiar smoothness of the hilt in her palm. The night was being kind to her; moon shadows danced through the branches and made the forest a chaos of movement. Even the sharpest-eyed shugenja would have trouble seeing her.

For the last five days, Tetsuko's Unicorn patrol had ridden the boundaries of their lands, searching for a band of bandits. They found vandalized homes, broken walls, and contaminated water supplies. While large towns could withstand such acts, small villages in outlying areas could be crippled by them. Ide Jikkyo, the patrol leader, was determined to find the outlaws and bring them to justice. Tetsuko, on her first patrol, was just as determined that she would not fail.

Concentrate, she told herself. She took another breath and, pursing her lips, gently let it go. Her senses calmed and became sharper, and the sounds of the forest became clearer.

Water dripped from the branches high above and made occasional plops in the darkness. Tetsuko could smell the scent of wet humus, damp leaves, and the clean air after rain. Forest creatures shuffled in the leaves. An insect rubbed its legs in a tentative buzz, found the sound to its liking, and began its nightly call. Here and there above her head, a tree branch creaked with tiny echoes. A bird took off from its perch, its wings beating the air with a soft *thwump thwump* that slowly faded into silence. Down the path, a twig snapped.

Tetsuko gripped the hilt of her katana. Her fingers wrapped around the leather bindings, sticky from sweat. She peered into the inky darkness. She could see nothing. The hairs along the back of her neck stood on end.

With no more thought, Tetsuko pushed off the tree and launched into the dark, hoping surprise would work for her. In midair she collided with a solid form. They both hit the ground with a thud.

"Oof!" the form said as it fell.

Tetsuko sprang up, raising her katana in a battle stance. Just as she was about stab the slender blade through the form, it rolled away from her and jumped to its feet.

"Don't you think you should know who you're going to kill?" a familiar voice asked in the dark.

"By Shinjo!" Tetsuko yelped as Jikkyo chuckled. "You almost got a katana in the belly!"

"Calm down," Jikkyo said. "I thought you knew it was me. I knew it was you fifty yards ago."

Tetsuko straightened up, katana still at the ready. The moon had emerged from the clouds, and she could make out the large, dark outline of the patrol leader against the pale light. Although her heart was still pounding from the fright, her breathing had slowed enough to allow her a grunt of disbelief. "How could you have possibly known it was me, in this dark?" she asked. "I could have been one of the thieves, following you."

"I doubt any of the thieves washes his hair with lavender," Jikkyo calmly replied.

Tetsuko's one indulgence on patrol was an occasional bath, scented with lavender from her grandfather's garden. Most people did not have the nose to catch the faint scent, especially hidden among the other smells of sweat, leather, horse, and wood smoke that all the patrol members carried on them. Jikkyo, however, was not like most people.

Jikkyo sidled up to her and put his hand on her shoulder. "Don't worry about this," he said kindly. "And certainly don't give up your baths because of it! I'd rather have you smelling like day-old lavender than Horse Dung Hishi."

Tetsuko managed a grim smile at the joke. Ide Hishi, one of the patrol members, was known for his pungent odor no matter how much he bathed. Which, she had to admit, was not much.

"Perhaps I should make Hishi a lavender bag for his bath," Tetsuko said, sheathing her katana. "Then you would not be able to tell me from him on a darkened pathway."

"Ha!" Jikkyo said with a snort. "The day I can't tell a well-scrubbed Battle Maiden from a smelly horse trainer is the day I cut off my nose."

Tetsuko laughed out loud, and she could feel the tension between her shoulders relax.

Jikkyo turned serious, and he said, "I saw no sign of the thieves down this path. Did you find anything?"

"No," she replied. "But they cannot have traveled far."

Jikkyo was silent. Moments passed.

Tetsuko stood at casual attention, waiting for her leader's reply. Years of training had made this stance as natural to her as breathing or riding; legs slightly apart and knees bent, balancing her weight evenly in case of a surprise attack. Her right hand rested lightly on the hilt of her katana. She took a deep breath and let it out slowly, shifting her weight from one foot to the other.

Tinged with humor, Jikkyo's voice came from the darkness, "Am I taking too long for you? Your legendary impatience is showing."

Tetsuko ignored the jibe. She wasn't surprised her leader had heard her movements. Will I ever be experienced enough to hear such sounds? she thought to herself with a sigh. Out loud she said, "I await your orders as always, Jikkyo-san."

"Even in this darkness a band of desperate thieves would be hard to miss," Jikkyo said finally. "Perhaps Fumi and Kin will have something to report." His mind made up, Jikkyo turned and started down the path, and Tetsuko followed.

As they walked, Tetsuko glanced from one side to the other, her hand on the hilt of her katana. The humid stillness of the forest pressed down on her, making it hard to breathe. Even the sounds of the forest, so clear before, were muffled, as if a blanket of despair had descended on the wood. A sliver of fear ran up Tetsuko's spine.

With a troubled frown, Jikkyo looked back at her. She smiled at him, and his face relaxed. He turned and continued on. Tetsuko's smile faded once his back was turned.

Her mentor and leader, Jikkyo had specifically asked for Tetsuko to be assigned to this patrol. It was a brave and honorable thing for him to do, considering the disgrace she had brought on herself by leaving the Battle Maiden school before her training was complete. Jikkyo had faith in her, and she was determined not to let him down. She would never betray weakness by voicing fear.

The trees began to thin. Tetsuko and Jikkyo emerged from the forest. The moon had come out in full force, and its white glow illuminated the path. Tetsuko caught a savory whiff of stewing meat and spices, and her stomach rumbled again. It was a relief to be finished with foot patrol duty for the night, and she was looking forward to a hot meal—the first one they had allowed themselves all week.

Jikkyo and Tetsuko strode into camp. "Where are Fumi and Kin?" Tetsuko asked, realizing the two were not at the fire.

"Not back yet," Moto Yuko replied as he squatted by the fire, stirring the large stew pot that hung over the flames. "They left after you. They had better be quick, though. We're hungry enough to eat this entire pot!"

Soon everyone was around the fire, eating hungrily. The rabbit stew was thick and hearty, exactly the right meal for a group of cold, wet, soldiers. For a long time there was no sound except an occasional slurp as the members of the patrol dug into the meal.

Tetsuko gazed around the camp as she sipped the thick broth from her delicately carved wooden spoon. Hishi had taken most of their soggy belongings out of their packs and laid them near the fire to dry. Garments, sleeping mats, bags, and sacks lay strewn around the ground. The horses were tied to nearby trees, happily grazing on the thick green grass of the clearing.

Jikkyo looked up from his bowl. "Well done!" he said to Moto Yuko, raising his wooden spoon in salute.

Yuko grinned, his long black hair tied back with a fragment of silk cloth. He reached into the pot and stirred the contents. Not only was Moto Yuko an expert hunter, he was also a good cook. Everyone in the patrol looked forward to the nights when it was his turn at the fire.

Beside him sat Shinjo Rinako. She was a seasoned cavalry veteran who had fought in the Unicorn armies during the Scorpion Clan Coup, just two years before. Rinako wore the scars of many battles beneath the silk of her travel-stained kimono, but she rarely spoke of them. She rarely spoke at all, if the truth be told. Tetsuko knew little of her, other than that she was a master bowman and that she had survived the deadly plague that was sweeping Rokugan.

Ide Hishi, the horse master, sat a distance from the fire. Even there, Tetsuko could smell his ever-present scent of horse sweat, leather, and dung. His bald head, bent over his wooden bowl of stew, shone brightly in the firelight. He was a pleasant man, fiercely devoted to the Unicorn mounts. He had spent his life in the stables, and both his sisters had been respected Battle Maidens in their day. Although he was of little use as a fighter, his skill with animals was indispensable to the Unicorn units that patrolled the borderlands. Tetsuko liked him.

Across from her sat Jikkyo. He was a few years older

than she, about twenty-eight or so. He proudly wore his long, shiny black hair tied loosely behind his back. He had a thin, well-kept mustache and goatee, which made him look older than his years. Even now, after days of hard riding and soaking rain, his kimono looked as fresh as it had when he had first removed it from his pack.

At this moment he sat with legs stretched toward the fire and back propped against a large rock. Sensing Tetsuko's eyes on him, he looked up from his stew and smiled at her.

"It's a relief not to be rained on, for once," she quipped. "I was beginning to wonder if I'd ever be dry again."

"For myself, I'll be glad when we catch these bandits and return to civilization," Jikkyo said.

"These thieves aren't smarter than us," Rinako said. "But luck is certainly with them. We would've caught up to them by now if we had found their abandoned camp sooner."

Tetsuko's cheeks flamed at Rinako's remark. The day before, when it was Tetsuko's turn to lead the patrol, they had walked right past the remains of their camp. It was not until a second pass through the area that they had discovered it. By then, the rain was coming down in full force, and any clues as to which way the thieves had gone had been washed away.

Tetsuko stood up, hands clenched at her sides. Rinako glared at her, contempt clear on her face. Before either of them had time to speak, Jikkyo jumped to his feet and said, "That's enough. This is not the time to let tempers overcome judgment." Trembling with anger and embarrassment, Tetsuko slowly sat down.

"As for you, Rinako," Jikkyo said, turning to the older woman, "your frustration is certainly understood. But we must work as a unit to complete our task. These criminals are armed and deadly."

He looked from one woman to the other. "Shinjo Yokatsu himself assigned us to guard the southern borders and all the Unicorn villages between here and the City Between the Rivers. We have no clear idea how many roving bands there are. We are in constant danger. Protecting the people who live here is our duty. Finding these bandits and bringing them to justice is our goal."

There was silence. Then Rinako rose, turned on her heel, and disappeared into the darkness. That seemed to be a cue for everyone to start moving. Hishi scrambled up and trotted off in the direction of the horses. Yuko quietly gathered the dinner bowls and made his way to the stream nearby. Jikkyo settled back, picked up his spoon, and dipped it into his now-cold stew.

Tetsuko stared into the bright, dancing flames and lost herself in thought. A drop of water from the leaves above fell into the fire, making it sizzle and pop. Sparks swirled in the warm draft and scattered like fireflies into the dark night sky.

"It was more than two hundred years ago when our ancestors returned from exploring the world," Jikkyo said aloud.

Tetsuko looked up from the fire. He had lifted his spoon, filled with meat and broth, and now gazed at it lovingly. He continued, "No matter how long we are here, or how much we become like the rest of Rokugan, I hope that we never lose our taste for red meat." With that he popped the spoon in his mouth, closed his eyes, and chewed slowly, a look of ecstasy spreading across his face.

Tetsuko smiled wanly. "Jikkyo-sama," she started, "I . . ."

"No," Jikkyo said, quickly swallowing. "It is done."

"But she is right. It was my fault. If I had been more alert, we might already be on our way home," Tetsuko said.

"Yes, you were at fault for not finding the camp," Jikkyo

replied. "But now you have learned. You will never forget this mistake. Not forgetting will make you more skilled. Do not speak of it again."

Tetsuko sighed. It had been cold, it had been wet, the day had been long, her eyes had been weary. . . . Excuse after excuse tumbled through her head, but none made her feel better. Her blunder had been severe, and another mistake like that could cost lives. Jikkyo was right. She learned.

Suddenly the tension and fear of the day weighed her down, and her eyelids began to droop. Bidding Jikkyo good night, Tetsuko pulled a damp sleeping mat from the pile of supplies and spread it out at the base of a nearby tree. She stretched out and closed her eyes. In the darkness, she heard the soft mummer of Hishi's voice as he spoke to the horses. Somewhere Yuko sang to himself as he washed the dinner dishes. Tetsuko smiled as she caught snatches of the song, a silly ditty sung to children to make them laugh. Slowly, her exhausted mind fogged over with sleep.

The sound of screaming startled her awake.

Tetsuko's eyes flew open, and she sat up, heart pounding. She looked wildly about her. The fire had gone down and was now only a glowing red spot against the darkness. Thousands of stars flickered and winked in the sky. It was the cold hour before dawn. There was no wind. Nothing moved.

"It must have been a dream," Tetsuko said to herself, breathing deeply to quiet the hammer in her chest.

She heard it again: a long, high-pitched scream that started loud and faded into a desperate wail.

Tetsuko jumped up and grabbed her katana. Jikkyo was only a few steps away, already awake.

"I heard a scream," Tetsuko said, "but I don't know where it came from. Did you hear it?"

"Yes," he replied in a low voice as Rinako appeared, a worried expression on her face.

"Where's Yuko?" she asked. Yuko, who was supposed to be on watch, was nowhere to be seen. "Where are Fumi and Kin?"

Tetsuko felt a stab of fear in her belly. They should have returned hours ago. Jikkyo seemed to read her thoughts. He dashed toward the horses and returned almost immediately. "Hishi is asleep near the horses," Jikkyo said, "but Fumi and Kin are not here."

The black trunks of the trees seemed to close in around her. The glow of the dying fire reflected off the trees, streaking them with blood-red light. A chill wind blew through the clearing, making Tetsuko shiver. Out of the corner of her eye, she saw a dark shape move through the trees, just beyond the camp.

"Jikkyo, look," Tetsuko whispered, but he had seen.

The form paused and then disappeared among the shadows.

Jikkyo pulled his katana from its sheath and hissed, "Tetsuko, guard the camp. Rinako, follow me!"

The two Unicorn samurai raced toward the form, leaving Tetsuko alone in the dying firelight.

The forest was dim and hushed. Tetsuko paced back and forth like a caged lion, her eyes scanning the endless darkness beyond the trembling light of their fire. A cold wind streaked through the clearing, followed by a low moan that sent a chill deep into Tetsuko's bones.

"Hishi," she whispered. She turned and ran to where the horses were tethered. Her mount, Cloud Dancer, neighed softly in greeting. The other two horses grazed quietly by the elegant beast's side. Nearby, the horse trainer was huddled beneath his heavy woolen saddle blankets.

Tetsuko pushed his shoulder and said "Hishi, you must awake. There is trouble." Instead of rousing, he rolled lazily onto his back. The blanket fell open and his arms flopped to his sides.

His neck had been slit from ear to ear so deeply that his head had nearly been severed. Blood covered him. His eyes were closed as in sleep, and he had a serene expression on his face.

Tetsuko jumped back and clapped her hand over her mouth. "By Shinjo!" she whispered. She looked wildly around in the dark, but there was nothing there except the shadows and the wind. She was alone.

The wind filled the wood with its terrible moan, and fear washed over the young Battle Maiden.

The last thing she wanted to do was to stay here, with death and fear all around her. Even so, Jikkyo had commanded her to guard the camp. But what if he and Rinako were in trouble? Tetsuko wavered between terror, duty, and loyalty, and then decided. She threw a saddle on Cloud Dancer's back and untied the other two horses, whispering soothing words to them. Then she quickly mounted and turned Cloud Dancer in the direction Jikkyo had gone. The other horses followed obediently behind as she galloped into the woods.

The forest had lost all its earlier friendliness. In its place was something angry and dark, darker than the shadows that had played with her mind on the path earlier. Dead branches clawed Tetsuko's face as Cloud Dancer crashed through the underbrush. Her lungs burned, and her eyes watered, but she rode on. Her armor began to rub bloody patches against her neck where her undergarment had shifted.

Tetsuko followed a trail of broken branches and trampled

undergrowth. The path was barely visible in the feeble moonlight. Time ceased to mean anything as Cloud Dancer struggled through the forest. Tetsuko had no idea how long she had been in the forest or how far she had traveled when, deep in the shadows of the trees, so far ahead of her that she could barely make it out, Tetsuko saw a red glow. Firelight.

She pulled Cloud Dancer to a halt and dismounted. The horse's sides heaved, and her coat was foamy from exertion, but she nuzzled Tetsuko's neck in understanding.

Slowly Tetsuko crept toward the low-burning campfire. It sat in the middle of a small clearing. She could make out five shapes sitting close to the firelight. Packs and bags were strewn about the ground. Her heart jumped as she realized that this was the bandit's camp. She crawled behind the base of a wide, old tree at the edge of the clearing. Its gnarled roots spread out like arthritic fingers, making a maze of lumps on the ground around her.

Two of the thieves were curled toward the fire to catch the last of its warmth. Three others sat silently nearby, watching the flames. One perched on a log, his face half-hidden underneath the soggy hood of a dark cloak. Leaning beside him was a golden-gilded katana. Even in the dark, from this distance, Tetsuko could see the magnificence of the weapon, with its barbaric, swirling designs etched on the blade. She noticed other weapons: an unsheathed katana lying near the fire, a wakizashi with a well-worn wooden sheath beside that, and off to the side, a broken tonfa.

Slowly, the hairs on Tetsuko's neck rose, and she shivered. The air had become heavy. Deep in her mind, Tetsuko heard the scream again, but this time it was faraway. It was no longer the call of someone in pain, she realized with a start. It was now the call of death.

Slowly, without thought, Tetsuko stood up, in full view

of the camp. The figures remained still. It was as if no one noticed that a samurai-ko in full battle armor had materialized beside a tree near their hidden camp.

The figure that Tetsuko had been watching leaned forward as if to rise. The hood of his cloak fell over his face, casting a dark shadow. Inch by inch he moved, and then toppled over and landed in a heap.

A log on the fire split, and the two broken pieces fell into the coals with a muffled crash, spitting embers into the air.

Tetsuko walked carefully toward the fire, katana drawn. Her eyes fell on the rest of the group, and she stopped dead. The camp was a shambles. The bags and packs she had seen from the tree were covered in gore. The ground was black with blood. Clutching her hand to her mouth, Tetsuko walked to one of the figures on the ground and nudged it with the toe of her leather boot. It rolled over, and the loose cloak softly fell away. It was a man, or had been, once. His eyes had been gouged out and his mouth slashed from ear to ear in a hideous, bloody grin. His blood-soaked cloak told Tetsuko that more horrors lay beneath it, but she turned away.

Tetsuko could barely breathe the thick air. As if in a dream, she stepped around the fire to the figure that had been sitting on the log. It lay face up on one side, its back against the log. It was a woman. Her eyes were wide in horror, and her mouth was twisted in a grimace. Clearly, whatever had killed her had taken her completely by surprise. A broken blade, covered with blood and gore, protruded from her chest.

Tetsuko stumbled backward. She reached the edge of the clearing and squatted there, vomiting, until her stomach was sore and the last of the night's rabbit stew covered the ground.

Dawn had begun far away, and the shadowy darkness of

the forest had faded to gray. She took deep breaths to steady herself and peered into the trees, unable to return to the horrors at the fire.

Suddenly the image of the golden katana appeared in Tetsuko's mind, gleaming with the light of the sun. She turned and, careful not to touch the gruesome bodies by the fire, took the magnificent weapon. It was perfectly balanced, and Tetsuko easily hefted it.

"By Shinjo," she breathed.

Ahead of her, half-hidden in the gloom of the predawn forest, Tetsuko saw the corner of a structure. She stood there a moment, confused by the appearance of a building in the wood.

The moaning began again, echoing among the trees.

Slowly, the golden katana at the ready, Tetsuko moved toward the building. The rice-paper walls had been torn away, and the wooden frame was splintered in many places. She crept around the building and found herself in a small village. Other buildings stood nearby, clustered around a central plaza—wooden frames, paper walls, and long, narrow porches. In the center of the weed-choked plaza was a kidney-shaped reflecting pool, slimy with algae. Tetsuko saw the glint of goldfish floating dead in the murky water. The stench of death was everywhere.

Tetsuko's attention caught on one building. The fusuma screen door was covered with violent slashes of red paint in a symbol that was all too familiar.

"Plague," Tetsuko breathed.

To spend even a few minutes in a plague village meant death.

Tetsuko ran across the plaza, calling to Cloud Dancer through the darkness and knowing that her steed would hear her.

Suddenly, from somewhere far away, screaming started. It got nearer and louder. Panic rose like bile in Tetsuko's throat. This time, the screaming wasn't in her head. It was all around her.

Figures at the edge of the clearing caught her eye— Jikkyo and Rinako. They stood upright and still, their hands at their sides like badly carved statues, their eyes staring straight ahead.

"Jikkyo!" Tetsuko yelled.

The proud man's head turned slowly toward the sound. He seemed frozen in place, but his mouth worked in a desperate attempt to speak. His eyes were wide with fear. Beside him, Rinako was stiff and unmoving, her eyes closed and her face twisted in terror. For a moment, Tetsuko thought she saw the outline of a monstrous claw, black and gnarled, clutching them.

With a shout she lunged toward the claw, slashing it with the golden blade. The claw faded, and the two paralyzed samurai dropped to the ground with a thud.

The doors of the buildings burst open, rattling the structures and causing paper walls to rip and fall. Dozens of creatures lurched slowly out of the buildings and shuffled stiffly toward Tetsuko. They were human, but their skin was a sickening shade of gray-green. Huge boils and lesions oozed plague infections. Men, women, and children all had the same dead look in their eyes. Each held some kind of weapon: sticks, hoes, rakes—whatever had been in their homes.

A zombie lazily swung a rake handle at Tetsuko. With a yell, she sliced the creature's neck. Its head fell into the dust and rolled underneath a bush.

Another creature stepped in front of Tetsuko, and her heart went dead.

It was Yuko. His armor had been smashed into bits, some of which still hung from his shoulders. His right arm was gone. His bowels spilled from a huge gash in his abdomen. On either side of him were Fumi and Kin. The top of Fumi's head was gone. Kin's heart had been cut from her chest. They all were covered with blood. The three creatures, all that remained of people Tetsuko had loved and respected, bore down on her.

Tetsuko stood unmoving, unable to raise her sword against them. She heard a hiss from behind her.

Jikkyo lunged forward. With one motion, he thrust his katana into Yuko's belly. "Tetsuko!" he choked. "Cut off their limbs! You must dismember them or die!" Jikkyo pulled his blade from Yuko's belly and struck the zombie's neck.

Yuko's head fell from his body and rolled into the fish pool. Before the headless body could take another step, Jikkyo made a deep cut in its right thigh. A second stroke sent the leg flying, and Yuko toppled to the ground.

Jikkyo's voice aroused Tetsuko from her stupor. With a quick prayer she stepped forward.

The thing that had once been Kin brought her sword down onto Tetsuko's right shoulder. The clumsy shot cut through armor and opened a gash.

"Yiiiieee!" Tetsuko screamed.

All regret forgotten, she whipped her katana above her head and brought it down on Kin's hip. It bit deep, and blood gushed from the cut. Kin stumbled and fell in a heap at Tetsuko's feet.

Tetsuko glanced at Jikkyo. He was struggling with Fumi, and the zombie was winning. It slammed a heavy club onto Jikkyo's head, sending the proud Unicorn leader crashing to the ground.

With one mighty swing, Tetsuko sliced Fumi's head

cleanly from his body. As the zombie crumpled to the ground, a creature grabbed Tetsuko from behind. It held her by each shoulder in a vice grip and lifted her until her toes grazed the ground.

Instinctively, Tetsuko bent her legs into her chest and kicked the thing holding her. It flew backward, sending them both rolling in the dirt. The grip on Tetsuko's arms loosened, and she managed to roll out of its reach.

All around her, the creatures were closing in. The stench of death was unbearable.

As the dead army advanced, Tetsuko heard a wild neighing from the edge of the clearing. Cloud Dancer! Tetsuko put her fingers to her lips and whistled sharply. The powerful steed crashed through the circle of zombies, and galloped to her mistress.

Tetsuko hauled Jikkyo to his feet and shoved him into the saddle. He collapsed like a limp doll against the horse's neck. Tetsuko reached for Rinako but recoiled in horror when she touched the woman's cold, dead skin.

"Go!" Tetsuko bellowed, jumping on Cloud Dancer's back behind her leader.

The majestic steed screamed, rearing and kicking the zombies aside. The hideous creatures fell like broken bamboo. Cloud Dancer charged over them. Zombies slowly rose and followed at a ghastly shuffle.

Cloud Dancer thundered out of the clearing, away from the village of death.

2 WHITE PETALS, FALLING

Ide Tadaji stood on the balcony of the imperial reception building, silently watching the play of moonlight and shadows in the garden. A gentle chorus of crickets accompanied the languid movement of a lone swan. She glided across the mirror-smooth surface of a small pond, the centerpiece of this particular garden. Along the pond's edge, carefully sculpted shrubbery rose and fell in controlled balance, giving the garden a sense of textured serenity. Beyond the pond, a dark forest of black pine served as a backdrop to the well-tended garden, giving the scene depth and a timelessness that pulled at Tadaji's heart. Familiar, so familiar.

Moonlight shone on Tadaji's brilliant golden kimono and the violet Unicorn mon embroidered on each breast. The deep purple obi around his waist was tied so expertly that its heavy gold embroidery was displayed perfectly in the center of his abdomen. Each time he took a breath, he could feel the small, ivory-handled tanto tucked securely in the folds of the obi. His ornate cane was another discreet weapon. Years of experience in court taught him that it was wise to be armed at all times—even at formal imperial dinners.

Tadaji's official Unicorn robes were of the highest quality, and they flattered his body. Despite his club foot, Tadaji was a handsome man. Time and life had etched tiny lines at the edges of his eyes and mouth, but he did not have the wrinkles that many people his age wore. He had been blessed with his mother's fine, wide cheekbones and creamy skin, which still stretched tight beneath his chin. His long hair had receded a bit at the temples, but his sleek topknot was still full and thick on his scalp. His eyes were clear and dark, with a hint of humor always lurking behind their seriousness. His body, somewhat soft from the comfortable life at court, was still healthy and strong from his daily walks.

Beyond the balcony's rice-paper door, he heard the rise and fall of conversations and laughter. How many receptions just like this one had he attended in his life at court? Dozens, hundreds, too many to count. He tried to remember a specific one, but gave up with a sigh. Why remember one when they were all the same? With a last glance, Tadaji turned his back to the garden, set the tip of his cane on the balcony stones, and strode into the reception hall.

It was a light, airy place with a high ceiling. Colorfully embroidered silk banners cascaded from the dark ceiling beams and rippled gently when someone glided past. Hundreds of tiny paper lanterns lined the walls, and soft candlelight made the room glow with a pearly sheen.

In the center of the highly polished wooded floor, the

imperial symbol was inlaid with emeralds and gold. Encircling it were smaller circles, each representing a clan of the Emerald Empire. Tadaji tapped his cane around the circle until he reached the symbol of his beloved Unicorn Clan: a ki-rin, carefully carved from amethyst and inlaid in the floor with expert precision. The shades of pink, lavender, and purple of the amethyst shimmered and moved in the candlelight, making the unicorn image rear and toss its head. "Preparing for battle, are you?" Tadaji thought to himself as he watched the play of light on the emblem. "Perhaps, perhaps. . . ."

His eyes moved from the Unicorn Clan insignia to those of the other Rokugan clans. Each was as expertly crafted as that of the Unicorn Clan, from gold, silver, copper, garnet, ruby, emerald, jade, and pearl. His gaze followed the circle until it came to an abrupt halt at a strangely blank space. This was something new; he had never before noticed a gap in the unbroken circle of Rokugan clans. Then he realized what it was. A wave of sadness enveloped him. While he was away, a very talented woodcarver had pried up the garnet Scorpion emblem and had filled in the hole with matching wood. The job was so skillful that Tadaji could not see where the image had been.

Tadaji felt someone's eyes on him, and the skin on his arms prickled at the feeling. He turned and saw a man standing alone in a far corner, sipping sake. He was a slender man, impeccably dressed in fine silks in the colors of the Crane Clan. His ice-blue eyes rested on Tadaji, and with a smile he bent his head in a bow of greeting.

"Well, Ide Tadaji has returned to the intrigue of the court!" The man's voice sounded like deep chimes. He raised his sake cup in salute, and with a smile Tadaji did the same.

"Kakita Yoshi," Tadaji said. "I did not know you were still

at the Imperial Palace. I heard you had left to return to Crane lands before I arrived. I was disappointed that I had missed you."

"I had planned to leave two days ago, but when I heard of your arrival I decided to stay to greet you. I am leaving tomorrow. My replacement is Kakita Umi."

Tadaji wrinkled his nose at the name, and Yoshi chuckled. "Yes, yes, she is sometimes abrupt, but her diplomatic skills are exemplary. And she *is* Hoturi's cousin."

The sake servant appeared and refilled each cup. The two men were silent until the woman melted back into the crowd. Then Tadaji said, "There have been more rumors lately than I remember from times past."

"In these times, rumor sometimes carries more truth than the truth itself," Yoshi replied, sipping the sake. "Since the plague swept the castle, nothing has been the same. It is as if the ground beneath our feet is no more than shifting sands and hidden holes."

Tadaji took a sip of his sake. The mellow flavor of good sake was missing from this liquid, replaced instead by a slight sweetness that Tadaji found not to his liking. He glanced at his sake cup, and Yoshi noticed.

"No, it's not the best sake, I'm afraid," he said. "Kachiko now reserves the best for her private meetings."

"Private meetings? With whom?" Tadaji asked.

"Shugenja from throughout Rokugan have been summoned to the emperor's bedside, trying to find a cure for this cursed plague. But others are allowed entry into the imperial chambers, others that no one at court seems to recognize. They arrive in the middle of the night and are taken directly to Kachiko."

"And there has been no change in the emperor's condition?" Tadaji asked.

"No one seems to know," Yoshi replied. "She forbids anyone from his side except herself. It is said that even the shugenja aren't allowed to see him."

At that moment an elegant woman broke away from the crowd and approached the two men. When she reached them, she bowed and said, "Greetings, honorable Ide Tadaji. I am Ikoma Natsumi, ambassador from the Lion Clan. I have been told much about you, and I am honored to meet you." Tadaji returned the formal greeting. She was a younger woman, no more than twenty-five. She wore a beautiful kimono of yellow ochre and sienna that pooled around her feet. Her long hair was roped about her head and kept in place with thin, silver sticks.

"Welcome to the Imperial Palace," Tadaji said.

"Thank you. I have been here for only a few weeks, but I am growing accustomed to life here." She paused, and then continued, "I would be honored if you would accept an invitation to tea, ambassador. We have much to discuss."

Curious, Tadaji nodded and murmured an acceptance. It was customary for ambassadors to hold private meetings, but personal invitations extended at state functions were unusual. Normally, such a breach of official protocol would not be tolerated, but Tadaji dismissed it to the Lion ambassador's inexperience. She would learn soon enough.

"My secretary will inform you of the day and time," Natsumi said. "Until then, Ambassador."

"Until then," Tadaji said. Then the lovely young woman left the two men alone once more.

"What do you think of that?" Tadaji said as they watched her go.

Yoshi shook his head. "She means well, but she does not realize what she has gotten into." Yoshi sipped his sake, and then continued. "It is bad here, my friend. A few weeks after

Tamura . . . after you left the palace, the plague arrived in a horrible wave. People dropped in the gardens, in the halls, everywhere. Many members of the imperial family were dead within a week. The emperor himself still lingers between life and death." Horror and disgust ran through Tadaji at the image of bodies filling the grand, beautiful palace.

"It was chaos," Yoshi said. "The shugenja tried to quarantine the palace, but people fled by the dozens, thinking to escape death. They destroyed gardens, ransacked buildings, and took anything they could carry."

Tadaji sipped the sake. "Yes, it reached the Unicorn lands as well," he said, "but it has not killed to the extent that it has here. Many at Shiro Shinjo died."

A look of sadness passed over Tadaji's face, and Yoshi saw it clearly. "And you, my friend?" he asked. "How have you fared these last months?"

Tadaji did not speak for a time. He stared into his empty sake cup. His thoughts traveled to his son, Ide Tamura, and the pride that he had in his strong, honorable child. "A light has gone from my life, Yoshi. I thought that my heart had died with my wife years ago. But I discovered that it was alive—until Tamura died. Now I truly have no heart left."

At that moment a commotion at the entrance made everyone in the room look up.

Empress Kachiko glided into the room, followed by her personal servants. Everyone bowed low, and silence filled the room. Kachiko surveyed the crowd, her hazel eyes framed by a delicate lace mask that only heightened her beauty. She wore an emerald green kimono embroidered with golden flowers, and the obi around her waist was made of golden silk woven with pure metal threads. Her long black hair was arranged in an elaborate twist on her head and secured with tiny gold pins in the shape of flowers. In her hand she carried a delicate fan of red silk.

She moved toward the Unicorn ambassador, smiling. "Welcome back, Ide Tadaji," she said when she reached his side. Her honeyed voice was soothing and melodic, and she was more breathtakingly beautiful than Tadaji had remembered.

Kachiko reached out and gently wrapped Tadaji's hands in her own. The intimacy of this action made Tadaji wince with discomfort. Her pearly white hands were as soft as down, her skin rubbed daily with scented oils. Her nails were long and hard, covered in red lacquer that shone like fresh blood.

Tadaji was startled by that image—why had he thought of blood? He looked into Kachiko's eyes and saw a flicker of something hard behind the flecks of sea-green. Immediately the look passed, replaced by kind sadness.

"When we heard of your son's death, all at the palace mourned for you and for Ide Tamura," she said. "He was a good man and a brave soldier, and the Emerald Empire has lost a cherished son." Tadaji watched Kachiko's full, red lips move as she spoke, and for a moment he saw an ugly smear of blood covering her face. He blinked, and the image was gone.

Quickly he bowed and replied, "Thank you, Your Majesty, for your kind words. He will be missed."

"In this world and the next," Kachiko murmured, squeezing Tadaji's hands.

Tadaji quickly looked up at Kachiko, startled. The kind, sad expression on her face had not changed. A shiver of fear ran down his spine. She smiled again, and with exquisite grace turned toward the center of the room.

"I thank you for attending this evening," Kachiko said.

"We are here for many reasons. One is to welcome back the honorable Unicorn ambassador, Ide Tadaji, to the Imperial Court. His presence has been sorely missed, and we are delighted at his return."

Tadaji bowed formally to the empress, and she nodded in response.

Empress Kachiko continued, "As you know, our beloved emperor still lies ill, and I stay at his bedside. But his illness has kept me from you, and I deeply apologize. Many of you have requested audiences with me, and I have been unable to honor those requests. I hope you will forgive me. I will take a few moments to speak to all of you, informally, but then I must return to Hantei's side. I know that you understand."

Kachiko made her way around the room, approaching the most senior ambassadors first. She had a kind word for everyone and made each person feel as if his or her words were the most important ones she would hear that day.

Tadaji watched her skillful performance with fascinated amusement. He knew her mind was anywhere but on the grumblings of the ambassadors. He also knew that when she turned her eyes on him, he would succumb to her spell. Empress Kachiko was the undisputed master.

One of Kachiko's servants approached Tadaji, who stood alone in a corner, his hands folded. The servant prostrated himself and said, "Honorable Ide Tadaji, Empress Kachiko has informed me that the emperor wishes for you to escort her to her chambers when the reception is complete."

"It is a great honor to know that the emperor has entrusted me with this task," Tadaji replied, wondering why Kachiko wanted to speak to him privately.

Soon Kachiko turned to the crowd and said, "Thank you for attending this reception. You do honor to the emperor, to your clans, and to all Rokugan."

In unison, the entire assembly bowed in silence to the great lady.

Tadaji bowed as well. Then he rose, shifting his cane to his left hand and extending his right arm to Kachiko. She placed her hand lightly on his silk sleeve. With her servants trailing behind her and her yojimbo, Aramoro, at her side, Kachiko and Tadaji stepped gracefully out of the room and into the garden.

As soon as they were away from the reception hall, Kachiko stopped and whispered something to Aramoro. He nodded and motioned to the ladies attending the empress. Bowing in turn, they withdrew and faded into the shadows of the garden. Tadaji's eyebrows rose in mild surprise, for he knew that Kachiko rarely walked without her attendants.

"There are times when ladies in waiting can be a hindrance, especially when one walks with a kind and honorable man," Kachiko said, smiling at Tadaji. She parted her lips slightly, allowing Tadaji to see the glint of her straight, white teeth.

"Thank you, Majesty," Tadaji replied. Although he was old enough to know Kachiko's games, he was a man, and like most men, he felt a tingle of pride at a compliment from an attractive woman. "I have missed the court and am glad to be back."

"I am pleased that you honor your life here at court," Kachiko said softly. "But the emperor gave you permission to remain at the Unicorn stronghold to mourn your son."

Although she kept her eyes on the path they strolled, Tadaji felt as if her gaze bored into his soul. There was an unspoken question: why?

Outwardly, Tadaji calmly pondered his response. Inwardly, his mind whirled. He could not tell her of the dreams he had been having for weeks. Of the nights he dared not sleep. Dreams that drove him back to the Imperial Palace, to face something that even his mind dared not reveal to him.

Tadaji forced a very natural-sounding chuckle from his throat and said, "Ah, my empress, you have caught me. The only thing I missed about court was the emperor's hot baths. I have had to make do these many months with a chilly stream and complaining servants whose backs broke with every bucket of water they carried."

Kachiko's laugh tinkled like bells through the night air, but she was annoyed at Tadaji's attempt to sidestep her question. She refused to allow a Unicorn, even a grief-stricken one, to push her aside.

"But I am sure even the emperor's baths were scarcely the enticement that brought you back?"

"No," Tadaji agreed carefully, and then said, "When word came that many in the imperial family were dead, I despaired. Then the news of the assassination attempt reached the Unicorn lands, as well as your bravery in saving the emperor from a certain death. . . ."

"I cannot be thanked for that," she demurred modestly. "My only thought was for the survival of the imperial family. He is the last, and he must live. Would that I could cure him of this horrible sickness that eats at him each day."

Tadaji searched her face, but it was indecipherable beneath her mask. She had always been difficult to read, and her ability to hide her feelings had kept her alive more than once. Married to an enemy after her family and clan were crushed, Kachiko had managed to survive. Although he did not trust her, Tadaji respected her.

"Have the shugenja not been able to discover a cure?" Tadaji asked, remembering what Yoshi had told him. "I understand that many have been summoned to the palace.

I would have thought that the Dragon shugenja, of all of them, would have found a cure by now."

Kachiko sighed delicately. "No, no one can explain it. His sickness shows all signs of the plague, but it has lingered long. Each day he seems neither better nor worse."

The two walked in silence for a time. A cloud passed over the moon, darkening the path. Tadaji felt a chill go through him. Beside him, Kachiko sighed.

He decided to bring up the concerns of his daimyo, Shinjo Yokatsu. "Many Unicorn patrols are riding along the borders of our lands," Tadaji said. "They have reported much unrest."

"Yes, we have received reports here and there," she replied. "The emperor's advisors assure me it is nothing to worry about."

"A number of small villages have been hit very hard, Majesty," Tadaji said. "First by the plague, and then by bandits who attack with the hope of finding food and goods. Many villages have been destroyed."

Kachiko looked intently at Tadaji. "Surely you speak falsely, Tadaji? No honorable citizen of Rokugan would dare attack innocents."

He couldn't tell if she were really surprised, so he played along. "I am afraid it is true," he replied sadly. "It is not just the Unicorn lands that have been troubled. Crab, Lion, and Crane villages are targeted as well. There is a sense of desperation in the land, Empress Kachiko. News of the emperor's illness has thrown the world off balance once again. I fear these attacks will become worse."

Kachiko dropped her gaze and stared off into space, delicately chewing her full, round lip in thought.

"The Unicorns are prepared to increase their patrols to other lands, Majesty," Tadaji continued, "but we need the support and permission of the emperor." Tadaji paused, knowing how insignificant the poor villagers were to Kachiko.

"The Unicorn is an honorable clan, but you are well aware of how my clan is perceived by many in Rokugan. We are of the Emerald Empire, but some of our brothers and sisters treat us as outsiders. Without the support of the imperial family, our actions could be misconstrued to be hostile, which is not our intention. We seek only to protect those who cannot protect themselves.

"And in these times, Empress Kachiko," he finished, "there are many who are too weak to protect themselves."

Kachiko glared at the older man. "Many are strong!" she said fiercely.

Tadaji bowed his head, surprised at her outburst and wondering what it meant. Kachiko never showed anger unless she intended a specific effect.

Aloud he said, "Forgive me, Empress, for upsetting you."

"Tadaji, it is I who should apologize," Kachiko said in a lower voice. She leaned toward him, and he could smell the scent of her freshly washed hair and feel the brush of her kimono.

He willed himself to ignore it. Stronger men than he had fallen into Kachiko's spell.

"The emperor's illness has me short-tempered. I did not realize the peasants in your lands were so . . . defenseless."

That stung. The empress had turned a request for aid into an indictment of Unicorn leadership. Kachiko played her game well.

Tadaji did so too. "Defenseless, yes, without their one true defender—Emperor Hantei. You asked me why I returned to the Imperial Palace, Majesty. That is why. I feel I can best serve the empire by serving the emperor—with more Unicorn patrols. I hope to speak to him on this matter."

They had arrived at the long, low building that held Kachiko's chambers. Inside, Tadaji could hear her servants moving about. Occasionally a woman would pass near one of the rice paper walls, casting a ghostly silhouette as she glided by.

They stopped before the wide steps that led up to her chambers. "I am honored by your presence and your support," Kachiko responded formally. "The emperor will consider your request."

"Thank you for the honor of your company, Majesty," he said, bowing low. "I am happy to serve you."

Tadaji's cane tapped softly on the stones as he walked back along the path, deep in thought. Much had been said, and nothing had been said. As he rolled the conversations over in his mind, the tip of his cane pressed on something and slid, catching him off balance.

It was Kachiko's fan. The fine silk was dyed a brilliant red, and in the center of the fan was a scorpion, painted in ebony ink. Tadaji picked it up and stared at it, certain the Scorpion who owned it had dropped it on purpose.

The color seemed to drip onto Tadaji's hand like spilled blood. He gasped and let go of the fan. Blood covered his hand, and he could feel its sticky warmth on his skin. The stench of death flooded his nostrils, and he choked. His head spun crazily, and for a moment he thought he was going to faint. Then the smell was gone.

He crouched in the middle of the path, head bent to his knees, and gasped for breath. When his lungs no longer burned, he looked at his hand. No blood. The fan lay at his feet. Tadaji took a deep breath and gingerly picked it up.

If Kachiko dropped the fan on purpose—and she did everything on purpose—she wished for Tadaji to return it.

It was bait for another of her traps. But if he did not return it, she would know he had stolen it. . . . The empress was a scorpion with an inescapable sting.

Swallowing his fear, Tadaji turned down the path toward the empress's chambers.

As he rounded a slight bend in the path, he heard a voice—Empress Kachiko's! She should have been inside by now, preparing for sleep. Tadaji stopped, all senses alert. She stood at the foot of the steps leading up to the porch, where he had left her, and she was speaking to someone.

Tadaji heard a male voice respond, but he could not make out the words.

Kachiko replied, "Send Zumo. No one will miss him. Tell him he must bring it back before dawn. It would be disastrous to wait another day." The male spoke again, and Kachiko said, "If she returns, send her away. The Lion ambassador must learn her place, no matter if she *is* the sister of Ikoma Ujiaki."

As Tadaji strained to hear more, he stepped forward. A twig snapped beneath his foot. "By Shinjo," he cursed under his breath.

"Who is there!" bellowed the male voice. In a flash, a man was in front of Tadaji, knees bent, katana drawn. It was Aramoro, the bodyguard.

"It is I, your servant Tadaji," Tadaji replied. "Empress Kachiko lost something on the pathway, and I merely came to return it to her."

"Who is it?" Kachiko's voice came.

"It is the ambassador, here to return a lost item," Aramoro replied, unmoving.

"What lost item?" Kachiko asked as she emerged from the shadows behind the large man. "Tadaji?"

"Forgive me, Empress," Tadaji said, bowing low. "I

found your fan along the path. I was merely hoping to return it to you, as I had left your side but a moment ago." He held up the fan, and Aramoro pulled it from his grasp.

Kachiko asked in a low, sweet voice, "How long have you been standing here, my friend?"

The hairs rose on Tadaji's neck. Nothing in her speech hinted at danger, but Tadaji was overwhelmed with fear. Slowly he raised his head, a look of mild incomprehension on his face.

"Long, my lady? Not long. I had just arrived when your guard met me on the path."

Kachiko looked calmly from Tadaji to the fan in her hand. For a moment nothing stirred. Then Kachiko smiled her beautiful smile.

"I see," she said. "Aramoro, see to it Tadaji arrives safely back to his chambers." With that, Kachiko turned and disappeared.

Tadaji slowly rose and started down the path toward the ambassadors' wing of the palace, with Aramoro a few paces behind. When they arrived at Tadaji's chamber he turned and gave the scowling yojimbo the appropriate thanks. He watched as the samurai strode off into the night.

Tadaji peered into the darkness for a moment, and then painfully climbed the three steps to the porch, slid open the paper door, and vanished inside.

Outside, beyond the building, a form crept from the darkness of the garden and dissolved into the cool shadows of the night.

3 A LENGTHENING OF SHADOWS

Tetsuko sat on the futon, twisting the silk sheets in her hands and staring into space. Outside the translucent rice-paper walls of the room, the daily routine of activity in the keep had begun. Soft, warm sunlight shone through the walls, hinting at a beautiful day. Servants shuffled quietly to and fro, carrying countless items to their private destinations. A distant neighing echoed on the morning air, and a happy neigh returned the greeting from somewhere close by. A unit of soldiers marched past, their footsteps crunching in unison on the gravel and the *clink clink* of their iron-banded armor sounding like a call to arms.

She remembered only pieces of the nightmare that had awakened her—dreams filled with oozing green pus and a low moan that would not stop—but her heart still pounded with fear. Gradually Tetsuko's heart slowed as the last shreds of the dream faded.

She sighed and rose from the futon. A low table had been set for breakfast, and Tetsuko absently poured herself a cup of steaming mint tea. A small basket of bread accompanied it, and she chewed on a slice as she rummaged through a large basket that sat near the futon.

It contained four kimonos, two pleated, divided hakamas that were worn over a kimono, and a purple obi embroidered with ki-rin in fine gold metal threads. She swiped the bread crumbs from her hands and tried on one of the kimonos. It fit Tetsuko as if it had been made for her, but she dressed with no thought to the fine stitches that held the seams of the dark purple kimono, or to the care with which the gold silk hakama had been made. Tetsuko never gave much thought to her clothing, although she was careful to keep what little she owned clean and well repaired. At that thought, she snorted as she wrapped the sashlike obi around her waist and purposefully slid her katana into it. "As if I own any clothing anymore," she thought with a pang, remembering the scattered packs that she left in the forest as she and Jikkyo escaped with their lives.

At the bottom of the basket Tetsuko found a pair of delicate silk slippers. She pulled them out, surveying the fine embroidery and the softness of the fabric. Then with a grunt of displeasure she flung them back into the basket and pushed her feet into her own leather boots, stained and worn and molded to her feet from years of hard wear. Now they were the only clothing she owned besides her armor and the precious leather leggings she wore beneath it.

Once she was dressed, she absentmindedly ran her hand through her chin-length chestnut hair. She was one of the few women in Rokugan who had ever cut her hair, and although she was not ashamed of it, she preferred to keep it tied back, away from her face and from the questioning eyes of those who noticed it.

Somewhere in the Utaku ancestry, barbarian blood mixed with Unicorn. Occasionally a child was born who showed signs of the wilderness past. Tetsuko was one of these throwbacks. She was of medium height, slightly taller than other Battle Maidens, but not unusually so. She was a serious woman who would be breathtakingly beautiful if she laughed or smiled. Her eyes were large hazel almonds, almost round but not quite, with thick lashes. But when she was angry her eyes darkened, flashing flecks of gray-green. Even those closest to her dreaded her fury when her eyes went the color of an angry sea.

Tetsuko, never one for being patient, was dressed and ready to go, but the servant who was supposed to take her to Shinjo Yokatsu had not yet arrived. She paced the small room, biting chunks of bread as she went, the heels of her leather boots stomping across the delicate bamboo floor.

Finally a timid knock came, and a servant entered and bowed prostrate. Without a word Tetsuko followed her out the door and through the grand Unicorn keep of Toshi No Aida Ni Kawa.

Quickly they made their way through the vast fortress, speeding down hallways and ducking through seldom-used rooms. Tetsuko had some trouble keeping up with the servant, who clearly knew her way around the castle and was taking Tetsuko along a few shortcuts to the great meeting hall.

They turned a corner and made their way down a long, wide hallway that cut through the center of the keep. Tetsuko's footsteps made an unnatural clomping sound on the highly polished wooden floor as they walked. A dark, vaulted ceiling soared high above their heads. But it wasn't the ceiling that halted Tetsuko in her steps as her gaze moved upward.

The walls on each side were set with enormous circular panes of thick golden glass. They were set side-by-side within an expanse of deep violet enamel. Each pane had been blown into a huge wheel many times larger than the arms' span of a man. Threads of gold swirled in the glass, breaking the light into a thousand golden shards that sparkled on the rich wooden floor at Tetsuko's feet. In the center of each pane, a master artist had painted the emblem of the Unicorn Clan, and the ki-rin heads seemed to shake in greeting as the two passed by.

Tetsuko gazed at the glass and thought of the hundreds of artisans, their names forgotten, who labored for years to create this marvel. Although no one remembered them, their souls lived on for centuries in the beauty crafted from their hands.

"Oh, Shinjo, make my soul strong," Tetsuko breathed as the golden light cascaded upon her.

The servant clucked impatiently, rousing Tetsuko from her musings. They hurried down the hallway toward a set of enormous, carved wooden doors that rose like sentinels. A man paced before them, his hands clasped behind his back, and his head bowed in thought. Tetsuko's eyes brightened in relief as she recognized Jikkyo.

As Tetsuko approached, Jikkyo looked up, and a wide grin spread across his face. He bowed formally. "Greetings, Utaku Tetsuko," he said cheerfully.

Tetsuko smiled and returned the bow. "I am happy to see your soul still walking in this world."

"Big things are happening, Tetsuko," Jikkyo replied.

"Shinjo Yokatsu has called all his military leaders to the keep."

Before Jikkyo could explain further, the heavy wooden doors swung open and a servant appeared. He knelt in front of the two and said, "Honorable guests. Your presence is required by Shinjo Yokatsu."

"Domo arigato," Jikkyo said, politely bowing. The servant shuffled aside, still on his knees, and they entered the room.

As Tetsuko's eyes adjusted to the dim light, she saw a large room with a high-beamed ceiling. The stone walls were covered with silk tapestries filled with scenes of battle and heroic deeds from the Unicorn's past. Rows of torches stood in ornate iron stands, casting round pools of light in even rows along the floor. The room smelled faintly musty, as if it were rarely used.

Down the center of the room stretched a long, low table made of dark cherry and polished to a deep shine. Dozens of people sat on silk cushions along each side of the table. There was a hush in the room, broken only by the soft thudding of Tetsuko's boots on the thick silk carpet that covered the floor from the door to the table. When the two reached the table's edge, they knelt and put their foreheads to the floor in unison. Jikkyo said, "Many greetings to the Most Honorable Shinjo Yokatsu, Master of the Four Winds."

"Greetings to you, Ide Jikkyo," came a reply from the far end of the table. "And to the young Utaku Tetsuko. Rise and be seated. We have much to discuss."

Tetsuko had the uncomfortable feeling they had interrupted a discussion that included them but wasn't meant for their ears. The sensation made Tetsuko feel as if she were a child caught doing something wrong. She sat down on the nearest cushion, fumbling slightly as she caught the hem of her kimono beneath her boots.

When they were settled, the strong voice that greeted Jikkyo spoke. "I am honored that each of you could attend this meeting," Yokatsu began. "By your presence, you honor both yourselves and the Unicorn Clan. We are entering strange times, and our clan will need your skills in the weeks and months to come."

Yokatsu cleared his throat, absentmindedly drummed the table with the fingers of his left hand, and turned his stern gaze slowly around the room. Yokatsu was one of the most respected daimyos in the empire, and as Unicorn Clan Champion, he had unquestioned prowess on the field. He was a stocky, well-built man, known for his love of riding and his unfailing devotion to his steeds. His rough face, lined with years of worry, wore a stern expression.

His title, Master of the Four Winds, came from his journeys as a youth. In all Rokugan, he was the only living member of his clan who knew the ancient land of his people—the Land of the Burning Sands. Yokatsu had an air of honest power about him, as if he knew the secrets of the world and understood how to use them honorably.

As his eyes moved down the line, Tetsuko held her breath. A muscle in her right thigh began to twitch, and she slapped her hand over the spot, digging her ragged, bitten nails into her flesh to stop it. His gaze fell on her, and Tetsuko felt his black eyes bore into her mind. She struggled to keep her face a calm mask, but her resolve crumbled. She blinked and bowed her head.

Her cheeks flaming in embarrassment, Tetsuko kept her head down until she felt Yokatsu's eyes move onward. When he began speaking again, she ventured a glance toward the front of the room.

"In recent weeks, disturbing news has reached us from all parts of Rokugan," he said. "Every one of you has a piece of the puzzle, and each piece is vital to understanding what is going on in the land. First, to the commander of the Unicorn forces stationed along the borders." He nodded to a short, well-dressed man beside him and said, "Shinjo Yutaka."

The man nodded in return, and then stood and addressed the assembled crowd. "For the last few weeks Unicorn troops stationed at Shiro Ide and Shiro Iuchi have reported Crab and Lion armies on the march. I have heard reports of Phoenix, Crane, and Lion armies on the march as well. The commander at Shiro Iuchi reported that a large band of what appeared to be Crab troops camped near Beiden Pass for four days and nights, but moved on. It is unclear at this point what their motives were, or even if they were truly Crab.

"Near the border of Dragon lands," he continued, "all has been quiet. Too quiet. There were a few Dragon troops patrolling the area, but now there are none. It is also said that ise zumi, the mysterious Dragon monks, have been spotted far beyond Dragon lands as well."

Jikkyo leaned over to Tetsuko and said in a low voice, "That is truly strange. There have been no ise zumi seen south of the Mountain of the Thunders in years."

"But it is not only Rokugani forces that are on the move," Yutaka said in a low voice. "I have received disturbing reports of Shadowlands troops attacking villages far beyond their borders. They seem to appear out of the air, in the darkest night, and consume a village without warning. Black creatures have been spotted as far north as the Hidden Forest and east, all the way to the sea." He sat down and bowed his head.

Tetsuko felt her stomach wrench. She clenched her fists to stop her hands from shaking. It didn't work.

Across from Tetsuko, a woman raised herself on her

knees and bowed to Yokatsu. He recognized her, and she spoke: "There are so many plague dead that the bodies are left where they fall. The stench of death crawls into everything for miles around. Entire villages have been destroyed, set to flame when all who lived there died. Not even the lowest heimin dare ransack these places.

"The poor wretches who escape death have no homes, no family, no food, no hope. Desperate for food and shelter, they band together in small groups and attack still-thriving villages. Lately there have been reports of these outcasts destroying entire villages, killing innocents in their beds and setting crops on fire. They are desperate, my lord."

Yokatsu nodded briefly and said, "Domo arigato, Moto Hirata." The daimyo turned to another woman near the front of the table and said, "Iuchi Kara." The woman nodded and began her report.

A sense of foreboding slowly descended upon the room as person after person rose and gave an account of some new horror. Even Yokatsu stopped drumming his fingers. He listened intently to each speaker. Tetsuko's mind spun with the stories of death and confusion, and the fear that she had felt earlier eventually settled into a hard lump in her stomach.

"Ide Jikkyo!" a voice seemed to boom in her ear, and Tetsuko's head shot up. Jikkyo rose to his knees, bowed, and reported the events of two nights before. Tetsuko's heart swelled with pride as her friend and leader held the whole room spellbound with his tale.

As Jikkyo described Tetsuko's valor, she blushed and lowered her head. The group at the table looked at the young Battle Maiden with awe, for it was hard to imagine this awkward, blushing woman brandishing her blade with such fury. Even Yokatsu looked upon her with a new respect.

Jikkyo finished speaking and bowed low to Yokatsu, signaling that his report was complete. Tetsuko realized with surprise that Jikkyo had forgotten to mention the thieves.

What should I do? she wondered fearfully. I cannot possibly speak to this assembly. My mouth will go dry, and I will not know what to say! To her surprise, Tetsuko felt herself rising to her knees and bowing toward the great daimyo.

He looked toward the young samurai-ko, and his eyes widened slightly. "Yes, Utaku Tetsuko?" he said in a clear, deep voice that quieted the room. "Do you wish to say something?"

Tetsuko swallowed hard and replied, "Yes, Shinjo Yokatsu, if I may. There are more to the events that Ide Jikkyo related." Tetsuko's heart was pounding so furiously that she was certain everyone could hear it.

"Very well, Battle Maiden," Yokatsu said. "What have you to tell us?"

Tetsuko took a deep breath and quickly related the events in the camp that led to her flight into the forest. Then she described the condition of the bodies she had found in the clearing. She could hear soft sounds of dread from around the room as she related the carnage at the camp. Even Yokatsu was not unaffected. At one point he grasped his water cup, threw back the contents, and wiped his mouth on the sleeve of his kimono.

"Then I heard a scream," Tetsuko finished, "and I found the village, which was not far from the camp. I saw Jikkyo and Rinako surrounded by zombies, and, well, you know the rest." With another deep breath, Tetsuko bowed her head.

For a long moment no one moved or spoke. Finally, Yokatsu said, "This is grim news. I have never heard of such inhuman butchery as this."

The only sound in the room was Yokatsu's fingers drumming the table in steady rhythm. "I fear that the Shadowlands forces have strong allies somewhere," he continued. "It is clear to me that a single clan alone cannot battle them with any hope of winning."

He turned to a young man seated near his right. "Yasamura, you will take a small force south to Hida Tsuru of the Crab, seeking an alliance. Then you and your troops will ride north, to the lands of the Dragon. They are aware of the growing threat. Perhaps they too will be willing to ally with us."

The young man's face lit up with a cheek-splitting grin. "You honor me with this assignment. Your trust and respect fills me with pride, and I will not fail you," he said in a rush, bowing low.

Yokatsu allowed himself a small smile at his son's exuberance, but it faded quickly as he turned to address the group. "As for the attacks by the outcasts, we will increase the patrols along the border." He reached into the folds of his kimono and drew out a piece of thick, folded rice paper. The large imperial seal that held it closed had been broken.

"This is a message from Ide Tadaji, the honorable Unicorn ambassador to the Imperial Palace," he said, tapping the edge of the paper lightly in his rough, battle-worn palm. "He has received permission from the emperor for Unicorn patrols to be officially stationed outside our borders, to the south and east. They will protect small, undefended rural villages from roving bands of outcasts."

Yokatsu slid the paper back into his kimono and said, "Let us adjourn and rest, for this meeting has been long, and I, for one, am hungry." The stocky man rose stiffly to his feet, and everyone in the room bowed low.

"Ide Jikkyo and Utaku Tetsuko, please remain," the daimyo said.

Tetsuko froze in the kneeling position as the rest of the assembly rose and, amid the rustle of silken robes, left the room. Tetsuko's right foot began to tingle painfully, and she wiggled her toes in a desperate attempt to keep her foot from falling asleep.

Finally the heavy doors closed, and Yokatsu said, "Rise, young samurai."

Together she and Jikkyo stood up, and Tetsuko's right foot crumpled beneath her. She yelped and fell back onto the cushion with a thud. A thousand pinpricks jabbed her flesh. She sat, knees bent, hiding her face in her lap like a child as she waited for the reprimand she knew would come.

Instead, she heard a strange burst of sound. Tetsuko looked up and saw the stern man, his mouth wide open, guffawing pleasantly at Tetsuko's misfortune. Jikkyo smiled and offered Tetsuko his hand. She grabbed it, and he clumsily hauled her to her feet. She half walked, half hopped, toward the great daimyo.

"Please forgive me, Utaku Tetsuko, I meant no discourtesy," Yokatsu said.

Tetsuko nodded, surprised at his apology. As she sat, she was careful to stretch her numbed leg in front of her beneath the table.

"A piece of advice from one battle rider to another," he continued. "Leather boots pinch the blood, especially when worn during long meetings." A new round of chuckles filled the room as Yokatsu laughed at his joke.

Even Jikkyo smiled.

With a final wipe of his eyes, Yokatsu let his laughter subside, and he became serious. "Of all the reports I heard today, yours disturbs me the most. Your encounter with the Shadowlands creatures says much about what may be happening in Rokugan."

Yokatsu peered at Jikkyo and said, "I have need for a samurai like yourself in the Unicorn army. You will report to Yasamura in the morning and ride with his troops to the Dragon lands."

Jikkyo's eyes widened in surprise and pleasure at this unexpected promotion, and he bowed low. "You do me great honor, Shinjo Yokatsu. I will do my best to honor you and the Unicorn Clan."

"I know you will, son of the Ide family," Yokatsu replied.

Jikkyo bowed again. Then Yokatsu said, "That is all, Ide Jikkyo. I wish to talk to your companion here."

After the heavy door shut behind Jikkyo, Yokatsu said to Tetsuko, "You and Jikkyo are friends."

"We have traveled many miles together," Tetsuko replied. "I feel grateful that he honors me with his friendship. I owe him my life many times over."

"And he owes you his, it seems," Yokatsu replied. Then abruptly he asked, "What made you plunge into the midst of the zombie horde, when every nerve in your body told you to run?"

Tetsuko blinked and answered without thinking. "I had to save them. There was no choice. It was my duty."

Yokatsu leaned back on one arm. He took in Tetsuko's rumpled kimono and the bright, hard fire that gleamed in her eyes. His gaze held gentle reproof of her headstrong youth, but also admiration for her samurai's heart. He seemed to wonder which would win out. At last, he said, "Jikkyo has been promoted to Yasamura's army, which means I have need for a patrol leader. I am assigning you the job."

Tetsuko gaped at him, unable to conceal her emotions. Then she bowed quickly, her cheeks flaming in embarrassment at the dishonorable display.

"You are reckless, but you are loyal," Yokatsu said. "Your first thought was to save the lives of those you cared about, regardless of your own safety. But you disobeyed a direct order to do so. In this case, you made the right choice. You may not be as lucky next time, when your impetuousness could affect more than the lives of the few who ride with you.

"You carry much pain with you, Utaku Tetsuko," he said sternly. "The pain can eat at your soul, or it can make you strong. The secrets in your heart may cost you your life, but do not let them be responsible for the deaths of others."

Yokatsu's face softened. "Now I am very hungry, patrol leader," he said, rubbing his stomach. "Leave me, and consider my words."

Tetsuko bowed and murmured a gracious "Domo arigato, my lord," and then quickly left the room.

Yokatsu watched her go, a bemused expression on his face. He had monitored Tetsuko in the Battle Maiden school, aided by his old friend Utaku Benjiro. Tetsuko had the single-minded doggedness of one who is expected to fail and has chosen to prove everyone wrong. Although her tactical skills were poor, she had practiced day after day on her techniques of fighting and martial arts. The last candle burning in the dorms would be hers as she studied far into the night.

Then she was cast out, disgraced. Most would have crawled away in shame, never to show their faces again. But Tetsuko bore her shame and returned to finish her training, despite the taint of disgrace. It took a strong will to face such odds, and Yokatsu respected that. But there were other things she could not face, not yet.

"I know much about you, Battle Maiden," he said aloud to the empty room. "But I wonder how much you know of yourself."

4 WHISPER OF SILK

irst, the drums began. Their pounding beat filled Tadaji's mind as he looked wildly around.

He was in his home of years before, the one he had shared with his beloved, Chisato. The house was dark and hazy around the edges.

Something reached out of the darkness and took his hand. An unseen ghost. It led him outside.

He followed, away from the safety of his home and down a forest path paved with black stones splashed with red.

Tadaji's terror grew as the ghost pulled him through the dark forest. From the shadows, thousands of eyes stared at him— thousands of eyes in the dark sockets of hundreds of disembodied heads. They floated cheek to cheek around him. Some were bare skulls, smashed and broken with battle wounds. Others dripped gore and dragged shreds of skin. Still others bore gaping, oozing plague sores so large that Tadaji could see bone, jaw, and teeth glinting through holes in the rotting flesh.

He tried to scream, but no sound came.

The heads opened their mouths wide and laughed, filling the forest with a chorus of unholy sound.

The ghost pulled him into a clearing. The drumming became louder. It matched the rhythm of Tadaji's heartbeat. He struggled to breathe.

The drummers stood in a circle facing a large fire. They were tall samurai, dressed in identical black armor, with no mon to identify what family or clan they were from. But it was not a fire; it was a fiery drum, the flames licking its edge as the warriors beat on and on.

Standing atop of the drum was Tamura.

He was no more than fifteen, and he wore the deep purple kimono that his mother had made for his gempuku, the traditional coming-of-age ceremony. His face was hidden in the flickering shadows.

As Tadaji watched, the flames caught the hem of the kimono and burst in a shower of blue sparks. He tried to race to his son, to save him from the flames, but the ghostly hands held him in an icy grip.

Tamura began to burn.

"I am dead but I cannot die," the boy said in a hollow voice as the roar of the flames rose higher. "I am here, in the spirit world, waiting in torment to move on to Jigoku. I cannot leave, for you sent me to my death and imprisoned me here. Only you can release me. Only you . . . only you . . ."

Tadaji could not see the boy's face, but in the flames a

white jawbone moved up and down where Tamura's mouth should have been.

"Hoturi is the key. Help him. . . . Help him. . . ."

The drumming got louder, filling Tadaji's ears.

Fingers of flame wrapped around the drummers, and in a flash they too had gone up in the inferno. But they never ceased their eternal drumming, only screaming their pain to the beat.

Tamura, by now a blackened skeleton, wailed with a sound that rent Tadaji's soul.

▲▲▲▲▲▲▲▲

Tadaji awoke with a start, his chest pounding in the rhythm of the drums and his body dripping with sweat. He gulped the water that his personal servant, Eda, had thoughtfully left by his bedside. He waited for his terror to subside.

It was his fault, he knew it. His stubbornness had sent his son to his death. Now, Tamura's soul was caught in the agony of the spirit world. His son's soul was cursed to remain there until Tadaji released him. But how?

When the trembling fear finally subsided, Tadaji sat up and looked around the room. Judging by the light, the day was almost done. Tadaji's presence was required at a state dinner this evening, and he was not looking forward to it.

He eyed a small scroll that rested on the table beside the bed. It was from Ikoma Natsumi, asking him to meet with her that evening after the dinner. He sighed and leaned back on his elbows. It was going to be a long evening.

His thoughts traveled to the Lady Scorpion. He had

been grateful when Kachiko had agreed to his request for Unicorn patrols in other clan lands, but when he had gone to formally thank her, she had been icy and distant. She usually saved that display for scorned lovers, Tadaji thought wryly, not for elderly ambassadors. It made him wonder.

Tadaji rose from the cushion and quickly dressed in a deep violet kimono printed with golden unicorns. Then he made his way toward the Imperial Hall.

His journey took him through familiar parts of the palace gardens, but much had changed. Many buildings were gone, set afire to repel the plague. Black scars on the ground marked where they had once stood. Others were damaged beyond repair and were being torn down. Here and there a gate to a beloved garden path would be blocked off, another sign of the devastation that swept the palace during the coup and the plague that followed on its heels.

Tadaji arrived at the Imperial Hall. Unlike other official rooms in the palace, this one was simple. The walls were made of creamy rice paper washed in watercolor waves of light blue. The soft bamboo mats on the floor were woven in shades of blue and sea green.

Most of the guests had already arrived. As Tadaji entered, the small crowd hushed for a moment and turned to see who had come. Tadaji, an ambassador's smile frozen on his face, bowed low to the crowd, who bowed back in return before resuming the low buzz of conversation.

He moved toward a group of people, who bowed again as he approached. "Greetings, Tadaji," a stately woman in a light blue kimono said.

"And greetings to you, Kakita Umi," Tadaji replied, bowing in return. "Welcome. Kakita Yoshi told me you were to replace him." He turned to Umi's secretaries. "And to you,

"Kakita Daro, and Daidoji Asira," he said politely, recognizing two of the Crane ambassador's senior staff.

They nodded their heads in return.

"Did you hear?" Umi began. "The empress will be unable to join us this evening. This is the third time she has canceled an appearance this week."

"That is indeed bad news," Tadaji replied. "I had hoped for a word with the lady this evening."

"About your Unicorn patrols, no doubt," Umi said, and a thin, tight smile played on her face. "It is said that these patrols will be allowed to enter other clan's lands freely. Is this true?"

"Yes," Tadaji replied, taken aback that she had heard this news so quickly. "We only seek to help Rokugan in its time of need."

Umi nodded. "We have no right to object, of course. Your troops travel under the emperor's own protection." Umi's eyes glinted as she spoke, waiting for Tadaji's response.

Tadaji gazed calmly at the woman. "Our mission is not to destroy but to protect, as you well know," he said evenly. "It seems other clans do not share our vision. In their zeal to kill and conquer, they have abandoned their own people. We have sworn to protect those who are unprotected, regardless of station or family.

"It is strange that you would be dismayed at the idea of Unicorns protecting Crane villages," Tadaji continued, "since many other armies are so interested in your lands these days. You might wish for a barbarian or two on your side if the Lions decide to march into your lands."

Umi lifted her chin in defiance and declared, "Our forces would crush them. We do not need help."

"Perhaps not," he replied. "But these are strange times. It is unwise to refuse something you may one day beg for."

"Beg!" Umi sputtered.

Before she could manage a biting reply, Tadaji bowed low, said, "Good evening to all of you," and gracefully moved away from the group. Tadaji made his way to the table and lowered himself onto a sumptuous silk cushions.

One of the glories of the Imperial Palace was this magnificent water table. It consisted of a stream of clear, cold water, about two feet wide and a foot deep, flowing through the center of the hall. Large, jagged rocks were placed in orderly disorder in the stream, and the water bubbled around them with a soothing sound. Well-fed goldfish swam lazily in the slow-moving stream, flashing glints of yellow. The bottom of the stream was lined with black pebbles, accented here and there with flat white stones. Delicate water plants waved gently in the light current.

A tinkle of bells signaled the first course. Servants appeared and placed before each guest a delicate porcelain dinner set—a bowl, a small plate, a set of chopsticks, and a sake cup. Servants piled spoonfuls of steaming rice into each bowl and filled the cups.

A large white water lily appeared at the end of the canal and slowly floated downstream, accompanied by the trembling notes of a flute. When the flower had disappeared through the small opening in the opposite wall, the music stopped. Boat-shaped lacquered trays appeared on the water. They were laden with strips of salmon, trout, and shark, and were joined end-to-end by chains of pearls. Each guest took what he or she wished from the trays as they floated past. Servants offered sauces and spices to each guest.

Tadaji took only a small portion, for he knew that there would be at least three more courses in the elegant meal. Each course, presented in its own fleet of boat trays, would float down the marvelous table, proceeded by an exceedingly intricate floating flower arrangement and accompanied by the sound of flutes.

Toward the end of the meal, a door opened and a tall, slender man dressed in a vibrant blue kimono entered the room. His long white hair flowed about his shoulders and complemented his pale skin. His eye caught Tadaji's, and the young man smiled. He made his way around the room and lowered himself on an empty cushion next to Tadaji.

"Tadaji, how good to see you again," he said in a clear, rich tenor voice.

"Hoturi, when did you arrive at the palace? Tadaji asked, pleased by the unexpected appearance of his friend.

"Just a few hours ago," Hoturi replied. "Toshimoko and I came, on serious business. Our formal reception will come tomorrow. We're not even sure what rooms we have for the night."

Tadaji smiled in amusement. The Crane daimyo seemed completely undisturbed by the fact that he had barged into a formal dinner late and had missed most of the meal. The young man's confidence and pleasant arrogance had always delighted Tadaji. Secretly, he had wished to be as easygoing and imperturbable as Hoturi.

The young daimyo glanced at Tadaji. "I heard about your son, and I am deeply sorry."

"It was Shinjo's will," Tadaji said sadly. "Tamura's caravan was stranded in a village decimated by the plague. Every soul in a town of five hundred died. The village was burned to the ground. He did not even have a proper burial." Tadaji's voice caught, and he looked away.

"This plague has taken the best of us," Hoturi said softly. "And now war is coming." He looked around the room, and then leaned toward Tadaji and said in a low voice, "There is rot in the land, Tadaji, worse than just plague. Even the air feels wrong."

The sound of bells signaled the end of the feast, and both men rose. "Yes, I have felt it too," Tadaji replied. "But here is not the place for this discussion. How long will you be at the palace?"

"It is hard to say," Hoturi replied. "Empress Kachiko has summoned me for an audience. It is well, for I have a pressing matter to present to her. I will not leave until I see her." A far-away look passed over his eyes and was quickly gone. He cleared his throat. "But I might as well enjoy myself while I am here. Perhaps you will join me in the baths sometime soon?"

"Yes, that would be very enjoyable," Tadaji said, smiling. He knew it would do him good to spend time with Hoturi. The younger man's easy spirit would do much to remove the darkness that seemed to choke Tadaji these days.

Hoturi smiled. With a flourish of his sky-blue robes, he turned and strode purposefully from the hall.

▲▲▲▲▲▲▲▲

The full moon shone brightly in the sky. Lion Clan Ambassador Ikoma Natsumi paused in the doorway of her chambers to enjoy its beauty. She waited. She knew it was not customary for ambassadors to hold meetings in their private chambers, especially late in the evening, but she had decided to ignore protocol. She wasn't the first ambassador to do so, nor would she be the last.

The moon slid away behind a cloud, casting the world in shadow. Natsumi sighed and went inside. A low table sat in the center of the room, flanked by two silk cushions. The tea sat waiting.

Soon Natsumi heard a soft tap on the door. She waited for her servant to allow the Unicorn ambassador inside. She heard no sound of the shoji sliding aside. Puzzled, Natsumi went to the shoji screen. When she slid back the paper door, however, nothing greeted her except dark shadows. Natsumi leaned out of the doorway. No one was there. No guest, no servant. Slowly she slid the paper door shut.

Someone grabbed her from behind. The assailant twisted her hands behind her back and clapped a gloved hand over her mouth. Someone else blindfolded her, and she felt herself being lifted by two pairs of hands.

Someone knocked loudly at the screen.

"Ikoma Natsumi!" came Tadaji's voice from the other side.

Natsumi wriggled her head free and screamed. It was a hoarse, gurgling scream, but it was enough.

The two assailants dropped the Lion ambassador just as the door burst open.

Tadaji rushed inside. He went straight to her prone form on the floor and pulled the blindfold from her eyes. "Natsumi!" What happened?"

"Two of them, they tried to kidnap me," Natsumi gasped.

Tadaji jumped up and looked around. Other than the two of them, the room was empty. There was nothing except the black silk blindfold in Tadaji's hand to suggest that anyone except Natsumi had been there.

"Ninja," Tadaji said as he helped the young ambassador to her feet. "It must have been."

"B-but," Natsumi stuttered, "but ninja d-don't exist."

Clamping his lips together grimly, Tadaji said, "These ninja did."

Tadaji guided Natsumi to one of the cushions and poured her a cup of tea. She drank it, trembling so badly that the cup shook in her hand. Tadaji meanwhile checked the balcony and secured the entrances. Satisfied the danger was done, he poured himself a cup and sat, waiting for Natsumi to calm.

Finally her breathing returned to normal and the shaking subsided. She looked at Tadaji with large, dark eyes and said, "Thank you, Ambassador. It is likely you saved my life."

"But why would anyone want you dead?" Tadaji asked.

"Because of what I know—what I suspect." Her voice dropped to a whisper. "Someone is trying to kill the emperor."

A cold knot of fear twisted in Tadaji's stomach. "Why do you say this?" he asked slowly.

"The first week I was here, I was granted an audience with Empress Kachiko," Natsumi began. "A formal welcoming, I assumed. But instead of meeting with her in the reception room, she asked me to come to her private chambers.

"As I sat waiting, I noticed a beautiful screen in one corner, painted with flowers so real they seem to bloom on the silk. When I went behind it to examine the work more closely, two men entered the room. I crouched behind the screen and stayed quiet.

"They were discussing the emperor's condition, and they spoke in strange accents. I heard one of them say, 'That's enough to kill him.' At that moment Kachiko came through the door, and they were silent. She greeted them and asked if they had seen me. They said no and left. Kachiko followed a few minutes later. Then I fled to my chambers."

The woman took a deep breath and released it slowly. "I

fear that someone Kachiko has summoned to the emperor's side is really here to kill him. I dared not speak to Kachiko, for I have no real proof."

Tadaji leaned back on his hands, trying to absorb this astounding story. If what this young ambassador suspected was true, Kachiko was in terrible danger.

"Until now, I was unsure of anything I had heard," Natsumi continued. "I had convinced myself I was wrong. But this . . ." her voice trailed off.

"Why doesn't your daimyo send you a bodyguard, or a secretary?" Tadaji asked. "That way, you will have someone with you at all times."

"I have already sent a message to the Lion stronghold," she said. "But the roads are treacherous these days. I don't expect anyone to arrive for at least a month."

Tadaji was silent, thinking. "What about another bodyguard?"

Natsumi said, "Who can I trust? I cannot tell anyone about this attack. I do not know who is behind it, and I do not have friends in court."

"You have one," Tadaji replied.

Natsumi gave the older man a trembling smile. "Domo arigato," she said, her voice breaking slightly.

"I agree that this attack should not be mentioned," Tadaji said slowly. "Not yet, anyway. In the meantime, you must have a guard until your own arrives. It will not be difficult to secure an official palace guard, and no one will question the request. Until you get one, I will send one of my own servants, Eda, to you."

Natsumi nodded. "I will make the request tomorrow."

"I must ask you," Tadaji said, "is this why you summoned me to this meeting? To confide your suspicions to me?"

Natsumi bowed her head. "Yes, it was," she replied. "I was told you were a man of honor and that you could be trusted."

"Who told you that?"

"Doji Hoturi," the woman replied. She saw Tadaji's startled look and quickly added, "Yes, it is unusual for a Crane and a Lion to have such a discussion. I met the Crane daimyo a few months ago, when the ambassadors of our two clans met in an unsuccessful attempt to discuss our situation. At first I did not trust him, for he is Crane. But as the official Lion diplomat, I was forced to receive him." She looked mildly surprised as she continued, "He told me that you were a man of honor and kindness and to seek you out if I needed help.'"

Only a novice ambassador would have breached protocol so blatantly as to speak personally with the daimyo of her clan's enemy. Instead of being shocked, though, Tadaji smiled.

"Hoturi is an honored friend," he said. "I am glad that he thinks so highly of me." Tadaji rose from the cushion and said, "I must return to my chambers. I will send Eda to you immediately. Will you be all right until then?"

Natsumi hesitated, clearly uneasy at the idea of being alone. "Yes," she said finally, also rising from the cushions. "I do not think they will return tonight."

She bowed and said, "Thank you, Ide Tadaji, for your help and your kindness."

Tadaji bowed in return. Deep in thought, he departed and made his way quickly to his rooms.

He didn't hear the soft rustle of branches near the pathway or see the dark figure that lurked in the shadows beyond the edge of the path, watching him carefully as he climbed the steps to his own rooms. The figure lingered for a few moments, watching the silhouette of the old ambassador against the low glow of the paper walls as he spoke to a servant.

Then the form crept silently into the deep shadows of the elegant palace gardens and was gone.

5   FIGHT FOR HONOR

Watch your back!"

Tetsuko wheeled Cloud Dancer. She pulled the reins with her left hand, and the bells on the horse's mane jangled. With her right hand she gripped her katana.

A clumsy blow fell on her shoulder. It glanced off her iron-banded armor with an ugly metallic clang.

Cloud Dancer pranced backward, neighing loudly.

Tetsuko turned to see a dirty, snarling horseman. He cursed at the miss and swung again, this time aiming for Tetsuko's head.

She arched backward, lying flat on Cloud Dancer's broad back. Just above her, the man's katana whipped past—a nicked and stained blade with a hilt of tattered silk. Probably stolen.

The man grunted in anger. The force of his miss made him flail wildly. His mount, unused to such motion, reared in confusion and fear.

Tetsuko flexed her thigh muscles and, with a fluid motion borne of years of practice, snapped herself upright in the saddle. She swung her katana at the man's head just as his horse came down on all fours. Her golden blade bit deep between the man's rusty helm and his mismatched armor.

He had seen the strike coming and dodged, pulling hard on the reins. The blade struck his neck but did not sever it. Blood poured from the wound and flowed down his armor. Still, the man was off balance.

Tetsuko saw her chance. With a loud "Yieeee!" she dug her heels into Cloud Dancer's side and thrust her golden katana straight into her opponent's belly. He shrieked.

The stolen horse had had enough. The whites of its eyes bulged in fear and hatred of its rider. With an ear-splitting neigh, it reared, ramming the man's head into its powerful neck and sending his battle-worn katana flying end-over-end through the air. The man bounced off the horse's neck and flew backward. He slid off Tetsuko's blade and, with a heavy thud, landed in the dust.

The horse galloped to the edge of the clearing and disappeared into the woods with a crash of brush and branches. Tetsuko watched it go. Then she turned to stare at the outlaw she had just killed.

Just a few moments before, her patrol had surprised a large band of thieves on the main road. It was a quick fight, with many injuries but few casualties. That was Tetsuko's order to her soldiers: do not strike to kill unless you must. "Our job is to bring justice," she had told her patrol, "not to administer death." Some in her patrol, especially the Battle Maiden Shinjo Shenko, didn't agree.

Tetsuko had waited anxiously for their first real encounter. Would they obey her orders? She surveyed the remains of their first skirmish. Of the twelve thieves, five were dead. Tetsuko counted seven others, wounded but alive, either bound or unconscious. None of her soldiers were dead. Clearly her orders carried some weight. The thought filled Tetsuko with relief and pride.

A woman in bloodstained armor rode up to Tetsuko. The woman had a smear of red on her cheek, and one shoulder strap had flapped free, but she managed a smile as her horse and Cloud Dancer nuzzled in greeting.

"Thank you, Shenko, for the warning," Tetsuko said.

"I was too far away to help, Tetsuko-sama," Shenko replied. "Please forgive me." She bowed, and then motioned her head toward one of the thieves, who was kneeling in the clearing, holding his head in his hands and moaning loudly. Nearby, a Unicorn shugenja named Moto Hakuro pled with the Fortunes to heal one of the wounded men, who were tied feet-to-ankles in a line on the ground.

Shenko eyed Tetsuko quizzically. There came an awkward silence. Tetsuko realized with a start that Shenko was waiting to receive orders. Tetsuko swallowed hard and looked across the clearing, giving herself time to think. What would Jikkyo do? a voice in her head asked frantically. Then another, stronger voice replied, No, what will *you* do?

Tetsuko took a deep breath and said, "I need to know the status of the injuries, on both sides, horses and humans."

With a quick nod, Shenko turned her mount and headed for a large tree at the edge of the clearing. There, the remaining patrol members—Utaku Eri, Iuchi Kaori, and Ide Umio—had gathered with their prisoners. Tetsuko dismounted and knelt beside the dead man, careful not to touch the body.

His kimono, now bloodstained and filthy, was made of plain green silk with no mon or pattern embroidered into it. No help there. Clearly he had been the leader, or at least the highest-ranking member of the group. His katana was the blade of a samurai, but Tetsuko had no way of knowing whether he had stolen it or it had always belonged to him.

Sighing, Tetsuko rose and went to the group. By this time the thief with the headache had been deftly bound, and all surviving members of the group sat nearby, glaring at their Unicorn captors.

Shenko strode up to Tetsuko and bowed. "None of our patrol were killed," she said. "Hakuro supplicated the Fortunes to heal three of us, including Kaori, who has a broken arm."

She motioned to a woman who sat on a large stone nearby. She had her right arm in a makeshift sling. "I am sorry to have weakened the group with my injury," she said slowly. "I fear I will be a burden to you now."

"Nonsense," Tetsuko replied. "Hakuro is favored of the Fortunes, and you will be fine in a few days' time." She glanced sideways at her shugenja, and then added, "That is, if he does not dip too often into the sake rations."

Hakuro, an indignant look on his face, replied, "The Fortunes smile upon me when I've a bellyful of sake!" he said, smiling.

They all laughed, and Tetsuko could see young Kaori visibly relax. This was her first assignment, and Tetsuko knew exactly how she felt—trying hard to please and being devastated when something went wrong. Tetsuko understood the power that a compassionate leader could have over others. She smiled inwardly as her mind went to Jikkyo for the hundredth time that day.

"Now, continue with your report, Shenko," Tetsuko said. "What of these despicable thieves?"

"Four died during the battle," the Battle Maiden said, "and one other as Hakuro supplicated for his healing. Six survived, hurting but alive."

"They are definitely the group that has been attacking the villages around here," Umio said, pointing to a nearby tree. Beneath it lay opened sacks and a good-size pile of silver cups, small household statues, and other valuable objects. It was clear the patrol had done a thorough search. "The objects were found in the horses' packs."

"Domo arigato," Tetsuko said, smiling at the young man. He bowed in return.

"Who are these thieves?" Eri asked, eyeing the bound captives.

"Let us see if we can find out," Tetsuko replied.

She squatted down beside one of the thieves. His long, gray hair hung in greasy strands from his balding head, and his thin, wispy beard was matted with dirt. He wore a filthy kimono, and his armor had made jagged holes in the once-elegant fabric. His watery, bloodshot eyes glared at her.

"Sumimasen," she greeted formally, a hint of sarcasm in her voice. "Excuse my intrusion. I am Utaku Tetsuko, Battle Maiden of the Unicorn Clan and leader of this patrol. Who are you?"

"Do not speak to me, you filthy gaijin," he spat through cracked lips.

His breath almost knocked Tetsuko over. Her eyes narrowed. "So that is how it is going to be, eh?"

The old man's face twisted in anger, but he said nothing. Tetsuko looked at the other thieves. Now that the battle was over, none of them seemed very threatening. Tetsuko could tell from their sallow skin and hollow cheeks that it had been a while since they had eaten. None of them would look at her.

Tetsuko stood up and spoke to them all. "Your actions

disgust me. You are cowards who prey on the weak and sick. But we are not here to kill you or to pass judgment on you. If you will not tell me who you are, that is your choice. The villagers whom you attacked two days ago will not need to know your names when I return you to them.

"But if you will not talk, perhaps your companions will," Tetsuko said. "Eri, Umio, see to it that these thieves thoroughly search the bodies of their former companions."

The old thief said, "We will not do it."

In a flash, Tetsuko whipped out her katana and pressed it against the man's throat. "Then you will join him," she hissed. "Make your choice."

The man glared at her, his eyes filled with hate and disgust. Then he bowed his head in defeat. One of the other thieves frowned at the thought of touching a dead body, but Tetsuko ignored it. "Watch them carefully," she said to Eri and Umio. "If they find anything, take it."

Tetsuko turned to the rest of the patrol. "Round up the stolen horses," she instructed, "and load as much as you can onto them." She looked up, shielding her eyes against the sun. It was midmorning, and the sky was clear and blue. "We will need to travel fast, for it will take us the rest of the day to get to the nearest Unicorn village. I want to be there before dark."

"What about the bodies?" Shenko asked.

"We will have to take them with us."

Looks of disgust and horror crossed everyone's faces. Tetsuko continued, "The thieves refuse to tell us who they or their dead companions are. We cannot bury them properly or perform the appropriate rituals."

Tetsuko's eyes fell on each patrol member in turn, and one by one they nodded in agreement. "Now, let's get started," Tetsuko said. "We don't have much time."

▲▲▲▲▲▲▲▲

As late-afternoon shadows deepened into twilight, the warriors rode in silence. They were stunned and depressed at the sights that had greeted them that day.

The first village they had come upon was abandoned. The two bloated, plague-ravaged bodies in the tiny town square were enough to explain why.

The second village had been worse. The plague had swept through it with breathtaking fury. Children lay dead in the dust. Dead farmers littered the fields. Some of the buildings had been set afire and were little more than smoldering ruins of blackened bamboo. Tetsuko couldn't tell if the fires had been set by the doomed villagers or by ransacking thieves. It did not matter. Everyone was still dead.

They had left these death villages quickly, and Tetsuko had no choice but to keep the patrol moving. They were in unfamiliar territory, but Hakuro assured her there were more villages ahead.

They rode on. Twilight moved into darkness. A few stars peeked from wispy clouds in the sky above. The narrow, muddy path had widened into a road. Patches of small white pebbles peeked here and there between the weeds, hinting at the road's former elegance. A shrine to some forgotten deity lay broken beside the road, its head lost among the weeds.

As the group rounded a bend, they saw the walls of a good-size village. The gates had been made from tree trunks hewn in half lengthwise and lashed together with sturdy rope. The walls were made of entire logs, at least a foot thick, lashed together with an intricate web of ropes and knots. Every log had been sharpened to a fine point at the top. Embedded in the edges of each point were dozens of finely made blades.

The group approached the gate. At Tetsuko's signal, the patrol halted. She rode ahead.

Cloud Dancer's bells jingled softly as the great horse trotted forward, and the sound calmed Tetsuko's racing mind. Although she had been outwardly calm all afternoon, inwardly she was overwhelmed with panic and dread. Her warriors looked to her for guidance. Their lives were in her hands. Yes, they had survived today's skirmish and a few previous ones, but that was in the past. Now came the true test: would the villagers who huddled in fear behind these heavy walls trust her, a Unicorn? Would they welcome her patrol? It was just as likely they would refuse the Unicorns' help. It was even possible that they would attack the patrol, no questions asked.

Tetsuko rode to the foot of the gate and reined Cloud Dancer to a stop. Tall torches on either side of the gate cast a smoky glow that did little to cut the darkness. Tetsuko shifted in the saddle, hearing the familiar sound of creaking leather. She waited.

She didn't have to wait long. From behind the wall came the sound of footsteps. Someone held a lantern up over the top of the wall. At the same moment, four archers in full armor popped up, and she heard the unmistakable sound of arrows being drawn back. The curved bows were aimed directly for Tetsuko. The archers' faces were covered with simple black masks.

Tetsuko's heart sank. She heard soft gasps coming from behind her. By Shinjo! She had had no idea that the patrol had wandered this far into what had once been Scorpion lands. She cursed herself for this blunder. As leader, she should have known, but it was too late now. Tetsuko straightened her back, looked directly at the bowmen, and rested her hand lightly on the hilt of her katana.

"Who goes there?" A voice shouted from behind the ramparts. The bowmen didn't move, their weapons still trained on Tetsuko.

"I am Utaku Tetsuko, Battle Maiden of the Unicorn Clan and leader of this patrol," Tetsuko said in her loudest, most commanding tone. "We have captured some criminals that have been attacking nearby villages." She hoped distance kept them from hearing the slight tremble in her voice.

Instantly, the lantern disappeared, leaving the smoky torches as the only light. The archers held steady. Cloud Dancer, sensing the tension, neighed softly. Tetsuko petted her neck reassuringly, keeping her hand in plain view.

"These were once Scorpion lands, Battle Maiden," a new voice said. It was rich and deep, but the tone was edged with anger and . . . something else. Fear, perhaps? "They are every bit as dangerous as once they were. Unicorns are not welcome here."

"These are indeed grim times," Tetsuko responded. "There is danger in every bend of the road. The Emperor himself has sent Unicorn patrols such as this one throughout the borderlands to roust out bandits who prey on those too weak to defend themselves."

"How dare you suggest that Scorpions are weak!" the voice thundered.

Damn! Tetsuko cursed under her breath. "You misunderstand me," she replied evenly, trying to sound commanding and apologetic at the same time. "It is clear your village is strong and well protected, but many smaller villages have been destroyed by these bandits."

Tetsuko straightened her shoulders and slowly lifted her hands, palms up. "We fought this group of thieves near here this morning. We brought them to two other villages, but they had been destroyed. I suspect these thieves have attacked you as well. It is for you, not me, to hand justice to these men."

Tetsuko sighed inwardly. "I have five wounded, tired, and hungry soldiers, and I ask for shelter and food for the night for them and myself. If this is too much to request from a Scorpion, I will gladly leave my captives and the bodies of their companions in the dust at your gate and move on." Tetsuko dropped her hands and held her breath.

For a long moment everything was quiet. Even the crickets had stopped chirping, and the wind was still. Then the huge, heavy wooden gates slowly swung open. Beyond, Tetsuko saw a village square surrounded by low buildings.

The last thing she wanted to deal with tonight was a Scorpion test of trust. Shinjo only knew what secret treachery was in store for them behind the wooden gate, but Tetsuko had no choice. She motioned for the group to follow her. With a quick press of her heels into Cloud Dancer's side, she passed through the gate and into the village.

The village square was covered with sandy gravel, and a small, neatly tended rock garden marked the center. Tall trees here and there were strung with lanterns, which gave off a weak light. Modest homes lined the square on either side. A small temple stood at one end of the square. It too was modestly constructed, with two carved wooden doors and a simple porch that wrapped around the front.

Before the temple stood a man, his feet slightly apart in a relaxed warrior's stance. He was of medium height, and his hair was arranged in a samurai's topknot. His simple kimono fit him well, and his obi was tied carefully around a wide but not yet pudgy waist. His Scorpion mask completely covered his face except for his mouth, which curled in a snarl. He rested his hand on the hilt of his sheathed katana, which was slung low on his hips. He had an air of icy authority about him as he watched the young Battle Maiden approach on her magnificent steed.

The man was flanked on each side by two warriors, dressed in the same simple kimonos. They too stood with feet apart, casual but ready. Tetsuko could feel dozens of eyes watching from the shadows around. Every last face would wear the mask of the Scorpion Clan.

Tetsuko reined in Cloud Dancer and dismounted. She strode purposefully to the group and bowed low to the leader. "I am Utaku Tetsuko, Battle Maiden of the Unicorn Clan," she said simply. She was in his territory now, and she knew that this game was all his.

The man silently watched her and said nothing at first. Then he spoke. "I am Shosuro Gonshiro, Scorpion Clan karo. This is my village, and all who live here are under my protection."

He pointed to her patrol. "Who are they?" he asked.

"They are my soldiers, and they are under *my* protection," she replied. "We have been in the wilderness for almost a month, chasing the thieves that we fought this morning." With that, Tetsuko motioned to two of the patrol members, Eri and Umio. They dismounted and led the prisoners forward.

Without a word, Gonshiro strode past Tetsuko and peered closely at the first prisoner, the greasy-haired old man. Without taking his eyes from him, Gonshiro motioned to one of his guards, who disappeared. Almost immediately he returned escorting a bent, elderly woman.

The old woman shuffled painfully to Gonshiro and followed his gaze to the prisoner's face. Her thin, gray eyebrows raised in recognition, and she slowly nodded. She said something to Gonshiro, and then the guard carefully led her away.

Without warning Gonshiro yanked the man off the horse and threw him to the ground.

"Filthy criminals," he spat as the bound man lay in the gravel, unmoving. He turned to Tetsuko and said, "This is one of the men who burned Lea's farm, a few miles beyond the village walls. Her husband, an honorable man, died in the flames."

Gonshiro searched the faces of the criminals who slumped on the backs of the horses. "But there were others, and a leader who commanded them to steal the rice and to burn the house. I do not see them here." His eyes narrowed in suspicion and contempt. "Did you let them get away?"

Tetsuko stifled the urge to spit a retort at the arrogant man. Instead, she motioned behind her, never taking her eyes from Gonshiro's face. Eri led two horses forward, their backs laden with large bundles. She pushed the bundles with the end of her katana, and they slid to the ground.

"There are the rest of your criminals," Tetsuko said grimly.

Gasps came from the buildings beyond the square at Tetsuko's pronouncement.

Gonshiro looked at her, and then barked a command. Immediately a bent old man emerged from behind a building and quickly untied the ropes around the bundle. The stench of death exploded from the sack and the samurai recoiled, his hand over his nose. He turned to the eta and said, "Search the bodies and bring anything you find to me."

"They have already been thoroughly searched," Tetsuko said, annoyed, as the man set to work. "Your people will be able to recover any of the things that were stolen from them."

"So, it is true that Unicorns soil themselves with the unclean dead," Gonshiro mused with a sneer. "I am not surprised."

Then his face twisted in anger. "Lea's husband's life was

stolen from him," Gonshiro thundered. "Her home, her food, even her clothing. She will never get these things back—not even from an unclean Unicorn who rides with dead bodies!"

Something inside Tetsuko snapped. She stepped forward, stood toe to toe with the Scorpion samurai, and looked him straight in the eye. He was slightly taller than she, and even the mask could not hide the deep lines of his face. Tetsuko realized with a start that he was an old man.

"I did not come here to be insulted by a truth-twisting Scorpion, and I did not ride all day with these stinking bodies for pleasure," she began in a low growl. "I am truly sorry for the horrors these men caused your village, but do not blame me or anyone else for your misfortunes. We have ridden for days to protect your ungrateful people, and I, for one, am beginning to regret it."

Behind her she heard the sound of riders dismounting and katanas being pulled from their sheaths.

"Get out of my face, Unicorn," Gonshiro whispered, "or I will slice you in half where you stand."

A shout came from behind. Tetsuko jumped back and drew her katana with one fluid motion, fully expecting an all-out attack. Instead, she saw the eta waving something in his hand. In a moment he was at Gonshiro's side, handing him a crumpled piece of fabric. Gonshiro slowly unfolded it. It was a mask, bloodstained and stiff.

"Scorpion," he breathed. "You killed a Scorpion samurai, and then dragged his decaying body through the countryside instead of giving him a honorable burial? How dare you, you barbarian filth!" He trembled with anger as the words spit from his mouth.

Still eye to eye with the old samurai, she said, "There were no masks on any of the outlaws."

"Liar," Gonshiro replied, hefting his katana and pointing it at Tetsuko's chest. She didn't flinch. Without taking his eyes from her, he said loudly, "Eta, where did you find this?"

"On the leader," came the timid reply. "It was hidden in the folds of his obi."

"See, Unicorn?" Gonshiro asked, raising the point of his katana to Tetsuko's throat. "Scorpions wear their masks at all times. You fought him, you killed him, and you hid the evidence."

"You have been in this isolated village too long, Scorpion," Tetsuko replied, anger trembling in her voice, "making up stories to amuse yourself. You are nothing but a forgotten coward, left here to rot by your treacherous brothers."

In a flash, the Unicorns were surrounded. Villagers wielding hoes and pitchforks stood shoulder to shoulder with soldiers holding katanas, all pointing at Tetsuko's ragtag, exhausted group.

Gonshiro froze in place. His blade did not waver in the air. The square fell silent. No one moved. Then the proud man slowly lowered his blade and stood straight.

"I will kill you, Battle Maiden," he said. "But not tonight." He took a step back from her and spoke to the assembled crowd. "Barbarian Unicorns are not fit to live. They kill Scorpion samurai as they kill animals and eat their flesh. They bring the dead to our doorstep, hoping that their tormented souls will stay here."

Gonshiro paused, and then continued in the silent hush of the square. "But this particular Unicorn killed those who attacked us and gave our people the chance to see justice served. I cannot ignore that, no matter how much she disgusts me. So I will make an offer. I will fight you alone, Battle Maiden, in two day's time. Fairly. To the death."

"If I refuse?" Tetsuko replied.

"Then we will kill you all, here and now, and burn your bodies to ash so that all of Rokugan can forget that you ever walked the world," he said simply.

Tetsuko had no choice. "You will allow me and my troops rest and food," she stated. "Our horses will be cared for properly. And if I lose," she said finally, "my patrol will be allowed to go on its way unmolested."

"You are in no position to bargain, Unicorn," Gonshiro said, enjoying the power he held over this Battle Maiden, "but your requests are fair. I agree.

"You are not prisoners, but honored guests, and will be treated as such as long as you do not leave the village," Gonshiro said, smiling a little at Tetsuko's fury. "Guests who will be closely guarded, that is." With that, the older man disappeared into the crowd and was gone.

6 BROKEN SUNLIGHT

A warm breeze wafted past Tadaji as he strolled slowly in the palace gardens, his eyes downcast and thoughtful. He had hoped to see some early morning songbirds with their bright colors and cheerful notes, but they had already fled the heat of the sun. Far away, the rough caw of a crow split the air and echoed into silence.

Anyone who might have wandered past Tadaji that morning would have seen a calm Unicorn. But inside, the old ambassador was alert and tense. His face was pale and drawn, and he had dark circles under his eyes.

A tiny bead of sweat trickled uncomfortably down Tadaji's neck as he reached a path that was blocked by a fallen log. Beyond it, the stone pathway ended in a pile of broken rubble surrounded by charred weeds and the stubble of thin, blackened trees. The burnt garden was quiet now, except for the occasional rustle of the leaves in the wind high above Tadaji's head. He imagined fire gutting the once-elegant garden, flames licking the trees, brush crackling in the rising heat, screams of animals as they fled. For a moment Tadaji saw the image of a huge, fiery drum in the center of the destroyed garden. He shook the vision away.

Centuries ago, the palace's lands had been crafted into a series of unique gardens interconnected by miles of meandering paths. Each path was as individual as a person, with its own look and personality. One was made of perfectly circular flagstones set a footstep apart. Another was a plank path that rose over a wetland garden of floating lilies and water grasses. Still another was constructed to look like a rushing stream, with flat, shiny stones that seemed to bubble through the landscape.

Tadaji's favorite path, however, was the one that he traveled today. It had been constructed of jagged stone fragments set at odd angles and unequal distances. Tadaji appreciated it because it was unexpectedly beautiful; the stones themselves were ugly, but together they formed something serene. The path reminded him of himself. Though some had considered him ugly and worthless, others had been able to see the beauty behind his own strange angles and unequal distances. They had helped build him into something unique, as some soul did long ago with a discarded pile of broken stones.

Tadaji's mind went back to the last time he had walked this path. It had been just a few months after the chaos of the coup, almost two years ago now, when he had summoned his son, Ide Tamura, to the palace. One warm evening, father and son had escaped the stifling confines of palace politics and strolled along the path.

▲▲▲▲▲▲▲▲

"Father, I have something to discuss with you," Tamura began as soon as they were out of earshot of the palace.

"And I you, my son," Tadaji replied. They seated themselves on a low stone bench near a bend in the path. Tadaji closed his eyes and breathed deeply, inhaling the sweet fragrance of the garden.

"You have been unhappy these last few months," Tadaji said. "I know how hard it must be for you to be assigned as permanent guard to the Shiro Utaku Shojo stronghold while other troops are sent abroad. Your letters speak of your fears and frustrations."

"There were times when I felt I would go mad," Tamura admitted. "But it is my duty." He straightened his shoulders with pride, and Tadaji felt his own pride in his tall, honorable son. He reached over and took Tamura's tough, war-callused hands in his own soft, well-manicured ones. Both grips were strong.

Tadaji smiled and said, "When you were a boy, you constantly begged me for the ancient stories of our clan's adventures in the wilderness. You have always longed to see the world, so I have arranged for you to be assigned to oversee the guard troops for a Racing Winds caravan."

"You did what?" Tamura exclaimed, jerking his hands from his father's grasp and jumping up, almost knocking Tadaji backward off the stone bench.

"It took months of negotiating and not a few koku's worth of geisha and sake to arrange this for you," Tadaji said with a note of impatience as he quickly checked his balance. "Do you have any idea how drunk a Unicorn military leader must get to agree to anything—especially letting go of one of the army's most trusted cavalrymen?"

Tamura stared down at Tadaji, trembling. His face twisted in anger. Then the younger man's expression slowly softened, and he sat down again beside his father.

Tamura said simply, "I am in love."

For once, Tadaji was stunned into silence. In a rush Tamura continued. "She is beautiful, Father, with silky hair that cascades down her back like water. Her eyes are like jewels, and her smile! My heart feels as light as a rice paper bird when she smiles at me. She is smart, and tender, and her touch sends cold lightning through me. She is strong too, and she rides like the wind."

As Tamura spoke, Tadaji's mind went far back into the past, to a sunny spring day when a young, crippled man glimpsed a beautiful young maiden in the gardens of the Dragon monastery where he lived. Yes, he remembered what love felt like.

When Tamura stopped to take a breath, Tadaji broke in and said, "I am truly glad you have found love," Tadaji said. "Does she share your feelings?"

"Yes, Father, I am sure of it," Tamura replied without hesitation.

"Well, then," the older man said, "it is good that she loves you too. It will make the wait easier while you are gone."

Anger flickered across Tamura's face. "Father, I cannot leave her," he said.

"Bah," Tadaji said, dismissing the comment with a wave of his hand. "Of course you can. You will be gone only a few months. She can do without you for that long."

"There is a complication," Tamura began, looking away.

"No complications!" Tadaji bellowed, slapping his hand on the cold stone bench. Tamura's eyes widened with surprise at his father's unexpected outburst.

"The Ide family has always served the clan and the empire," Tadaji continued more quietly. His voice was smooth, but there was anger beneath his words. "I have served in the Imperial Palace since I returned from the Dragon lands, sent away in disgrace because my twisted foot was an embarrassment to my family. I found my path, and I have traveled it well. I had no guidance from my father. He was ashamed of me. It was difficult, very difficult. Each day of my life I thank Shinjo that Iuchi Daiyu took an interest in me. If it hadn't been for him, I would have died of despair long ago.

"All my life I was told that no woman would want me," he continued. "I was blessed again when your mother, Doji Chisato, saw past my deformity and loved me for who I was. She was patient while I learned how to battle through the politics of court, using my wits and my voice to make words that calmed anger and smoothed bruised egos.

"You were the greatest gift that she ever gave me. I vowed that I would do whatever I could to make your life what you wanted it to be—"

"But Father—" Tamura interrupted.

Tadaji cut him off. "I have worked very hard to make this assignment happen," Tadaji said with a frown. "You have the battle skills that are needed to command the guards. Your quick wit and smooth tongue will enable you to talk through problems before they lead to bloodshed.

"I had to call in many favors to get this for you. It is a remarkable chance to show your talents. When you have successfully completed the assignment, you can marry your love and live in comfort until the end of your days."

For a long moment, neither man spoke. Then Tamura slowly rose to his feet and said softly, "I love you, Father, and I respect all that you have done." His voice grew stronger and more confident. "But all my life you have made it easy for me. You helped me get into the bushi school. You negotiated my position with the Unicorn cavalry. Now you have constructed my path again. You know nothing of my life, and I won't have you continue to build it for me."

The shock of Tamura's refusal stunned Tadaji. For a moment, no words escaped him. Then his eyes narrowed. "The caravan is set to travel the entire length of Rokugan," he said. "You will visit places that you have never seen, experience things that you may have the chance to again—especially if you wed."

For a brief second, the anger in Tamura's eyes was replaced by a fleeting moment of excitement. Tadaji knew that look. He had seen it every time the boy had listened to the Unicorn stories, his mind far away, dreaming of adventure.

Tadaji rose and leaned on his cane. "I hope you will willingly agree to do this. If you do not, you will be defying both your clan and Shinjo Yokatsu, who agreed to this."

Then his eyes softened. "Tamura-maru, if she loves you, she will wait, and when you return we will celebrate your wedding with joy."

For a moment Tamura wavered. Longing, anger, frustration, and sadness crossed his face in waves so clear that Tadaji could see each emotion as it passed. Then a look of calm descended upon the young man's face and stayed there.

"No," he said simply. "I refuse."

Tadaji's chin dropped to his chest, and he closed his eyes. Then he slowly raised his head and looked his son straight in the eye.

"If you do not report to the stables in two days, you will be arrested for refusing a commission," Tadaji said.

"You cannot do that to me!" Tamura yelled. He lifted his arm to strike his father, but Tadaji stood straight, his eyes still boring into Tamura. The young man's arm trembled like a willow branch in a storm, all muscles tensed. Then with a growl, Tamura abruptly dropped his arm to his side and hissed, "We shall see, old man." With that he turned on his heel and stalked away, leaving Tadaji standing alone, in the dark, on the broken-stone pathway.

▲▲▲▲▲▲▲▲

Someone approached from behind.

Tadaji startled out of his reverie. He wiped a tear from his cheek and turned around, sliding his hand between the folds of his obi to grasp the hilt of his tanto.

Hoturi appeared around the bend. When he noticed Tadaji, the younger man looked up, surprised.

"Ah, Tadaji!" he said, smiling. "I did not expect to see you here this morning."

"I walk here sometimes, when the weather is pleasant," Tadaji replied.

Hoturi motioned toward a stone bench beside the path, and Tadaji nodded. Slowly the two men sat.

"You seem unwell, my friend," Hoturi began, genuinely concerned. "Your eyes have the look of someone who has not slept in many days."

Tadaji looked away, fearful to confess his dreams to his friend but longing to unburden his mind. Finally he said, "My dreams are troubled, Hoturi. I cannot escape my grief, even in sleep. Tamura comes to me in dreams of fire and pain. I cannot help him."

Hoturi looked at his friend, whose sorrow was plain on his face. "You are a strong, honorable man, as was Tamura," Hoturi said. "He loved you and honored you beyond all others. I cannot believe he would harm you, even in dreams. I am honored you trust me with your confidence."

"Domo, Hoturi," Tadaji said with relief in his voice. "It is good to speak of it with a friend."

They were silent for a few minutes, each enjoying the quiet of the garden. A dragonfly buzzed past on some urgent errand. Finally Tadaji cleared his throat and said, "I am surprised you are still here, Hoturi. I would have expected you to deliver your message and be on your way."

"Her gracious lady has yet to grant me an audience," Hoturi said. "I hope she decides to see me soon. Grave business requires my attention elsewhere."

"I had heard that a Lion Clan army was headed to Crane lands," Tadaji said. "Is that what brought you here, my friend?"

Hoturi smiled grimly and shifted on the hard stone bench to face the older man. "Partially. When the Lions first sent their armies toward Crane lands, we were prepared. It is not news that the Crane and the Lion continue to fight. I came here to speak to the emperor about this thunder on our horizon.

"That was my mistake," he continued, tapping his fingers on the stone bench. "A day after I began my journey here, Matsu Hametsu and his Lion army pushed toward Kyuden Kakita. The Crane defenders had fought well, but they were outnumbered, and the plague had broken out again. We had sent a message to the Phoenix Clan weeks before, telling them of the Lion threat, but had heard no reply. Then as the Lion attacked us, Shiba Tsukune and a small army of Phoenix warriors and shugenja appeared to aid us. The battle was quick and bloody, and the Lions were soundly routed."

"So the Phoenix have allied with the Cranes," Tadaji said. "This is wonderful for your clan." Tadaji peered closely at his friend. "So why do you still seem disturbed?" he asked in a concerned voice, seeing that worry still lined the young man's face.

Hoturi sighed. "It will take more than this alliance to save my clan from destruction, I fear.

"The Cranes are greatly weakened," he said. "Many samurai are dead from the plague. Villages have been destroyed by plague and bandits. Kyuden Kakita is guarded by a small force, less than a third of what is needed to protect it from attack. No one outside the Cranes knows this. If more Lions march, we will be destroyed."

He straightened his shoulders and continued. "I came here hoping to convince the emperor to help the Cranes in the battles to come. I fear that if the palace does not support us, we will surely fall."

"It is not the Emperor but Kachiko you must deal with," Tadaji stated matter-of-factly.

"Yes," Hoturi said. After a moment, Hoturi roused himself from his musings. "She is the one I must speak to, and she has kept me waiting long enough. I am anxious to return to Kyuden Kakita."

Tadaji rested his gnarled hands on the tip of his cane, thinking. Finally he said, "Since the Unicorns returned to Rokugan two hundred years ago, we have often had to stand alone against all that has been thrown at us. We have learned to take care of ourselves. In that learning we have come to realize something else: the value of a trusted friend."

Hoturi stared into the distance as Tadaji continued. "A darkness is coming. It will be worse than the coup, worse even than the plague in its most horrible days. Of all the clans of the empire, the Unicorns know the fear and desperation of standing alone in a fight.

"You are a Doji, as was my beloved wife. You are an honorable warrior and a trusted friend. Seek an alliance with the Unicorn Clan, Hoturi. I can speak to Shinjo Yokatsu. He will agree to a meeting if I request it."

Hoturi leaned back, the worried expression on his face unchanged. "An alliance with the Unicorns," he said carefully, but Tadaji could see a glint of hope in his eye. "Our families have been allies for generations," he continued, "and I can think of no other clan I would rather trust at my side in these uncertain times."

Footsteps tread heavily toward them. Hoturi sprang to his feet, hand ready at the hilt of his katana. Tadaji stood more slowly, leaning on his cane.

The empress's bodyguard Aramoro came into view. Tadaji's eyes narrowed suspiciously at the towering yojimbo, who ignored the older man and strode to Hoturi.

Bowing low, Aramoro said, "Honorable Doji Hoturi, the emperor, through Empress Kachiko, requests that you do him honor by attending her in the royal chambers in one hour."

"Domo arigato. Please tell the lady that it is I who will be honored to appear at her request," Hoturi replied formally, nodding in return. "I will arrive at the appointed time."

Without another word, Aramoro bowed again and left.

Hoturi and Tadaji exchanged glances. Hoturi let out a short, humorless laugh.

"I see that the great lady has finally found a moment to

see me," he said sarcastically. "I hope she will listen to me as well."

A nagging feeling of discomfort tugged at Tadaji, and he said, "Watch yourself, my friend. Kachiko is acting strangely these days, and few have seen her."

"I will be careful," Hoturi said. "But I must leave you now. I want to visit the baths before my grand appearance. Would you like to join me?"

"Thank you, but no," Tadaji replied. "I would like to enjoy the gardens for a while longer before I return indoors." Humor danced in Tadaji's eyes as he shifted onto his good foot. "Besides," he said, "I do not have a beautiful lady to bathe for today."

Hoturi laughed aloud at the joke, and Tadaji's face broke into a relaxed grin. Tadaji's sense of humor rarely surfaced these days, and Hoturi seemed glad to see it.

Despite their age difference, Hoturi and Tadaji had always shared a deep friendship. When Hoturi was twelve and his mother died, he had been inconsolable. Tadaji's kind words and strong will helped the grieving Hoturi cope with his loss. Hoturi had been delighted when Tadaji had married his mother's cousin, Doji Chisato, and Hoturi had seen Tadaji's joy when his only child, Tamura, was born.

When Tadaji was overwhelmed with grief at the death of his beloved Chisato, it was Hoturi who had been the greatest comfort to Tadaji in his pain. Their friendship had been forged in loss, and each man trusted the other without question. Even the coup and the recent troubled times could not break the bond of friendship they shared.

The two men bowed formally to one another. "Someday, I will send Kakita Toshimoko to Shiro Shinjo," Hoturi said. "He is a good man, and a fine samurai. He has a great respect for the Unicorn as well. He has a story of a horseback duel with a young Unicorn Battle Maiden that will make you laugh until you cry."

Tadaji chuckled. "You must also tell me how it goes with Kachiko. Perhaps we will meet for sake and a game of Go after your meeting?"

"I look forward to it with pleasure. Until then, my friend," Hoturi said, bowing once again. Then the strong daimyo, full of the promise of a long life, turned and disappeared down the pathway.

Tadaji watched him go, the smile still on his face.

The sound of drums came from somewhere far away. Tadaji's rational mind told him they were merely the drumbeats of palace musicians practicing on the grounds. But fear suddenly overwhelmed him.

As the drums continued, Tadaji thought of Tamura. He had forced his son to travel with the caravan. It had ultimately been his death sentence. Tadaji's grieving mind filled with confusing emotions. They turned to colors, which danced and throbbed in front of his face. He tried to touch them, but as he reached out his hand, they laughed and pulled away.

Then the colors formed a recognizable shape. Tadaji saw Hoturi before him once again, pulsing with light. Hoturi reached forward, in his one hand a katana and in his other a small red object.

It was a statue of a horse, and it glowed with a crimson light that nauseated Tadaji. The sickness in his belly grew, and bile rose in his throat. The drumbeats intensified, pounding behind Tadaji's eyes in a throbbing, steady rhythm. Then the object split with a silent burst. Tadaji cried out and was immediately, violently ill.

When he finally straightened, he wiped his mouth on the sleeve of his kimono and looked up. The drumbeats had stopped. There was nothing before him except the calm garden. A gentle wind whispered past his face. He stood and let the breeze fan him.

A voice came to him on the wind. A voice he recognized. His heart stopped cold.

"Only you, Father . . . can save him. . . ." the voice said with a sigh. "Only you. . . ."

7

HONOR AT SWORDPOINT

The evening lamps were lit when Tetsuko descended the wooden steps of the inn and made her way through the village square. The twilight was cool and crisp, and she welcomed the chance to clear her thoughts and think about what lay ahead.

True to his word, Gonshiro had made sure that the Unicorns were not treated as prisoners, allowing them to wander the village freely but under the watchful eye of his personal guards. Tetsuko glanced around the square. Yes, there was one guard, sitting casually in the open-air sake bar on the corner. He watched her as she strode down the narrow, deserted market street, but he made no move to stop her.

Even though the village wall gave the impression that the town was large and prosperous, in reality it was quite small. Four streets radiated from the square, each lined with neatly kept houses and communal buildings. Tetsuko walked the market street, with small, shuttered booths on either side. Her destination lay at the end of the road.

The house was set apart from the rest of the village buildings. In front of the house was a simple garden of five large rocks surrounded by coarse sand. The sand was raked into intricate swirls and curves. A thin pathway led to the steps of the porch, and small lanterns lined the path to light the way.

Tetsuko's knock was answered by a pretty young girl, barely old enough to be called a woman. She wore a simple servant's kimono and a plain black mask. As she bade her enter, Tetsuko saw that the house was one large room that could be divided into smaller chambers by rice paper screens. There were no screens up now, and the room was large and airy. The floor was made of bamboo slats smoothed and waxed to a clean shine. The walls were unadorned, and there were no works of art or decoration to be seen anywhere. Tetsuko thought that odd, considering Gonshiro was the leader of the village and quite possibly the ranking samurai in the area.

The servant led Tetsuko to a small deck that overlooked another rock garden. In the center, a small fountain bubbled in a good-sized pool. Raked pebbles of the garden, followed the contours of the pool, reminding Tetsuko of the ripples from a rock tossed into still water.

Gonshiro sat cross-legged on a large cushion near the edge of the deck. His back was to Tetsuko. He wore his hair loose about his shoulders, its whiteness stark against the dark green of his kimono. His katana was lying neatly beside him, its shiny lacquered sheath glinting in the lantern light.

With a timid bow, the girl left.

Tetsuko's instincts told her to be wary in the presence of this Scorpion, so she stood still, waiting.

"Come, sit with me," Gonshiro said without turning around. He beckoned to the space beside him. There was another cushion placed near his. Between them sat a low table laid with a delicate porcelain beaker and two sake cups.

"How did you know I was coming?" she asked, no surprise in her voice. "I told no one, not even my companions."

"It is the evening before a battle you do not want to fight," he said simply. "You have never been challenged to a duel to the death. Your enemy is an unknown samurai who has shown you enough respect that you think you might be able to reason with him. I would try to talk to him if I were you, young Unicorn samurai-ko."

"I do not trust you, Scorpion," she said, her eyes narrowing in response to Gonshiro's accurate guesses.

"Ah, it is well that you do not trust me," Gonshiro replied. "You should not trust anyone else, either. For everyone lies." He waved impatiently toward the empty cushion. "I do not have all night, little Unicorn," he continued wearily. "If you have come to talk, please do so and be done."

Tetsuko bristled. "I am Utaku Tetsuko, Unicorn Battle Maiden," she replied with a steel edge to her voice, "not 'little' to anyone. If we are to talk, you will honor me with the respect that I have shown you since we arrived here."

Gonshiro said nothing. Tetsuko could hear the sound of flowing water in the silence. Just as she was about to turn on her heel and leave, he said softly, "My apologies, Battle Maiden. Will you sit with me?"

She paused a moment longer, and then approached Gonshiro and lowered herself onto the empty cushion. He glanced briefly at her as she sat, making note of the heavy leather boots she wore beneath her simple purple kimono. Tetsuko noticed that the mask he now wore matched the deep green of his kimono.

Gonshiro poured two cups of sake. "Choose one, Battle Maiden," he said. "I will not poison you. Tonight."

Tetsuko took one. She watched as Gonshiro raised the second to his lips and took a deep sip.

"Now, Utaku Tetsuko," he said, finally. "What is it you wish to discuss with me?"

"This duel is folly," Tetsuko began, coming right to the point. "There is no need for a fight to the death. I have no argument with you, Scorpion, and I suspect that you have none with me."

"Who are you to tell me that there is no reason to fight?" Gonshiro asked, an edge of anger in his voice. "You who killed a Scorpion in cold blood and then deliberately desecrated his body so that he could never leave this world. There is no forgiveness in hell, Battle Maiden. There will be no forgiveness here, either."

"Why are you so concerned over one criminal?" Tetsuko exclaimed, slamming down her sake cup and sloshing the liquid onto her hand.

The old man shifted on the cushion. "For a Unicorn you are excitable and speak overmuch," Gonshiro said. "Aren't the barbarous Utaku Battle Maidens supposed to be silent and thoughtful?"

Tetsuko's first instinct was to whip out her katana and show this arrogant samurai how silent and thoughtful she could be, but instead she bit her tongue and said nothing.

He sipped his sake slowly, clearly unperturbed by her outburst. "For many years, I was a strong samurai, karo," he began. "When I reached my forty-fifth year, the daimyo released me from his service and commanded me to govern this village. I came willingly, for I was ready for a quiet life. And a quiet life I had, for five years, until the coup."

Gonshiro paused and took another sip of sake. "Before that, this village was prosperous and its people happy. We sold our crops throughout Rokugan, as did many other small Scorpion farm villages. Then, as quick and bright as a flash of summer lightning, all that I had loved, all that I had fought for was gone."

Gonshiro's voice had risen, and the sake cup trembled in his hand as he continued. "Those of us who remained outside the battle felt our defeat more keenly than any young samurai who had seen bloodshed. No one would buy from us or from any other Scorpion village, no matter how innocent its people had been of the crimes of our clan. Our crops rotted in the field, and the people starved. We have been weakened by the plague and attacked repeatedly by the rogues who wander the land."

"Two days ago, you Unicorns appeared on our doorstep and announced to us that you captured our tormentors and that I—that we Scorpions were now under your protection. My archers did not cut you down where you stood because we longed to hand justice to those who attacked us."

"So we have the thieves to thank for our lives?" Tetsuko said incredulously, marveling at the logic of the Scorpion samurai. Everything she had ever heard about this clan was true, she realized. Their minds twisted around reality in ways that were beyond understanding.

Gonshiro chuckled. "Yes, I suppose you do, but I would not bother sending them a thank-you scroll. They are all dead."

Tetsuko's eyes widened as she stared at the old samurai. "Scorpion justice is swift," she finally said picking up her saki cup once again.

"Scorpion justice is final," he replied, returning her look as he refilled his cup.

The two were silent for a few minutes, but Tetsuko couldn't relax. A muscle in her thigh began to twitch. She put down the cup. "Call off this duel," she said, looking closely at the old samurai. "There is no point to more bloodshed. We put our own lives on the line so that you could deal with the criminals in your own way. That should count for something, even to a Scorpion. Unicorns have vowed to protect those who are beset by the evil forces that are moving in Rokugan. We want to help you."

With lightning-fast reflexes, Gonshiro sprang to his feet, grabbing his katana and pulling it from its sheath in one swift move.

"How dare you claim to help this village with your barbaric ways, the stench of raw meat on your breath, the filthy dried skins strapped to the backs of honorable animals?" he growled. "You even have the gall to wear filthy leather boots instead of proper silk shoes. You disgust me."

In an instant Tetsuko was on her feet, her own blade drawn.

"You murdered a Scorpion samurai," Gonshiro hissed, "and if that were your only crime I still would fight you to the death. But I also swore to defend this village with my life, and I will not allow others, especially Unicorns, to take my place. I fight for the honor of my samurai brother and for the people I vowed to protect. If you strike me down, so be it. But I will die defending the only thing I have left in the world, and that will be my justice."

They stood glaring at one another. Gonshiro's sword hand trembled, and Tetsuko knew that he longed to slice her in two. She also knew that this battle was more than an exercise for an aging samurai who has seen his glory days fade into memory. He wanted revenge, and Unicorn blood would do fine. She was trapped, and they both knew it.

Slowly, without taking her eyes from Gonshiro, Tetsuko lowered her blade and rose to her full height. Gonshiro took a step back, startled at the commanding presence of the young samurai-ko.

"Your insults mean nothing," she said forcefully, her rich voice carrying across the garden. "Empty words. Fight for your village, that I can respect. If you fight for the Scorpion Clan, you are a traitor and a fool. For that I will gladly cut you down."

With a quick swipe of her boot, she sent the low table flying across the deck. Porcelain shattered on the floor, staining the wood with the last of the sake. "But do not ever underestimate a Unicorn, and especially not this one," she said. Without another word she turned and left, leaving the old man staring after her.

A look of surprise and the beginnings of a grudging respect spread across his face.

▲ ▲ ▲ ▲ ▲ ▲ ▲ ▲

That evening, after the moon had set, a single lantern burned in the inn where the Unicorns were housed. Tetsuko sat alone, cleaning her road-weary armor. She did not speak. The simple meal that had been brought to her remained untouched. None of her companions knew where she had been, but they wisely left her to her work.

When the Unicorns awoke the next morning, Tetsuko was already dressed, meditating in the center of the sparse room they had been given. The violet lacquered scales of her armor gleamed as if they were newly made. Her futon was tightly rolled in the corner of the room, untouched. Tetsuko was silent as they ate their breakfast of cold rice and water. No one dared speak to her.

Later, the Unicorn patrol made its way to the village square. A large crowd had already gathered. It parted silently to let the group through, all eyes on the young Battle Maiden in violet armor. Without looking right or left, she went straight to the middle of the square and sprung lightly over the rough rope. The rest of the group gathered in a tight knot at the edge of the roped-off area.

A few moments later, Gonshiro arrived. Without a word he went to stand in front of Tetsuko. They bowed to one another. Then they both raised their swords.

Tetsuko stood still, sword raised, feet apart, watching. She could feel her blood racing in her head, making the vessels in her temples throb. But she could feel no pain, no heat from the morning sun that beat down. Her ears could not hear the murmur of the spectators on the other side of the rope. There was only her mind, her body, and Gonshiro.

He stood about four feet in front of her. His elaborate breastplate was made of slats of red lacquered iron hinged together with cording. The armor strained slightly against his widening belly, hinting at the fact that it had been a few years—and a few meals—since he had donned his armor. On his head, as on hers, sat a helmet. His sword was poised above his shoulder and was still. The sunlight glinted off its tip and briefly flashed in her eye.

Tetsuko ignored it. The words of Benjiro, her sensei, flowed in her head: Relax your mind and open it to the broader plane. Feel your body from your shoulder to your feet. Think of what you know of your opponent and use the knowledge to your advantage. Tetsuko forced her body to relax.

She bent her knees slightly, as the old Battle Maiden had

taught her, and settled into the familiar battle position. She had practiced iaijutsu duels dozens, maybe hundreds of times at the Battle Maiden school. Those matches had used bokken, wooden practice swords. A true iaijutsu duel was quick, bloody, and deadly. Each samurai focused and prepared for one, dramatic strike. One samurai would win. The other would die.

Tetsuko had learned to study her opponents and use their weaknesses to plan her attack. Almost every time she had been victorious, but she had never fought a Scorpion samurai one-on-one in any battle, and she had never fought an iaijutsu duel to the death.

A scorpion stings without warning, Benjiro's voice said again. Expect everything.

Tetsuko saw the almost imperceptible movement as Gonshiro adjusted his weight to his right foot. She deflected the swift blow that followed almost before he threw it.

The villagers fell silent.

Gonshiro moved back, and Tetsuko stepped forward. With one quick motion, she swung at his head and hands at once.

Gonshiro sidestepped the move. With an ease born of experience, he swung his sword and landed a stinging blow to her shoulder. It cut through armor to the bone.

At the last minute he checked his swing.

Tetsuko jumped back, stunned that his blow did not strike her dead. She regained her focus, not feeling the burn of the cut or the warmth of blood.

It was very rare for an iaijutsu duel to continue for more than a few seconds. But one look at Gonshiro's wide, gleeful eyes and his relaxed manner told her this battle was to be different. He knew she did not want this duel, so why did he prolong it?

As her blood poured through the wound and stained her armor, Tetsuko paused. "I ask you again, Scorpion," she said, loud enough for the spectators to hear, "call off this fight. I have no quarrel with you or your village. Let my patrol return to its work in peace."

"Never, Unicorn filth," he replied.

Honor demanded that she accept defeat. His blow should have killed her. To ignore it would be a supreme disgrace. But something deep within her rebelled at the idea that she would surrender her life to this scheming Scorpion. In a flash she realized the truth: there was no honorable death in a dishonorable fight—for either of them.

Gonshiro misinterpreted her hesitation and growled, "No, Maiden, you will not yield!" He rushed her.

Tetsuko jumped back and deflected his wild swing with a thrust of her own. Flipping her wrist, she threw a lightning blow to his head.

Gonshiro tried to dodge the blade, but he was not fast enough. He stumbled back, his sword point drooping as blood coursed through a clean slice in his helm.

Tetsuko took a deep breath. With a speed she hadn't realize she possessed, she grabbed Gonshiro's arm and twisted, forcing him to drop his sword. Then she pushed him backward.

With a howl he fell onto his knees. Tetsuko stepped forward and put her sword tip to the center of his abdomen.

"Do it, Battle Maiden," he whispered. "I do not deserve to live. I am Scorpion, bringer of death and dishonor to Rokugan. Do it!"

Tetsuko stared at him.

"You wanted this," she said brokenly, the tip of her katana still pressed into his chest. "You forced me into a duel because you are disgraced, too cowardly to commit seppuku like any honorable Scorpion." She tried to pull the blade away, but Gonshiro grabbed the end of the sword in his strong grip.

"I will die an honorable samurai's death," the old man said thickly. "You have no choice. My guards have orders to kill you and your soldiers if you dishonor me by letting me live."

Tetsuko looked up and tried to focus. Her soldiers were surrounded by a group of Scorpion guards, their katanas drawn. The face of every Scorpion villager was hidden behind a mask. Along the walls of the village, archers were poised to fire.

Tetsuko looked down at Gonshiro once again. He stung me after all, she thought.

Slowly, as if in a dream, Tetsuko lifted her katana.

Gonshiro opened his eyes and smiled his Scorpion smile. "Yes," he whispered.

Tetsuko plunged the sword in a mercy blow through Gonshiro's neck. His head rolled in the dust, still smiling.

Blood spurted in a fountain of red from the wound. It covered Tetsuko's hands, her armor, and her soul.

8 SAKE FOR THE HOUR OF LONELINESS

Since the news of the Lion attack on Crane lands, the palace was on edge. The air was tinged with fear and anxiety.

Even the usually polite ambassadors felt the tension. Kakita Umi had become openly hostile to Ikoma Natsumi. It was an embarrassment to see the usually stoic ambassador dishonor herself and her clan. Natsumi bravely stood her ground against the furious assault of Umi and others, and it was clear the inexperienced ambassador could certainly hold her own in a fight.

In an attempt to defuse the volatile mood in the palace, Natsumi arranged a diplomatic meeting with Umi. It was clear from the outset, though, that the Crane ambassador had no intention of smoothing things over. She thirsted for the Lion ambassador's blood, and everyone in the room could see it.

Ikoma Natsumi and Kakita Umi stood before one another, surrounded by secretaries, guards, and servants. Natsumi wore a calm expression. Umi was furious and did little to hide it.

"How dare you speak of your Lion army as honorable?" Umi spat, all traces of diplomacy gone.

"My clan has been the defender of the Emerald Throne for generations," Natsumi replied evenly. "Our honor is un-questioned, and I will defend it with my life." Her eyes glinted as she continued, "The Crane are quick to gather gold and favors. It is not the Lion's fault that they do not show the same speed on the battlefield."

Umi trembled in anger. "The Lion Clan's lack of skill in court is well known," she said, making no attempt to hide her contempt for the young ambassador. "The hot-headed pride of your clan will be your defeat, and you may well pay for this Lion treachery with your life."

The Crane ambassador turned abruptly and left in a whirl of silk. Natsumi watched her go, and then bowed in a pointed insult.

Her secretary, Kitsu Mitoru, approached her and bowed. Sighing, Natsumi returned the bow.

"We must watch out for that one," he said as the two of them made their way through the press of people that had attended the meeting. "All know of her temper and of her hatred for you."

"She is angry, and I am the representative of the Lion Clan," Natsumi replied. "Surely she understands that I have no control over my daimyo, as she has no control over hers."

"The mood in the palace is dark," Mitoru replied. "I am fearful that anything can happen."

Natsumi thought of the attack in her quarters and

silently agreed with her secretary. Aloud she said, "We will be cautious."

As the two continued through the palace, they came upon Umi, who stood with her staff. Natsumi bowed in polite greeting to the Crane ambassador and then moved on. The young Lion could feel the Crane's dark glare follow her until she was out of sight.

▲▲▲▲▲▲▲▲

"Father!"

Tadaji awoke with a start. It was sometime deep in the night. Moonlight glowed through the rice-paper walls of his room. He breathed heavily, his heart slamming in his chest and his sweat-soaked body stuck uncomfortably to the damp silk sheets. He closed his eyes.

"Tamura," he sighed, and a sob caught in his throat.

For a long time he lay there, letting his mind go blank as the Dragon shugenja had taught him years ago. Slowly, he relaxed.

Soon Tadaji rose from the soft futon and walked through semidarkness to a low shelf. He pulled a thick cotton blanket from a neatly folded pile of clothing, quickly wrapped it around himself, and sank onto a large cushion beside his dining table. Three sake cups sat in a row on the table, each filled to the brim with liquid. He had placed them all there before he slept, for he knew he would awaken in the night, as he had done since Tamura's death.

Tadaji picked up the first cup. "This is to battle the demons who have already left their mark," he said, and threw it back with one gulp. Then he leaned back on his arms, feeling the burn of the sake as it flowed down his throat.

Tadaji shook his head, and then raised the second cup of sake to his lips. "For the demons who visited tonight," he said as he swallowed.

He picked up the last porcelain sake cup and stared at it for a few moments, admiring its delicate color.

"The third is to battle the dreams not yet come," he said aloud as he poured the sake into his mouth. Then he crawled back between the now-dry sheets of his bed. With a whispered prayer, Tadaji closed his eyes. The sake deadened his mind in a dreamless sleep.

▲▲▲▲▲▲▲▲

The next day, word came that a huge Crab army was bearing down on Beiden Pass. The news threw Umi and the other Cranes into enraged turmoil. Tadaji expected to see Hoturi smoothing the feathers of the embattled Crane ambassador or simply lending her the strength of the Doji family. But the day faded into night, and there was no sign of him.

Three days after Tadaji and Hoturi parted in the garden, Tadaji sent a messenger to Hoturi's apartments. That evening, when Tadaji was dining alone in his rooms, the messenger returned.

"Honorable Ide Tadaji," the messenger began, bowing low. "Kakita Toshimoko has sent this message for you." She handed him a scroll sealed with the Crane emblem, then bowed and left quickly.

The hastily scrawled message read:

> *Most honorable Ide Tadaji, Unicorn ambassador,*
> *Your message disturbed me. I too have not seen*

Hoturi since he left for his audience. I did not worry until this afternoon, when my own messages to the palace were returned unanswered.

Hoturi has spoken of you as a trusted friend, and I am honored by your concern. As you may know, our situation is grave. The Cranes here grow anxious, for our clan desperately needs us. I cannot disobey my daimyo, but neither can we remain here much longer. If we do not hear from Hoturi by tomorrow, I will be forced to move without him.

Kakita Toshimoko

Tadaji slowly rolled up the rough paper. So Hoturi has not been seen by even his second-in-command. A chill crept up Tadaji's spine.

For hours, Tadaji paced his chamber. The steaming mint tea that Eda had brought grew cold in the cup. Feeling like a caged animal, Tadaji threw on a kimono, grabbed his cane and left.

The evening was cool, and a strong night breeze bit through the thin silk of his kimono. Tadaji wrapped the fabric tighter around him as he headed toward the palace buildings. It was very late, and the grounds were deserted. He had no destination in mind, but his feet carried him around the Great Hall, past the Ambassador's Hall, and down the meandering pathways through the darkened, empty palace grounds.

Finally he awoke from his thoughts to find himself standing in front of the imperial stables. He stopped short and shook his head wonderingly. His troubled mind had brought him to the one place in the entire Imperial Palace that would feel like home to a Unicorn.

The emperor's stable was not nearly as grand as those at the Shiro Utaku Shojo, but it was impressive enough. It was a long, low structure, built on a foundation of stone. The stable was the only building in the palace constructed entirely of wood, built by Unicorn carpenters more than a hundred years before. During the coup and the destruction that followed, many people had sought shelter here, thankful for its strong timber walls.

Tadaji heard a soft neigh, and a longing for home filled his heart. He eased open the heavy double doors of the stable and squeezed inside.

Tadaji breathed in the familiar scent of hay, horse, and dung. He stood for a moment, letting his eyes adjust to the darkness. At first, all was black. Then he began to see shapes: the long row of stalls along both walls, a pile of sweet hay, a stack of heavy sacks filled with imported Unicorn feed.

The enormous stable had been built to house more than two hundred horses, and the stalls were large enough to accommodate even the mightiest Unicorn mount. Tadaji smiled, knowing that the Unicorns purposefully built a grand imperial stable in which their mighty war horses looked fine, but the horses of the other clans looked tiny and weak. This ancient insult was the source of much humor among the Unicorn cavalry.

He passed many bare stalls, cleaned and scrubbed, before he found an occupied one. He didn't recognize the horse, who looked up from her manger as he passed, eyeing him with curiosity.

He slipped into her stall, talking quietly to her and stroking her flanks in the way he had been taught as a child. She was probably one of Kachiko's pleasure mounts, for she was far too small to be a war beast and too large for a child's pony. Her back was silky, the result of many hours of brushing, and Tadaji was thankful that an animal that was so seldom used got such good treatment.

He moved toward her head, stroking and petting her, and she neighed softly, nuzzling the old man's neck in the semidarkness. Homesickness pinched Tadaji's heart at that simple gesture. He leaned his head on the horse's smooth neck, feeling her strong muscles. He breathed in the horse's scent, which to him was like rare perfume.

Tadaji had no idea how long he stood there, eyes closed, letting the smells and atmosphere of the quiet stable calm him, when suddenly the double doors burst open. A figure holding a lantern strode purposefully through the stables, scattering hay and causing the horses to stamp and neigh in surprise.

Startled, Tadaji sank into the shadows of the stall. The man quickly passed, the lantern light dancing crazily on the stalls and floor as he walked. In the moving light Tadaji was stunned to see that it was Hoturi, with a look of single-minded determination on his face.

It was on the tip of Tadaji's tongue to call out to his friend, but something kept him silent. Instead, he crept out of the stall and followed in the shadows behind Hoturi.

The Crane daimyo made his way toward the end of the stables where the war mounts were housed. Hoturi slammed the paper lantern onto a table beside one stall. Then he shrugged out of the large pack on his back, let it drop to the floor, and disappeared into the stall. The horse neighed and stomped in surprise and fear at being so abruptly treated, but a curt word from Hoturi silenced him.

Tadaji paused in the blackness just beyond the pool of lantern light. Hoturi quickly threw a blanket and a saddle onto the horse's back and led him out. The ambassador was surprised to see that the majestic animal strained and pulled against the reins, unwilling to leave the comforts of the warm stall.

"Damn you, ungrateful beast!" Hoturi growled, pulling harder at the reins. Finally Hoturi managed to drag the horse out. Then he began loading his pack onto the animal's back, grunting and cursing when the horse tried to shy away from the rough treatment.

Tadaji couldn't stand it any more. "Hoturi!" he exclaimed, moving into the wan circle of lantern light. "Friend, it is good to see you! Where have you been these last few days?"

Hoturi whirled around at the sound of Tadaji's voice, and the older man's jaw dropped in complete surprise.

The young daimyo's face was twisted into a dark scowl, his lips pursed in anger and impatience. His hair, usually impeccably coifed, was disheveled and uncombed. Although his kimono was clean, it was wrinkled and unkempt, as if this always-fastidious man had slept in his clothing for more than a few days. But it was Hoturi's eyes that made Tadaji gasp. They glared with a burning hatred, the pupils so large that they turned his gaze black. The whites of his eyes shone bright in the low light, reminding Tadaji of a horse's eyes when fear takes it.

"Tadaji!" Hoturi exclaimed. "What are you doing here?"

"I could not sleep," Tadaji replied, shrinking slightly from the anger in Hoturi's voice. "I could ask the same of you."

Hoturi glared at his friend for a moment longer, and then turned and continued loading the horse. "I am in a hurry. It would be wise if you returned to your chambers."

"Wise!" Tadaji exploded. "You have been missing for days. Now you reappear in the dead of night, with no explanation, just to disappear again."

"What I do is my business, Tadaji," Hoturi replied. "It is not up to you to keep an eye on me like a worried hen."

"Did things go badly with the Lady Kachiko?"

Hoturi paused and slowly turned to Tadaji. The young Crane's eyes were filled with anger.

Tadaji returned the stare defiantly, but his mind was in a whirl. "Hoturi," Tadaji said softly, in the voice he used to calm heated diplomatic arguments. "It is I, your friend. You can speak openly to me." He took a step toward Hoturi.

"I know who you are, old man," Hoturi growled, "but I have no time to discuss things with you. I saw Kachiko, and now I know what I must do." Hoturi pushed him away.

Tadaji stumbled backward into the table beside the stall. The table's legs gave way. The lantern fell to the floor and went out, plunging the stables into darkness.

Hoturi quickly mounted. He yanked the reins and dug his feet into the horse's side, making the horse rear slightly.

Tadaji picked himself painfully off the hard floor as Hoturi tore through the stables.

Morning was approaching, and the large, open doors of the stable made a dark gray square in the shadowy interior. As Hoturi passed through, he paused.

For the rest of his life, that image was seared into Tadaji's mind: the silhouette of rider and horse, strong and proud against the blue-gray of the coming morning. Then the Crane turned and was gone.

9   BLOOD FROM THE SHADOWS

Tetsuko sat in the main room of the inn. The shugenja Moto Hakuro hovered over her.

"Do not move," Hakuro commanded as Tetsuko fidgeted. "The Fortunes cannot heal you if you will not stay still."

"Bah," Tetsuko said with a snort, but she sat more quietly as the man finished his ministrations. Finally he wrapped Tetsuko's wound with clean cloth and sat back, satisfied.

"This might heal if you don't agree to any more iaijutsu duels for a while, Tetsuko-sama," he said gravely, bowing.

Tetsuko threw him a withering glance.

The shugenja merely smiled at his commander. He knew about her impatience and her temper, but he also knew he owed her his life.

At that moment a woman bearing a tray of food entered the room. She was an older woman, perhaps fifty, with a tall, stately build. Her ebony hair was streaked with gray and fell gracefully down her back. She wore a plain gray kimono edged with black. The top half of her face, from her forehead to her nose, was covered with a simple gray mask. Through it, her deep-set almond eyes studied the injured woman.

"You are the innkeeper," Tetsuko said, recognizing the clean, threadbare kimono the woman wore day after day. The woman was like her town: proud but threadbare, holding things together as best she could with what little she had.

She nodded, her face expressionless as she placed the tray on a small table near Tetsuko.

Tetsuko smiled and motioned for her to sit. With an uneasy look, the woman bowed, and then complied.

"I am Bayu—I am Tokiko," she said.

When Tetsuko and the patrol had arrived, Gonshiro had commanded the woman to house the six Unicorn soldiers and their mounts. She had been none too pleased, pursing her lips and eyeing the travel-worn Unicorns with open contempt. She had made them all strip and bathe before they were allowed to enter their rooms, and all of their leather possessions—including Tetsuko's boots—had been taken to the tumbledown stable behind the inn's main hall.

"Tokiko," Tetsuko said, nodding to the woman in formal greeting.

"With the death of Gonshiro, I am now leader of this village," Tokiko said matter-of-factly.

"I am truly sorry about the death of the samurai," Tetsuko said. Her head throbbed. "He was an honorable man."

"Honorable?" Tokiko replied softly, her voice rising slightly. "He was arrogant and self-important. He looked on the villagers with contempt, as all samurai do."

"But he fought for the honor of the village," Tetsuko said. "He could not live with the disgrace of allowing Unicorns to help the village he had sworn to protect."

A half-smirk twisted at the corners of Tokiko's mouth. She dropped her hands into her lap and said, "Gonshiro did not care whether we lived or died. He saw our village as his prison. It was his punishment, not being called back into active duty for the coup."

Tetsuko stared at the woman, thoughts tumbling. The pain of her arm and head added to the confusion in her mind. "Then why . . .?"

"Why did he insist on a duel? To steal a shred of honor for his name, as if that would do it." Tokiko sighed.

"Gonshiro was banished to our village," she said. "He did something terrible, we do not know what. When our clan was broken, even seppuku was not an option, for what honor is there in a clan without honor? Gonshiro acted as if he were exiled here. His only use for the villagers was for what they could bring him in koku and food.

"When the plague came and so many were lost, Gonshiro became like a madman, sitting quietly one moment and raging the next. He begged his guards to kill him, but they refused. As villagers died by the dozens, he tried to commit seppuku, but his cowardly heart would not allow him to do that.

"He was away when the outlaws struck. They burned two farms outside of town and ransacked part of our market. They broke into his house and took some of his things. When he returned he was enraged. He had four men put to death, convinced that they had somehow helped the thieves enter the village. He immediately ordered the wall to be built, forcing our farmers to abandon their fields while the work was done. Many crops were lost.

"When you appeared, bearing the bodies of the thieves, Gonshiro saw you as his chance to escape disgrace once and for all. It was sheer luck that one of the outlaws happened to be Scorpion. It gave Gonshiro a reason to force you into an iaijutsu duel. If he told you that he fought for us, he lied. The only thing he ever fought for was himself."

Tetsuko sank deep into the soft futon. "If I had refused, he could have committed seppuku as an honorable samurai disgraced by refusal," she said slowly. "If I didn't kill him, his guards had orders to kill me and my soldiers where we stood."

"He would have done it too," Tokiko spat. "But he never intended to leave the village square alive."

Tetsuko shook her head in disbelief at the way Gonshiro had trapped her. "Everyone lies," she murmured, feeling drained.

"But why tell me this?" Tetsuko asked as she stretched her arm above her head, testing the healing talents of the shugenja.

Tokiko gazed out of the open doorway of the inn. Finally she said, "I have not always been an innkeeper. When Gonshiro came, I lived in the house you know as his. My family has led this village for ten generations."

The woman looked away. "My daughter, Anshira, lived with me. She was a beautiful girl, in her fourteenth year. Her gempuku was to have been that summer. When Gonshiro took my house as his own, he sent me to a farm and kept Anshira as a servant. A Bayushi servant! Gonshiro enjoyed the idea of a Bayushi forced to obey his every command.

"Villagers sometimes heard screams coming from the

house, but they could do nothing. He had a guard posted to me at all times so that I could not speak to her, even on market day."

Tokiko paused. "The last time I saw her, her belly had grown round. She walked with the stoop of an old woman, and I could see faded bruises on her face. My heart wept for her. So in the crowded market I slipped her a tanto, a small blade that she could easily conceal. Two days later the plague came, and Gonshiro told the village that she was its first victim."

The older woman raised her head, and tears glistened on the mask that covered her face. "I will never know what really happened, for the plague swept through the village immediately after that. The farm workers died, and my crops rotted. The innkeeper died as well, so I left the farm and moved here to be closer to my people. By that time Gonshiro had begun to go mad. He did not even notice I was here."

The room was quiet as Tetsuko absorbed the disturbing tale. Although she had known full well that men like Gonshiro walked the land, she had never before been a part of the black world that one had created. Victims of the coup, she realized, bled in even the smallest parts of Rokugan.

"Utaku Tetsuko," Tokiko said, rousing the Battle Maiden from her thoughts. "You have done us an honorable service, but we have no way to thank you. Our village is in ruins, our people hungry. My people respect and honor you. Would you consider staying here a few days to help us, before you move on?"

Tetsuko searched the Scorpion's face for any sign of treachery. After her experience with Gonshiro, she hesitated to trust anyone who wore a mask. But Tokiko's eyes returned her gaze with honesty.

"Yes, we will stay," Tetsuko said finally, "As long as we can have food and a place to lodge while we are here."

"Domo," Tokiko said, bowing. She did not smile, but there was relief in her eyes.

For the next few days, Tetsuko rested in the inn as her shoulder healed. Scorpion villagers began to see violet-clad Unicorn samurai repairing buildings, picking vegetables in kitchen gardens, or carrying water from the village well. On both sides, fear and anger faded into the first glimmers of respect.

Each afternoon, the patrol gathered in the main room of the inn after their duties were done. They were usually accompanied by a villager shyly bearing a small gift: a basket of apples, a small dish of freshly caught fish, or a bowl of sweet wild blackberries.

On the afternoon of the fifth day, Tetsuko was sitting with Tokiko and the rest of the Unicorns when a stranger walked in. The conversation quieted as the dusty man, dressed in a travel-stained kimono, bowed to Tetsuko and Tokiko.

"Greetings, Tokiko," he said in a gravely voice. Although his hair was still dark, his face was weathered and lined with wrinkles and his hands were red and tough from years of work in the fields. As he bowed low, Tetsuko saw that his hands trembled.

"Greetings, Arata," Tokiko said, nodding in return. "What brings you into our village? We had heard that you had left the area months ago."

"I did, gracious lady," Arata replied, "I have only recently returned, but I have news for you."

"What kind of news, Arata?"

"Bad news," the man said. "The Shadowlands forces are coming."

Everyone in the room gasped at this statement.

Tetsuko's eyes flew open, and she said, "What do you know of this? Speak!"

Arata looked at her and seemed to notice her for the first time. His eyes narrowed into slits as he said with a sneer, "Tokiko, since when have you begun consorting with filthy Unicorns?"

"Silence, Arata!" Tokiko said, glaring at the old farmer. "These Unicorns are allies and friends. Now tell us what you saw, please."

Arata gave Tetsuko another scathing look, and then sighed and turned to Tokiko. "Five days ago I saw an army of large creatures attack a village east of here," he said. "Hundreds of them swarmed like ants, killing and burning everything they saw.

"I came upon the carcass of a horse," he said. "The poor beast was viciously torn apart. I will not describe what I saw, but it was truly terrible."

Fear washed over Tetsuko, and her mind filled with images of the thieves by the fire.

Arata continued, "I found a tiny cave and hid. The army marched past the cave that night, and I heard things." Here the man paused and gulped a cup of water that a servant pressed into his hand.

"What things?" Eri said, on the edge of her seat.

"Grunts and squeals, wailings and whispers," Arata replied, wiping his mouth on the sleeve of his kimono. "The sound of a mighty host crashing through the forest, much bigger than the army I saw in the village. It took most of the night for them to pass. And they were headed this way."

The room was quiet as everyone digested this news. Tetsuko took a deep breath. The faces of both Scorpion and Unicorn looked to her for leadership, and she swallowed hard.

"Tokiko, how prepared is this village for a battle?"

"Not very," she replied. "Few have been trained in warfare, but we will defend our village with our lives if need be." She looked at Tetsuko with worry. "Do you really think we are in danger?"

"I hope not," Tetsuko replied, "but if we do lie in the path of this army, it is certain that they will attack. And I do not think we will be able to defend this village alone against a Shadowlands army the size that Arata describes."

Tetsuko rubbed her forehead with her fingertips, trying to get a clear thought. Whatever decision she made in the next few seconds would affect her folk and every person in the village. The idea that she commanded that much power made her feel ill. She remembered the admonishment of Yokatsu: You may not be as lucky next time, when your impetuousness could affect more than the lives of the few who ride with you. Now was the time, and she must choose a course of action or wait for death to come.

Finally, Tetsuko said, "Yasamura's army is traveling east of here, headed north toward Dragon lands."

"Yes, Tetsuko-sama," Shenko replied.

"Shenko, find Yasamura and tell him of our danger," she said. "You must convince him to come to our aid before it is too late." Shenko bowed, and then quickly left to prepare for her journey.

"Tokiko, we must ready the villagers for whatever may come. Ask them to gather in the square in two hours, and we will make our plan." Tokiko nodded to the young samurai-ko.

"Eri, I need to know how many weapons we have and what we can devise from the village supplies. Hakuro, there is at least one other shugenja in town. Work with her to prepare in whatever ways you must. Umio, take two men with you and inspect every inch of the wall. I will meet you in the square when the villagers gather."

The Unicorns bowed and rushed out the door to obey her orders.

Tetsuko stood and flinched at the pain in her shoulder. She wondered if this battle would be her last.

Putting that thought away, she headed out the door to prepare for the grim battle to come.

10 THE STAIN OF CHAOS

Late afternoon sunlight sifted through the trees on the imperial grounds, casting long shadows on the pathway before Tadaji. After the events of the night before, he had not slept or eaten. Finally, Eda had ordered him to the baths, and he had been grateful to comply.

Tadaji was on his way toward the main baths when a servant galloped around a corner, running headlong into him and knocking them both to the pebbled pathway.

"Watch where you are going, boy!" Tadaji exclaimed. He struggled to rise from the ground.

"Forgive me, Ambassador," the messenger said breathlessly, helping Tadaji to his feet only to drop abjectly prostrate. "My clumsiness is a terrible disgrace. I beg your mercy."

"What reason have you to be in such a hurry?"

"Gracious lord, I am on an urgent errand. There has been a murder in the palace!"

Tadaji stared at the boy, unsure if he had heard him clearly. "Be off, then."

The boy rose, bowing deeply in thanks, and then dashed away down the pathway.

A scream rent the air.

Quickly, Tadaji followed the sound. It had come from the direction of the Lion ambassadors' quarters. As he approached, he saw a crowd gathering in front of Ikoma Natsumi's chambers.

The crowd parted, and two eta appeared.

A weight of fear fell upon the gathering. They looked on in horrified silence and made room for the eta to move through.

The eta carried two bamboo poles with a large piece of heavy silk stretched between. Something large and heavy was lying on top, covered in a dirty, bloody cloth. One eta stumbled, and the cloth fell from the stretcher.

Tadaji recoiled in horror. Beneath the cloth was the body of Ikoma Natsumi.

With a curse, the eta stopped. One of them grabbed the cloth and threw it back onto the stretcher. They bore their ghastly burden out of the crowd and disappeared.

Tadaji trembled slightly, unable to speak or think. He moved slowly through the crowd.

Someone said, "Only Shadowlands creatures kill in such horrible ways."

"Shadowlands creatures, here?" another asked, terror gripping her voice.

"No, it was the Crane," someone accused. "Who else had reason to murder the Lion ambassador?"

"Wasn't the daimyo here a few days ago? Has anyone seen him since?"

Murmured nos rippled among the crowd, and the air crackled with a new fury.

Tadaji was about to say something, but then he remembered Hoturi's behavior. He pushed his way out of the group, which buzzed like a hive of angry bees. Soon, news of this grim discovery would race through every room and garden, and the facts would instantly be replaced by rumor and speculation. But what were the facts?

The memory of Tadaji's meeting with Natsumi came rushing back to him. There had been no more attacks since that night, and Eda had stayed with Natsumi until a guard was secured. The young Lion ambassador had seemed more at ease after that, and Tadaji had gradually forgotten the incident.

He closed his eyes. Images danced across his lids. The first was Tamura, begging for help. Then it was Hoturi, looking at Tadaji with friendship and respect. Finally, he saw Natsumi's face as her fear-filled eyes pleaded to be believed.

Another memory came to him. It was a memory of a night in the imperial gardens, escorting a beautiful empress. That night, he had heard a cryptic exchange between Kachiko and her ninja brother-in-law and had seen a vision of death and blood so real that he had retched from the feel and smell of it.

It was a vision brought on by a red silk fan embroidered with the symbol of the Scorpion.

▲▲▲▲▲▲▲▲

A few hours later, Tadaji strode through the imperial gardens, a look of determination on his face. He made his way through familiar pathways, but his eyes did not glance about in memory.

He soon came to the section of the gardens that had been most affected by the destruction of the coup and the plague. This was the Place of Peace and Harmony, which contained shrines and small temples to deities and ancestors. Although the emperor was the son of Amaterasu, the Sun, each clan worshiped in its own way. This garden had been the place where ambassadors, staff, and visitors from throughout Rokugan could pray and meditate. The Scorpion shrines and temples had been some of the most beautiful in all of Rokugan. It was no wonder that this place had been the first to burn, or the one most completely destroyed.

The entrance was lined with large rocks, blocking entry. Beyond it lay a tangle of fallen branches and charred underbrush.

Tadaji glanced around to see if anyone was near. The garden was deserted. Carefully Tadaji climbed over the rocks and disappeared into the burnt, dead garden.

He fought his way through the destroyed vegetation and fallen trees until he came to the remains of a small building. Tadaji was surprised to see that the paper and bamboo structure had survived the worst of the flames. Although two walls and the roof were gone, two other walls still stood. Tattered shoji trembled in the soft evening breeze. The once-white paper was now black with soot, but Tadaji could still make out the watercolor paintings that had graced this Unicorn temple.

Tadaji carefully picked his way inside the building, toward the spot where the enormous altar stood. The altar had been made by Unicorn artisans more than a century before. It was a large block of violet marble, carved in intricate patterns of vine-work. Now it was covered with branches and debris, which Tadaji carefully removed. He stood for a moment, admiring its beauty as he had done countless times before.

Then Tadaji lit the lantern he carried with him and placed it on the once-elegant altar. He pressed himself against the cool stone and ran his fingertips lightly over the carvings. After a few moments, his hands found what they were looking for. He reached into his obi and drew out a thin rod made of metal, with a ring at one end. The other end was carved in an odd shape. Tadaji inserted the rod into the tiny hole and twisted it until he heard a soft click.

With a grim smile, he pulled the key from the hole and slid it into the folds of his obi. Then he pushed the altar, and a section of it swung silently forward, revealing a set of stone steps that led down into darkness. Tadaji took the small lantern and slowly descended the steps, his heart pounding. They were narrow and steep, and Tadaji kept his palm on one wall as he carefully made his way downward.

Unicorn craftspeople had built this temple and altar in a time of uncertainty for them in Rokugan. They had only recently returned from the wilderness, and their position in the empire was precarious at best. As a gesture of goodwill, the emperor had invited them to construct a temple in the palace garden. The Unicorns built an elegant structure quite worthy of the Imperial Palace, but they also built a series of tunnels beneath the temple.

The catacombs had been made originally as a secret escape for the Unicorn ambassador and the daimyo should they ever need to flee the palace. The tunnels twisted upon one another in such confusion that anyone who didn't know his way would immediately be lost. They emerged along the seashore miles away. Few folk knew of their existence. The Unicorn ambassador was one of the few.

Tadaji reached the bottom of the stair and sat on the last step to catch his breath. The lantern light revealed a small stone room with a single door made of heavy wood. It had an ornate metal handle with a keyhole. Tadaji inserted the key into the door. It turned smoothly, and the heavy door swung open into a tunnel that stretched into darkness.

Tadaji put down the lantern and pulled a ball of white silk string from his obi. He tied one end tightly onto the door handle, and then jerked it twice to test the knot. It held. Holding the ball loosely so that it would unwind as he walked, he raised the lantern and stepped into the tunnel.

Its smooth stone walls arched only a few inches above his head, and the flat stone floor beneath his silk shoes was cool and dry. Tadaji turned right and began walking, leaving a white silk trail behind him. He let his memory carry him through the catacombs, turning right, and then left through tunnels that looked identical. Soon he came to a small alcove and stopped. There was nothing but a light layer of dust and a few cobwebs, still intact and waving in the breeze that Tadaji made as he passed.

He knelt and placed the lantern beside him on the floor. Then he gazed at the stone wall, counting to himself. He reached out and pressed one of the blocks that made up the wall. It moved slightly. A faint sound of stone scraping against stone echoed in the tunnel, and another block slowly pushed itself out of the wall above Tadaji's head. It pivoted to reveal a dark space behind. He reached into the space and felt around in the darkness. His hand touched a familiar shape. Sighing with relief, he gently removed the object and pushed the stone shut.

It was a small wooden box. The lid and sides were intricately carved with strange symbols and letters. Their beauty had always moved Tadaji. They were interspersed with carvings of the Unicorn mon, forever linking the clan with its barbarian past.

He carefully opened the box. Inside, lying on a bed of

violet silk, was a remarkable carving of a horse. The horse had been made from a block of deep red amber, a precious stone from the wilderness of the barbarian lands. The stone, said to be the hardened sap of a tree, was such a dark red that it sometimes appeared to be black.

The delicate carving fit in the palm of Tadaji's hand. He gently held it, rubbing his fingers along its silky smooth surface. When he raised it to the lantern light, he could see crimson and red glints deep within it. He smiled and said a prayer of thanks to the Ujik-hai artisan who had made such a work of art.

Tadaji knew the story of the carving by heart. Ide, the ancestor of Tadaji's family, was a peaceable man. He was chosen to be the voice of Shinjo in all dealings with strangers. It was said that this object was given to Ide by a Ujik-hai in thanks for settling a dispute. When the Unicorn returned to Rokugan, the Crane Clan was the first to welcome them back into the empire. One of the first marriages in the Unicorn Clan was between an Ide and a Doji of the Crane. The carving was given as a wedding gift, symbolizing the joining of Unicorn to Crane and to Rokugan in peace and honor. Through the generations, the carving was passed between the families whenever they were joined by marriage. It was said that protection from harm was bestowed on whomever possessed the beautiful statue.

The statue had returned to the Ide family with his marriage to Doji Chisato, and it was to have been passed down to Tamura and his wife when they wed. But when the coup threatened Rokugan, Tadaji hid the statue, fearing it would be stolen or destroyed in the chaos. Then when the plague swept the land and Tamura died, Tadaji had been too grief-stricken to retrieve the precious artifact from its hiding place deep within the Unicorn tunnels.

Now he was the last Ide of his line. His beloved Chisato was dead. Tamura was dead. It was clear to Tadaji what he must do: give the statue to Hoturi, the most powerful Crane of the next generation. Its protective powers would shield the young daimyo from harm. To help Hoturi would be to help Tamura. It was Tadaji's only hope to be released from torment.

"For you, my son," Tadaji said aloud, carefully placing the scarlet horse back in its box and tucking it into the folds of his obi. His words echoed eerily down the tunnel and bounced back to his ears, making him think for a moment that someone had spoken to him. But he was alone, and no one knew he was there.

With a sigh, he turned and slowly began rolling up the silk string. He had walked only a few steps when he felt the taut string become slack in his hand. Puzzled, he continued to follow the silk string as he rolled it, then suddenly stopped dead. A frayed, chewed end dangled from his trembling hand.

Tadaji ran a few steps forward, the lantern light bobbing along the walls as he frantically searched for the end of the thread. It was not there. He searched his mind to remember each turn he had taken, but he had not paid attention to where his feet had taken him. He dashed through one tunnel, then another, unwilling to admit to himself that he was lost.

Finally he could not deny the truth. He stood in the center of a tunnel as fear enveloped him. The frayed edge of the useless string dangled from his sweaty hand. It was cooler in this particular tunnel, Tadaji noticed, colder than the others had been. He could see his breath in the air, and a chill crept over him. The cold bore down on Tadaji like a great weight, and a gust of wind snuffed out the lantern, plunging Tadaji into darkness.

Tadaji tried to take a deep breath, but the air in the tunnel was so cold it cut his lungs like a thousand tiny knives. From far away Tadaji heard Tamura's voice echo through the passage, "Only you, only you, only you . . ."

The tunnel began to glow with an eerie blue-gray light.

Suddenly Tadaji was standing on a cliff overlooking a valley. The sky was orange, and a sun blazed high overhead, casting everything in a blood-red glow. The land beneath his feet had been laid waste by war. Its blackened and cracked surface stretched to the horizon.

Thousands of figures crawled like army ants over the valley. They moved back and forth in waves across the dead landscape. The scene became clearer. The figures were not men but animals—thousands of cranes, crabs, unicorns, lions, dragons, and phoenix tearing at one another in a bloody frenzy of death.

A troop of phoenix attacked a small group of lions, ripping open their bellies and scattering their organs. Black crows waited with glee for the feast to begin. An army of crabs attacked a flock of majestic cranes. The crabs, their huge claws snapping, tore the birds apart. Blood-soaked feathers burst into the air and floated lazily back to the ground.

In the west, an army of dragons, unicorns, cranes, and phoenix stood together. Before them rose a majestic lion, stained red and black. His mane had been shaved in disgrace, but his face was still proud as he opened his mouth and roared. The motley army faced an enormous crab force clicking their claws horribly as they raced toward them.

Soon thousands of dead bodies lay strewn on the blackened ground. Their blood flowed like rivers through the landscape, carrying the dead in its terrible current.

Near one river of blood, a final battle still raged. A huge, snow-white crane struggled to rise from the ground. It looked at Tadaji and pleaded for help, its red eyes sparkling like jewels. A scorpion crouched beside the crane, and stung the bird with a quick movement. The crane flinched, then lay still.

The stench of death hit Tadaji in the face like a blow. He stumbled back, lightheaded from the smell. The air grew warmer. The vision drew back and faded into darkness.

Tadaji bent down, retching from the lingering scent of death, but his stomach was empty and he heaved uselessly.

When he stood up, he found himself in the small room at the foot of the staircase. His small lantern burned low on the bottom step. He looked around uncomprehendingly, the battle vision still fresh in his mind. But there was no mistake. He clawed at his obi and was relieved to feel the square box still secure at his waist.

Trembling, Tadaji made his way slowly back up the staircase. He slid the altar back in place above the stair and left the bloody vision of death and horror in the darkness behind him.

11   RED BLOOD, BLACK DEATH

Tetsuko leaned on the doorjamb of the inn and looked out onto the darkened village square. It was late, but the chill in the air told her that morning was not far away. The moon and stars had been hidden behind thick, dark clouds all night, making it hard for Tetsuko and Umio to see as they had ridden through the surrounding area, scouting for signs of the enemy.

They had just returned, and Tetsuko had ordered the entire village roused. Although she was outwardly calm, fear had such a grip on the young woman's heart that it was all she could do not to jump onto Cloud Dancer's back and flee. However, she would not let anyone see this fear on her face.

Tetsuko felt Tokiko standing behind

her. "It is worse than I expected," Tetsuko said aloud without turning around. "Much worse."

"How much worse?" Tokiko asked.

Tetsuko didn't reply. Instead, she watched the square slowly fill with villagers. Most of them were dressed in hastily donned kimonos, their hair disheveled from sleep. Drowsy children hung like limp dolls over their parents' shoulders. Eri, Hakuro, Umio, and Kaori, all clad for battle, kept order in the crowd.

Tetsuko's heart sank as she watched the villagers. They were secretive and wary, as all Scorpions were, but they were also people. They did not deserve to die. Over the last few days, a strange respect had grown between these Scorpions and the Unicorns. It was a respect born of desperation, yes, and of necessity. But with each friendly smile and quiet "domo arigato," a bond was forged.

Tetsuko took a deep breath and turned to Tokiko. Without a word, Tetsuko shook her head slowly, looking straight into the older woman's eyes. Tokiko's eyes widened in fear. She understood the unspoken answer.

Tetsuko walked out onto the narrow porch of the inn, and Tokiko joined her. Someone had lit a few torches, and they cast a wan, eerie light onto the upturned faces of Scorpion and Unicorn. They waited to hear what Tetsuko had to say. The samurai-ko surveyed the small group. Fear once again gripped her. She was responsible for these people.

I cannot do this, her mind screamed.

Yes, you can, Benjiro's voice reassured her. You are strong, and I have trained you to be even stronger. You survived the death of your lover and your child. You survived the zombies and a death duel. Now you must use the strength that Shinjo has given you to help others survive. You are Utaku. You are Unicorn. And you are Rokugani.

Tetsuko swallowed. "I am sorry to have awakened you from your sleep," she began, "Please forgive me for this insult. What I have to say cannot wait until morning.

"For the last few days we have been preparing for a battle against the forces of the Shadowlands. I thank each of you for your tireless help and work. Yesterday afternoon Umio and I left for a scouting mission, to discover how much of a threat we were actually under."

Tetsuko paused and took a deep breath. "We saw the army that approaches, and we are in grave danger."

The silent crowd stared at Tetsuko through their masks. She had not gotten used to the masks that the Scorpions always wore, but she had begun to recognize individuals by their mask designs. As she surveyed the crowd, she saw some that she recognized. All friends.

"The army is vast," she continued. "We could not tell what kinds of creatures were in the army, but it is safe to assume we will face beings that we have never seen before. Umio and I killed two goblin scouts not far from the village, but another one got away." Tetsuko shivered as she remembered the brief, bloody skirmish and the strength of the twisted, black creatures they defeated.

"I will not deceive you," Tetsuko continued, rubbing the twitching muscle in her thigh as she spoke. "Our chances do not look good. Anyone who wishes to leave should do so now. It will be too late once the sun has risen. . . ." Tetsuko trailed off, looking down at her mud-caked boots, waiting.

When she heard no sound, she looked up. No one had made a move to leave.

"What about Shenko and the Unicorn army?" someone called.

"We have not yet heard from the army," Tetsuko replied grimly. She remembered the last time she saw Shenko, galloping out through the village gates, the message carefully tucked in the folds of her kimono. "There is still a chance they will come, but we should not count on it." Tetsuko didn't voice her worst fear. Shenko was a strong, capable warrior. Nothing had happened to her.

Tokiko stepped to the railing and addressed the crowd. "I am proud and honored by your trust and bravery against such fearful odds. Domo arigato." She bowed, and then she turned to Tetsuko. "You entered this village as outsiders, unworthy to be called Rokugani in the minds of the loyal and dedicated Scorpions who live here. After you defeated Gonshiro, you could have left, but you did not. Instead, you remained to help us until it was too late for you to go.

"Now you stay to defend Scorpions in a fight we cannot win. You did not abandon us, so we will not abandon you. We will follow your orders and defend our village." From the crowd, nods and murmured approval came to Tetsuko's ears.

Her heart filled with pride and sorrow. She bowed low to the Scorpion leader, too moved to speak.

Tokiko bowed in return.

Tetsuko faced the crowd once more. "We must prepare," she said. "There will be no more sleep tonight." She quickly outlined her plan.

Once she was finished, the villagers left to make ready, leaving the Unicorns alone in the square. None of the Unicorns spoke, their minds heavy with thoughts of the battle to come.

Tetsuko cleared her throat and said, "You all have proven to be loyal, valiant, and honorable warriors. You have shown me respect and honor, and I thank you." Tetsuko bowed to them, and they returned the gesture. "We will probably die today," she said, "so prepare for death in whatever ways you must. But remember, it will be an honorable death, and our people will tell stories about us for centuries—the Unicorns who fought with Scorpions against the Shadowlands. What a tale this will make!"

A few wan smiles greeted this statement, and some of the fear in the soldiers' eyes faded.

"The villagers will look to each of you for guidance, so trust in your instincts and fight well."

With that, the patrol members bowed again and quickly left the square.

Tetsuko watched them go. Then she turned and disappeared into the inn, the heels of her leather boots clomping on the bamboo floor.

▲▲▲▲▲▲▲▲

A cold wind whistled in the air. The gray fog of predawn slowly lightened to a sickly yellow-green, tainting everything with a weird, deathlike pallor.

Tetsuko and the Unicorns were on horseback, as were a few of the villagers. Many villagers had taken up positions along the village wall. In the square, about two hundred stood, armed with whatever weapons they could find or make: pitchforks, scythes, daggers. . . . Some were stationed behind makeshift shield walls and small fortifications of stone and bamboo. Every villager over the age of ten was at the ready, with grim determination waiting for the onslaught. Not one of them had fled or hidden.

Unable to sit still, Tetsuko dismounted and climbed a rickety ladder to the platform that ran along the inside of the wall. Bowmen were stationed on each side of the village gate, where they had been the night the Unicorn patrol had arrived. In the last two days, they had hurriedly trained many of the villagers to shoot. Now they all stood, newly made bows in their hands and stacks of fresh arrows at their feet.

Beyond the wall, Tetsuko could see nothing except the tops of the trees and the narrow road that wound its way into the forest beyond.

She approached one of the guards and said, "Shosuro Oniji, do you see anything through that spyglass of mine?"

Without turning his head from the spyglass, the man replied, "This is a wonderful device, Unicorn. I can see for miles around, and everything is as clear as if it sat in front of me. However, I see nothing but trees and valleys as of yet."

Tetsuko gave the man a tight smile and said, "So, there are a few redeeming qualities about the Unicorns, eh?"

Oniji lowered the spyglass and looked down at Tetsuko. He was easily six inches taller than she and seemed accustomed to intimidating people with his height. This grim Unicorn, with her short hair and leather boots, was not intimidated in the least. Respect shone in his eyes. He bowed his head and replied, "One or two, perhaps."

Tetsuko smiled but said nothing. She looked out over the treetops, straining her eyes to see any movement.

"Utaku Tetsuko, there is something I would like to confess to you," Oniji said.

"Confess?" she responded, raising an eyebrow. "What is it?"

"I had been in Gonshiro's service since before he came to this village," Oniji began. "I agreed to come here with him, for I too was heartsick and defeated after the coup. He was cruel to the villagers, yes, but he was always fair to me. He respected me because, unlike the farmers here, I was a soldier."

"Make your point, Scorpion," Tetsuko said impatiently. "I have no time for the life story of a dead man."

Oniji bristled, but continued. "Very well, I will come to the point. The thief that you killed and brought to the village was not Scorpion."

"What?" Tetsuko glared at the tall man with such intensity that he shrank a bit beneath her stare.

"He ordered me to plant the mask on the man's body as a way to force you to remain in the village. I did so, for he was my leader and friend."

Tetsuko stared at Oniji as the impact of his words sank in.

"He was riddled with despair and anger," Oniji continued, looking out over the trees beyond the village walls. "He longed to die. He could not challenge you to a duel unless you had done something wrong, so he decided that killing a Scorpion samurai turned thief was good enough."

Lies and more lies, Tetsuko thought. She fell for the poisoned words of an old Scorpion, and now her entire patrol would pay the price for her inexperience.

"Why tell me now, Scorpion?" she spat. "Do you expect my forgiveness?"

"No, Battle Maiden," Oniji replied, keeping his voice even. "I do not want or need your forgiveness. But you have earned my respect, and for that I honor you with the truth."

Tetsuko shook her head. It was Scorpion honor to tell her that she and those she commanded were to die for a lie? But she knew that in his twisted Scorpion way, Oniji had shown her honor by his words.

"Thank you, Oniji," she said finally, knowing that anger now would be useless. "There is no honor without honesty."

A movement near the distant treetops caught Tetsuko's eye. Far away, at the edge of the horizon, a dark cloud had begun to rise from the ground. As it grew closer, Tetsuko smelled a sickly-sweet odor, pungent with the scent of decay. Beneath the cloud, thousands of dark forms darted among the trees.

Oniji dropped the spyglass and grabbed his bow.

Tetsuko turned to the villagers and yelled, "To arms! The army of blackness has come!"

With a sound like thunder, the black mass burst from the trees.

Swarms of goblins, the twisted race that Fu Leng created to serve him, led the army. They were mockeries of humankind, with pointed features and misshapen limbs. Tattered kimonos and bits of armor hung from knobby shoulders. Their shrieks filled the air as they raced toward the gate.

Lumbering behind them was a troop of ogres. They were huge, hulking beasts, slavering through their great yellow tusks and bellowing as they advanced.

In their wake, walking slowly but deliberately, came row after row of zombies. Most of them had been plague victims, and the hideous markings on their skin still oozed with the deadly disease. They were clad in the armor and mon of every clan in Rokugan. Tetsuko saw with horror that some zombies wore dirt-smeared kimonos in violet.

Tetsuko raced down the ladder and jumped onto Cloud Dancer.

Oniji shouted, "Fire!"

A rain of arrows sailed over the wall.

While one set of archers let fly regular shafts, others lit pitch-covered arrows and shot them over the wall. Women poured boiling water on the heads of foul goblins, which clutched and scratched the beams with their long, pointed claws as they climbed.

The air keened with squeals and shrieks of pain. For a time, it seemed as if the villagers could hold the entire Shadowlands army at bay. Then a huge *boom* rent the air. The heavy wooden gate rattled with the impact.

The gate had been bolted with the trunk of a tree, but it was only a matter of time before it was crushed beneath the onslaught. Tetsuko swallowed hard and gripped the hilt of her katana.

Boom . . . Boom . . . With an ear-splitting crack, the timbers broke apart, sending huge chunks of wood flying in all directions.

Tetsuko braced for the troops of creatures that would bolt through the opening. For a moment, all was still. Then a man astride a mighty black war horse crashed through the gate, waving a silver katana and screaming at the top of his lungs.

Tetsuko's mouth dropped open in surprise. She blinked and shook her head, disbelieving what her eyes were telling her. She knew this man.

It was Hoturi, the Crane daimyo. He wore sky blue and the mon of his house. It was unmistakably him, leading this unholy army.

When he was clear of the debris, he checked his mount. His eyes gleamed as he surveyed the ragtag villagers before him. His gaze fell upon Tetsuko, and a scowl darkened his face.

"Unicorn! How dare you ally with the Scorpion, despoiler of my people?" His horse turned in an angry circle. "I have ridden throughout Rokugan to find allies to defend my lands. Meanwhile you . . . you lend your sword to these traitors?"

The wound on her shoulder throbbed and burned, and Tetsuko grimaced. "What allies you have found, great lord."

"My father will be avenged." Hoturi broke the gaze and turned to the huge hole in the gate. With a shout, he waved his katana. The goblins and ogres advanced, their weapons drawn. Behind them, a large troop of zombies slowly clambered through.

"Forward!" Tetsuko screamed, waving her golden katana in the air. "Attack!"

She pulled Cloud Dancer's reins. Horse and rider jumped forward as one, attacking the first goblin they came to.

All around Tetsuko, the Unicorn cavalry yelled a war cry as they dived into the fray. Above them, a goblin surmounted the wall, and then another, followed by a troop of the slavering beasts, thirsty for blood.

Oniji tried his best to keep the archers together on the wall, but it was soon apparent that they were doomed. The archers dropped their bows and drew their katanas. One by one, the defenders were cut down. Their bodies were flung from the ramp onto the ground below.

As the battle raged on, the screams of villagers mixed with the grunts and squeals of monsters. Wave after wave of goblins crawled through the broken gate, gleefully cutting down villagers.

The folk fought on, brandishing homemade weapons with a skill born of desperation. They were no match for the Shadowlands forces. The ground was littered with corpses. Body parts drowned in a sickening mix of human and inhuman blood.

Buildings were set afire. Flames spread through the village. In the eerie yellow-green fog, the fire looked like a terrible monster with a thousand lethal tongues. Some villagers ran screaming into the flames, knowing they would be turned into zombies if their corpses remained intact.

A band of goblins swarmed Cloud Dancer. Tetsuko

wielded her katana with such speed and power that soon only one goblin was left standing. It tried to crawl up Cloud Dancer's flanks.

The horse reared. She screamed in horror and pain as the black claws gripped her flesh.

Tetsuko turned, ignoring the searing pain in her arm. She skewered the creature through the chest as it grabbed for her head. It shrieked and fell off the horse into a heap on the blood-soaked ground.

Tetsuko, her chest heaving, glanced across the square.

There, Umio and Eri were surrounded by ogres. Their mounts pranced and screamed as the two Unicorns threw blow after blow onto the heads of the enormous monsters. Umio disappeared beneath the crowd of grunting, drooling beasts.

Tetsuko dug her heels into Cloud Dancer's side and raced for her friends.

From somewhere nearby, the clear call of a battle horn split the air.

The Shadowlands army seemed to pause, listening.

Seconds after the call faded, the shouts of warriors rose. A new force charged through the broken gate. Blast after blast of the horn filled the air with their battle call.

The screams of the Shadowlands army changed from sounds of triumph to screeches of fear.

It was Yasamura's Unicorn army, roaring through the destroyed gate. Violet kimonos and armor flooded into the square. The cavalry viciously attacked the creatures that swarmed the village.

Relief filled Tetsuko, and she said a quick prayer of thanks before her attention turned back to the fight before her.

One ogre had gripped Eri's horse by the neck. The

animal's screams tore the air. Eri struggled to get a clear swing at the monster. Before she could, the horse's neck snapped with a terrible crunch. Eri and the horse were flung to the ground. She managed to jump clear of the weighty body and sprang up, sword drawn.

The ogre grimaced so widely that the light from the flames made its tusks glow orange. It pulled a huge club from its belt and raised it above its head.

Tetsuko charged it from behind, slicing her katana beneath a shoulder blade and deep into the creature's back.

It brought the huge club down with a sickening thud, missing Eri by mere inches.

Cloud Dancer pranced out of reach. Tetsuko swung again, this time catching the ogre in the lower abdomen. Thick, dark blood spurted from the wound.

The ogre did not seem to feel it at all, slowly raising the club again and swinging it mightily.

The thickest part of the club caught Tetsuko in the belly and flung her clear of the horse. She hit the ground and rolled, jumping to her feet. She gasped from the blow and from the savage pain that pulsed through her shoulder.

The huge beast laughed, planted its feet, and lifted the club to squash Tetsuko with one heavy stroke.

Eri dropped to her knees and slit the tendons above the ogre's ankles.

With a bellow, the ogre swung wildly, missing Tetsuko. It fell to its knees.

Simultaneously the two Battle Maidens plunged their swords into the creature's chest, one from the front and the other from the back, slicing its heart and organs in the dual thrust. Tetsuko jumped out of the way as the ogre crashed headfirst into the ground. Blood poured from its body in huge, dark clumps.

Tetsuko raced for Cloud Dancer and mounted painfully. Her left arm was oddly cold and numb. She whirled the horse in circles, trying to decide where to go to next. The square was filled with Unicorns, their violet armor gleaming as they cut away at the Shadowlands army.

Eri jumped onto a riderless horse and dashed toward a group of Unicorn cavalry. She helped them drive a band of screaming goblins toward the flames. Fire had spread to the whole village, covering the area with a choking smoke.

Tetsuko coughed violently, clasping a blood-streaked hand to her face.

Ahead of her, a lone Unicorn battled a horde of goblins. His mighty mount reared and kicked at the beasts as he sliced and parried desperately, but he was outnumbered and in trouble.

Tetsuko pressed her knees into Cloud Dancer's side and raced forward. "Yieee!" she yelled as she plunged into the fray. Her katana took the head off one goblin before he even knew she was there. Tetsuko swung a blow at the face of another, but it glanced harmlessly off its armor.

With a guttural growl, the beast hurled its sword at her head.

"Everyone wants to take my head today!" she bellowed. She cleanly sliced its sword arm to the bone.

It screamed, clutching the stump as blood spurted in a red fountain.

A second blow from Tetsuko's katana sent its head following that of its companion. The goblin's body fell to the ground with a thud.

The Unicorn leader still had his hands full. A goblin struck his armor with a blow that would have numbed the arm of a lesser man. He flinched, but did not fall, throwing a fast strike to the creature's head.

With a pained yell, it fell back. It hurled its nasty-looking sword at the man's body.

The Unicorn cleanly blocked the attack. He was so intent on this fight that he did not see the tall, blue-clad horseman who galloped toward him from behind.

Tetsuko saw. With a yell she pressed Cloud Dancer forward. She intercepted Hoturi just as he reached the Unicorn and attacked him with a well-placed blow to the head.

The blow clanged off the rider's helm, getting his attention. With a laugh, he deflected the shower of blows that Tetsuko rained on him. He sliced her in turn with an ease that left her breathless and bloody.

Tetsuko's katana clattered to the ground, and she fell from Cloud Dancer. Blood spilled from her body in a dozen fiery places. She rose to her feet, trembling.

Hoturi lifted his katana above his head to deliver the death strike.

Then Tetsuko felt a crushing blow to the back of her head, denting her helm and making her ears ring crazily. A second blow followed the first, crashing against her wounded shoulder and sending blinding pain through her entire body.

She pitched forward, fading into oblivion. The smell of burning flesh enveloped her.

12 INTO THE SILKEN WEB

"Ide Tadaji?" The timid voice came from outside Tadaji's rooms.

It was a gray afternoon, with rain clouds threatening to burst at any second. Tadaji sat alone in his room, oblivious to the coming storm. Before him, a few sheets of creamy rice paper were strewn about the table. His delicate calligraphy pen lay forgotten in its carved ivory case. A small glass vial of ebony ink sat at his elbow.

Distracted from his writing, Tadaji stared intently at the scarlet horse in his ink-stained fingers. Its color fluctuated from light pink to a deep black-red and seemed to glow with internal light. As he stared into its crimson depths, his nostrils filled with the stench of decay and death. His mind returned to his vision of twisted bodies on a black landscape. He trembled as one who is cold and cannot get warm, but his eyes continued to be pulled into the blood-red stone.

"Ide Tadaji?"

Tadaji blinked and shook his head to clear it. He quickly wrapped the horse in a square of thick black silk and placed it in its box. He picked up his calligraphy brush, dipped it into the ink, and leaned over the papers.

"Yes, come in," he called, clearing his throat and staring at the characters on the top page.

The servant slid aside the screen, entered, and bowed.

Tadaji looked up, feigning annoyance at the disturbance, and said, "What is it you want?"

"Forgive my intrusion, honorable ambassador," the woman said, not looking up from her prone position on the bamboo floor. "But Empress Kachiko has asked me to tell you that the emperor requests the honor of your presence in her private chambers in one hour."

"Thank you. Please tell her most gracious empress that I will accept the emperor's invitation."

"Thank you, honorable ambassador," the servant said, rising to her feet but remaining bent at the waist in a deep bow of respect. She quickly backed out of the screen, which rattled with the force of the wind as she closed it.

Tadaji smiled to himself. He had requested to see Kachiko only yesterday, instructing his servant to deliver his message to no one but the lady. He suspected the empress would pay attention to an urgent request to discuss the impending war between the Lion and the Crane. She would be uncertain as to where Unicorn loyalties lay, and she would wish to gather as much information about his clan's leanings as she could.

He wanted information as well, but not about the war.

His business with Kachiko concerned a dead Lion ambassador and the whereabouts of his friend Hoturi.

He rang a small bell on the table.

Eda entered. She was an elegant, elderly woman, with long white hair pulled back in a severe knot at the nape of her neck. Above her immaculate servant's kimono her face was a mass of wrinkles and lines. When he first became ambassador, she had been assigned to be his official palace servant, and she knew his moods and needs better than anyone.

"I am to meet with the empress in an hour," he said simply.

She nodded in understanding and disappeared, soon returning with a basket and a wooden bowl of warm, scented water. She placed them at his feet, along with a small white towel. Bowing again, she left.

He scrubbed his face and cleaned the ink from his fingernails. Then he stretched his legs out in front of him. Matter-of-factly, he pulled up the hem of the kimono and began to unwind the white silk bandages that covered his crippled foot. All Tadaji's life, someone else had tended his foot, from his mother when he was a boy to a special palace servant when he became an ambassador. He had always hated his crippled limb. It had been the source of anger and sorrow all his life.

But after Tamura had died, the plague had ravaged the land, and Tadaji had returned to his home in mourning, this indulgence seemed petty. He paused, remembering the first time he had unwrapped his foot alone in his room. On that cold, rainy afternoon, he and his body had finally come to terms with one another. From that moment on, he took care of his foot himself.

Tadaji briskly removed the last of the wrappings and

tossed them on the floor. He dipped the towel into the rose-scented water, gently pried each toe up one at a time, and bathed them. It really did look like a club stuck to the end of his muscular, healthy leg. The twisted toes bent like claws against the sole of his foot. His heel was round and red. As a boy, Tadaji had begged his father to cut his foot off. Now he accepted it as a part of him, and it relaxed him to tend it.

For a few moments, he carefully lowered the foot into the bowl, massaging it idly and letting the warm water loosen the tight, aching muscles. While his foot was soaking, he reached into the basket and pulled out a fresh bandage. He then slowly dried and wrapped his foot, taking care to wind the silk in exactly the same way as it had been before. It was an old ritual, and he smiled a little at the habit of it, but it somehow calmed him. He would need all the calmness he possessed for the audience to come.

Sighing, he rose and quickly chose a simple gray kimono embroidered with the Unicorn mon in purple silk. He slid his feet into black silk shoes, custom-made for his crippled foot. In them, he could walk smoothly, with only a hint of a limp. He opened a long, narrow box that sat in the corner and pulled out his most prized possession, his cane.

It was a masterpiece of the woodcarver's art. Intricate vines, so precisely rendered that some thought them living, climbed and twisted around the handle, which was made of solid gold. Here and there along the length of the cane, delicate golden flowers peeked out from behind the vines. It had been a gift from Tamura's mother, Chisato, many years before, and he cherished it. He needed it especially at state occasions, when he wanted to add a bit of flash to his appearance. He would need it today.

Soon the servant appeared to escort him to the Lady Scorpion. When they arrived, she bowed low and motioned for Tadaji to enter. He took a deep breath, gripped the cool golden handle of his cane, and went in.

Kachiko's private chamber was a light, airy space that held the feel and scent of an intelligent, wealthy woman. Carefully tended floral arrangements were placed in strategic spots throughout the room for the best visual effect. Bright silk hangings covered the walls with landscape scenes rendered in such tiny stitches that they were invisible. A beautiful low table stood in the center, carved with fanciful beasts and vines. It was surrounded by sumptuous silk cushions in deep colors that complemented the flowers in the room. And in one corner, Tadaji noticed the beautiful screens that Natsumi had hidden behind when she overheard the mysterious visitors to Kachiko's room.

Kachiko stood in one corner of the room, staring out of a small, round glass window that Tadaji did not remember seeing before. The gray storm light played on her profile, making her white-powdered skin seem more translucent that usual. Her long black hair draped elegantly about her shoulders. Small pearls on invisible strands of silk twined through her hair and glowed warmly. Her kimono was pale pink, shot with threads of silver. Tiny bells sewn along the edges trembled faintly, making a quiet tinkling sound as she breathed. She held one long, willowy hand to her throat as she watched the coming storm. She seemed lost in thought.

As Tadaji approached, Kachiko turned, her hand still resting at the base of her throat. She wore a simple mask of lace, but the mask could not conceal her luminous beauty. Her eyes were clear and bright, with a wide sensuality that caught Tadaji off guard.

He bowed low and paused, collecting his thoughts. Many powerful men had crumbled beneath the gaze of those eyes. They seemed to bore into his soul, discovering all of his deepest secrets. Those eyes were among Kachiko's best weapons, and already Tadaji felt wounded by them.

"Empress Kachiko," he murmured. "I am honored to be in your presence," he said formally, bowing.

"Ide Tadaji," Kachiko responded, bowing in return. She turned to Aramoro, who stood silently near his mistress. "You may go now," she said, fluttering her hand toward the door.

With a glare at Tadaji, the yojimbo bowed, and then left.

When the door was closed, Kachiko beckoned Tadaji forward. "Come here," she said. "I want to show you something."

Tadaji drew near Kachiko, his own face a mask of calm interest.

"Look at the window, Tadaji." She leaned backward slightly, letting her silky hair brush him.

Tadaji caught a whisper of her scent. He struggled to ignore her presence beside him, instead focusing on the extraordinary round glass window.

The surface of the pink-tinged glass was smooth, with no imperfections that would make the view wavy or blurred. Along the edges of the glass, the artist had formed thousands of tiny threads of gold into an interlacing pattern that shone as only purest metal could. In the center of the circle, imbedded in the glass, was a life-size golden scorpion. Tadaji placed his fingertips gently on the arachnid, feeling the bitter cold of the hard glass.

"An exquisite specimen of Unicorn art, don't you think?" Kachiko asked softly. "It was given to me at my gempuku. I recently had it installed here." She ran her index finger around the edge of the window, tracing the lines of gold in their elaborate patterns as the tiny bells on her sleeve tinkled softly.

"When the Unicorns first returned to Rokugan," she began, "a certain Scorpion, a powerful samurai, was taken with this barbarian artwork. He commissioned a master Unicorn glazier to make a set of windows for him. The man worked for five years on a set of ten, and when they were complete, they were hailed as the most beautiful objects that the Emerald Empire had ever seen.

"As soon as the Scorpion saw them, he immediately gave the artisan's family a fortune in koku. Then the Unicorn artisan disappeared. The Scorpion lord did not want the artisan to ever create anything as beautiful for anyone else again."

Startled, Tadaji stared at the glass as Kachiko continued, "There is only one window left of the set, and this is it. Each time I look at it, Tadaji, it reminds me of the power of beauty. And—" she paused—"the beauty of power." At that she moved away from the window.

Tadaji had never heard the story of the windows, but he didn't doubt there was truth in it. It sounded too much like something a Scorpion would do.

Kachiko took a few steps away from him. The silver bells tinkled gently as she moved. As he suspected, she began the conversation with the message he had sent. "So it seems Matsu Tsuko seeks to engage Shiba Tsukune in a personal war, after the defeat of her Lions by Phoenix shugenja."

Without missing a beat, Tadaji said, "Yes, Majesty. I am concerned about the growing threat. Were you aware that Tsuko has led several large armies into Doji Province?"

Kachiko nodded. She moved to the table. It was set with a tray of steaming tea and delicate cakes drizzled with honey. Kachiko lowered herself onto one of the cushions in one clean, graceful movement, motioning for the ambassador to do the same. He bowed and sat, laying his cane on the floor beside him. She poured the tea herself, and then handed Tadaji a steaming cup.

Kachiko sipped her tea. "It is a shame the Lion ambassador is not with us to explain the actions of her clan's forces. I was deeply upset at her untimely death."

Tadaji was unsettled by the calmness with which she mentioned Natsumi's murder. Without changing the expression on his face, he said, "Yes, it was a shock to the entire palace. Who could have done such a terrible thing?"

"The only reasonable explanation is that a Crane did this act," she said distastefully. "Crane Ambassador Kakita Umi left the palace before she could be questioned." Kachiko looked up at Tadaji from beneath her long, black lashes. "One witness, an old stable hand, swears he saw Hoturi leave in a rush only a few hours before Natsumi's body was found. He claims Hoturi was talking to someone before he left—perhaps an accomplice. If that man could be found . . ."

Tadaji took a sip of scalding tea. He should have known they had been watched in the stable, but he had let his guard slip that night. Cursing himself inwardly, he kept his face straight and his voice even as he replied, "I cannot believe Hoturi would do such a thing. There must be some other explanation."

"Perhaps," she said, taking a bite of cake. "You were well acquainted with the Lion ambassador. Perhaps you know something?"

Tadaji kept the mask of calm interest intact on his face. "Natsumi was a loyal member of the palace staff," he said slowly. "I believe she was concerned for the emperor's life, as we all are. She seemed to think that he is in danger."

"We are all in danger, I am afraid," Kachiko replied. "Did she tell you what her suspicions were, exactly?"

Tadaji felt the familiar grip of fear squeezing his stomach. Over the years at court, he had learned to heed this warning in his gut. "No, but she was clearly worried. I merely tried to give Natsumi some advice. Hoturi had suggested that I could be of some assistance to her."

"Hoturi was certainly in a foul mood when he left the palace," Kachiko remarked idly.

"He told me that he had an audience with you, Empress," Tadaji said, looking down as he chose a cake from the tray. "I was with him when Aramoro fetched him."

"You were?" Kachiko said. So she had not known—or had she? "Did he tell you why he requested to speak with me?"

"No," he lied smoothly. "But I know he was concerned about Tsuko leading a Lion army into Crane lands. This must mean that war has been declared."

Kachiko sipped the last of the tea from her cup. "The Lions are bent on destroying the Cranes at any cost." She poured herself fresh tea. "And what do the Unicorns think of this?" she asked.

So he was right. She wanted information about the Unicorns. He was prepared. "I have not heard from Shinjo Yokatsu in weeks," Tadaji replied, keenly aware of how easily the lies fell off his tongue today.

"Unicorn forces have been seen moving toward Dragon lands," Kachiko said, watching him carefully. He was silent as she continued. "It seems the Lion is not the only one bent on war. . . ."

So she thought the Unicorns were on a battle mission! He must be very careful now. "Unicorns do surprising things, as you know," Tadaji said, smiling as he tried to make a joke. "We are very unpredictable."

"But you are not stupid," she said with a tone of anger in

her voice, "as it appears the Cranes are. There are reports of a Crane army moving toward Unicorn lands. Your clan must be very powerful to be able to repel a Crane army and attack the mysterious Dragons at the same time."

Tadaji couldn't repress the small gasp that escaped him at this news. A Crane army! Had Hoturi disparaged his offer of alliance, choosing war instead? Tadaji choked on a crumb of cake, coughing hard for a moment and gulping the now-cold tea.

Alarmed, Kachiko motioned for a servant, but Tadaji shook his head.

"Please forgive me. This is news I have not heard."

"I can see that your clan has kept you as much in the dark as the Lions did to Natsumi," she said thoughtfully.

"The leaders of our clan, like those in the rest of Roku-gan, sometimes feel their palace ambassadors should not know all of their plans," he replied.

Kachiko looked intently at him, searching his face for signs of the lies he told. Years of practice in the Imperial Palace gave him the ability to hide his true mind, and he was confident she would be unable to read the real thoughts behind his mask of puzzled anger.

"Well," she said finally, "I'm sure all will be revealed in time." With that, she rose from the cushion, signaling the end of the discussion. Tadaji rose as well, pushing himself off the floor with his cane.

"That is a beautiful piece of work," Kachiko remarked, nodding at the cane. "I have always admired it."

"Thank you, Kachiko," Tadaji replied, bowing. "It was a gift from Tamura's mother, many years ago."

"Tamura," she said. "Tell me, did you ever discover who his love was?"

Taken aback, Tadaji replied honestly before he had a

chance to think. "No, I did not. But if she still walks among the living, I hope someday to meet her."

"Good luck then, Ambassador," Kachiko said, bowing. "I wish you well."

"And you, Empress Kachiko," Tadaji replied, bowing in turn. He pivoted, feeling Kachiko's eyes bore into his back as he made his way slowly out of the room.

Kachiko went to the Unicorn window and looked out. The storm had passed, leaving only muddy puddles of water in the garden and on the pathway beyond. She watched the old ambassador as he picked his way carefully along the muddy path.

"You think you know much, old man," she said softly. "We shall see."

13 SCENT OF DISCORD

The massive stone walls of Shiro Utaku Shojo felt comforting as Tetsuko lay in bed, listening to the storm that howled outside. She stretched her naked back against the torso of the one who lay behind her, feeling his warm skin against hers. He folded his arms around her, and she breathed the scent of sandalwood that always clung to him. He pressed his hands on her slightly swollen belly, gently rubbing the tight skin as she twined her fingers in his. "It will be a girl, bright and strong like her mother," the young man said, and Tetsuko sighed with the happiness that filled her heart.

A window high in the stone wall burst open, sending a blast of cold air into the room. The window began to open wider, like a monstrous mouth, and beyond it was a hole of cold blackness. Ice crystals swirled through the yawning hole and fell on her in a shower of white and blue.

Now Tetsuko was alone in the bed, the smell of her lover still filling her nostrils. She grabbed frantically at the cold, empty sheets beside her. She cried out his name, but there was no answer. Ice cascaded onto her bed, and a single crystal landed on her shoulder, sending a shock of cold heat piercing through her arm.

Then it was spring, and she was two years old, and her mother had placed her on a horse's back, alone, for the first time. Tetsuko cried for fear, and her mother scolded her. "Dry your tears, brave girl. You are Utaku. This animal is part of you, and you are a part of it. Do not ride on her, ride with her."

Tetsuko, trembling, nodded as she stroked the huge neck with her tiny hands. Her small, stubby legs didn't even reach around the sides of the huge beast, but she pressed her knees against the horse's sides as best she could.

She lightly pulled the reins, saying, "Forward, Wind Racer, ride with me!" in her high, childlike voice.

The magnificent beast turned and with slow, deliberate steps, moved forward. Excitement tingled through Tetsuko as she rode in rhythm with the horse's gait, as if the huge animal were a part of her. She closed her eyes and pictured the two of them galloping like the wind, her long black hair and the horse's black mane whipping in the wind together. Instantly the horse picked up speed.

"Yes, my daughter, speak to the horse with your mind as I taught you," her mother called as the child and animal rounded the circle.

Tetsuko opened her eyes and leaned forward in the saddle, still gripping the reins, and moved with the horse. As she raced past her mother, she saw her smiling at her tiny daughter, guiding the huge horse with a steady hand.

Now it was summer, and the sun shone so brightly that Tetsuko closed her eyes against the glare. She was on a bed, and the rough cotton sheets were stained with blood. She screamed against the pains that ripped through her body in waves. Gripping wads of cloth in both hands, she pounded her fists against the soft futon mattress as a voice somewhere commanded, "Push!" Then someone placed a tiny bundle into her arms and Tetsuko folded back the covering to see her child's face. But there was nothing there except a black shadow and the stench of death. Tetsuko screamed and threw the bundle to a faceless young boy, only fifteen or so, who stood in the corner, waiting. He was dressed in a deep purple kimono. He burst into laughter as he carried the bundle into a wall of flames.

Then the flames engulfed the room, and the walls exploded in a burst of red and orange sparks. Tetsuko screamed for help, but her voice was drowned out by the roar of the fire. Drumbeats vibrated through her mind, pounding with the pulse of the blood in her veins. She gasped for air. Her body was consumed by the heat. Then, in the center of the inferno, rain poured down in sheets of cold relief. Cool water put out the fire on her body, filling the air with gray steam. The steamy fog rose thicker and thicker, and Tetsuko felt herself falling down, her body weightless as it plummeted. Exhaustion enveloped her as she landed on something soft and warm.

For a time she slept. Then her mind awoke, and Tetsuko was comfortable, more comfortable than she'd felt in a long time. The soft mattress beneath her felt like a cloud, and the silk sheets wrapped around her like a cocoon. Tetsuko smelled the scent of sandalwood. A sob caught in her throat. She tried to swallow, but her mouth was dry. A form moved toward her, the mist swirling behind him as he walked. He smiled and held out his arms. Tetsuko smiled in return. As she stretched her hands to him, a searing pain shot inside her head, through her left shoulder, and down her arm. The dream instantly shattered. She gasped, fighting the nausea that the pain had brought.

"Good, you can feel pain," a familiar male voice said. Tetsuko tried to rise, but the lightning cut her head, and she fell back on the soft pillow.

"Tamura?" she said groggily, still in her fever dream.

"No," the voice said. "Do not try to move, Battle Maiden." A masculine hand pressed a cool cloth to her mouth, squeezing a few drops of water on Tetsuko's cracked and dry lips. She licked the cool liquid, and then whispered, "Where am I?"

The cloth went from her mouth to her face, wiping her sweaty brow. "You are in Yasamura's camp," he replied.

Memories came flooding back. The patrol. The duel. The village. The battle.

Tetsuko sighed heavily, eyes still closed, and lay still, careful not to move her injured shoulder. "How long have I been here?"

"Let's see," the voice said. "The battle at the village was fought six days ago."

"Six days!" Tetsuko exclaimed, and her eyes flew open. She was in a small, circular tent. It was night, and a single lantern burned on a low table beside her futon. A square of incense glowed in a small bowl beside the lantern, and Tetsuko caught the scent of sandalwood as the smoke drifted lazily by. Her eyes fell on the one who nursed her, and despite the pain in her arm, she broke out in a weak smile.

"Jikkyo," she breathed. Jikkyo grinned at her in return as he continued to bathe her forehead with the wet cloth.

"Don't scare me like that again, Tetsuko. Your wound was grave, and we were unsure if you were going to survive."

"My patrol?" she asked, closing her eyes as the cool cloth eased the pounding in her head. "What became of them?"

Jikkyo looked at her with a mixture of sadness and anger. "I am truly sorry, Tetsuko, but only two survived, you and Shenko."

Tetsuko turned her head to stare into the lantern light beside her.

"It is a deep and dark thing when those you command fall," Jikkyo said into the silence. "But now is not the time to grieve. You are seriously injured, Tetsuko, and even the shugenja who rides with us was unsure if he could save you." Jikkyo caressed Tetsuko's now-cool skin with the tip of one battle-roughened thumb. "Iuchi Akahito said that if you had lost any more blood, you surely would have died," he said softly, as a father who had almost lost a child.

Then Jikkyo cleared his throat, and his voice became more businesslike. "I was instructed to inform Akahito as soon as you awoke," he said, tossing the cloth into the bowl beside the bed. "I will return later." Tetsuko closed her eyes as Jikkyo gently brushed a damp strand of her chin-length hair from her face, and then rose and left.

Tetsuko had started to doze when a large presence bustled into the tent. She slowly opened her eyes and turned her head on the pillow to face the tall, imposing man standing before her. He bowed and dropped to his knees, looking intently at her.

"So, you are finally awake. This is good," he said in a mellow voice. "The fever has passed. Close your eyes, Battle Maiden."

Obediently, Tetsuko closed her eyes and immediately felt the shugenja's cool hands on each side of her head. Her skin began to tingle. A prickly warmth seeped through her skin and into the place where the blow had hit home. Her skull seemed to fill with a warm, soothing fluid that released all the pain and tension, and she sighed.

"Good, good," Akahito murmured, moving his hands lightly over Tetsuko's scalp.

Tetsuko felt herself slipping into welcome oblivion. She let herself fall once again into a fog where there was no time, no death, and no pain.

When she woke again, it was daylight and the tent was empty. She sat up slowly, testing her head and her shoulder for any sign of pain. Although her shoulder was numb, her head felt much better.

"Whatever he did, it worked," she said to herself.

A bout of dizziness hit her, and with a groan, she fell back onto the pillow.

"Tetsuko?" Jikkyo's voice came from outside the tent. "Are you awake?"

"Unfortunately, yes," she called out weakly.

The tent flap flew open, and Jikkyo entered, smiling. He was dressed in a dirty kimono, mud-smeared and blood-stained, and he smelled of horse and old sweat.

Tetsuko wrinkled her nose when he came close. "Phew! Have they kept you so busy that you have not had time for a bath?" she said. "Tell Yasamura he drives you too hard."

Jikkyo sat cross-legged on the cushion beside Tetsuko's futon and poured a cup of water from the pitcher that sat on the low table. He handed it to Tetsuko, saying, "Yes, I probably smell bad." Tetsuko gulped the water, and then fell back onto the pillow. Jikkyo continued, "I told everyone that as soon as you were out of danger I would spend a day scrubbing myself. Looks like I have to hold up my end of the bargain."

"There is some lavender in my pack. Feel free to use it," Tetsuko responded, and Jikkyo chuckled.

"What? And be mistaken for a Battle Maiden on a dark path? Never!" Relief filled Jikkyo's face as he gazed at Tetsuko. "It is good to hear you joke again, Tetsuko-san," he said. "I feared I would never again feel the sting of your tongue."

"No such luck. I am here to torment you once again, friend," Tetsuko replied, pressing her palm to the side of her head, "if this chaos in my head does not finish me off first." Her stomach chose that moment to rumble loudly, and Jikkyo leaned out of the tent and spoke to someone outside. Soon a tray of tea and steamed fish sat before them.

As they ate, Jikkyo told her what had happened. Yasamura's Unicorn army had marched to Crab Lands, seeking alliance with Hida Tsuru. Things were uneasy with the Crab, and they refused the offer. Yasamura then had turned north toward Dragon lands when they ran into a small Shadowlands force. The Unicorns defeated the creatures easily, and Yasamura ordered the army onward. When Shenko caught up to them, exhausted and almost unconscious, Yasamura realized the Shadowlands force they had defeated was but a fraction of the dark army that now moved south. Cursing his bad judgment, he raced south again.

"We could see the Shadowlands army swarm your village that morning, we were so close. Yasamura commanded the troops to move faster, for we knew you were doomed. When Shenko told me what you faced, I was certain I would find no more of you than what you found at the thieves' camp that night."

Tetsuko shivered at the memory.

Jikkyo took a deep drink of water and continued. "It was

clear the commander of the Shadowlands force sent only enough troops to defeat you. That was the only thing that saved us that day. Yasamura was in a rage, blasting on the war horn and commanding us to charge. I have never seen the Unicorn cavalry attack an enemy with such force and hatred, and it was a sight to fill my heart with both pride and fear."

"It seemed as if the village square was suddenly filled with cavalry," Tetsuko said.

"But we were too late," Jikkyo said, sighing and bowing his head. "The creatures had already breached the gate and the village had been set aflame. We destroyed the Shadowlands troops that still waited outside the gate, and then raced inside. By that time, however, there wasn't much left." Jikkyo paused and looked at Tetsuko. "How much of the destruction did you see?"

"Well, I remember blood, and bodies, and flames," she murmured, thinking. "I tried to save them, I tried to be a good leader. But in the end, all I could do was pray that their deaths would be quick."

Jikkyo looked at Tetsuko as she stared into the distance, struggling to remember the day. She couldn't remember what the creatures had done to the villagers. He knew her injured mind would recall the terrible scene someday, when she was stronger.

"It was not your fault that you faced a force ten times the size of the village." Jikkyo said. "Even if you had two hundred well-trained samurai at your command, you could not have hoped to survive."

Tetsuko remained silent.

Jikkyo continued his story. "I searched for you, but I soon despaired that you still lived. Then I noticed your boots sticking out from beneath the body of a huge ogre.

Only one warrior in all of Rokugan would wear such ugly things on her feet. You were still alive, only Shinjo knows how. By then the flames were out of control, and we had no choice but to flee ourselves or be consumed, so I threw you over the back of my horse, grabbed Cloud Dancer's reins, and ran."

Jikkyo chuckled as he poured himself and Tetsuko more water. "Yasamura was concerned that the main Shadowlands force would return and attack, so he ordered the army to keep marching," he said. "That was the worst time, when you were clinging to life by a silken thread. We could not stop for more than an hour or two to tend you. Akahito pleaded with Yasamura to make camp or your death would be on his hands, and he yelled back that the death of one reckless Scorpion-loving Battle Maiden would be insignificant against the decimation of his entire army at the hands of the Shadowlands."

Tetsuko sipped the cool water, fascinated that these two powerful Unicorns would have fought over her. "I suppose Akahito won, since I am still here and apparently still alive."

"An Ide shugenja does have a few tricks to force even the son of the Unicorn daimyo to bend to his will," Jikkyo agreed. "Two days after the battle, Yasamura gave in and made camp. We have been here ever since."

"What?" Tetsuko's eyes widened, and she sat up in bed. "This entire Unicorn army has been waiting here, just for me?"

"Yes and no," Jikkyo said. "We had many injuries during the battle; the Shadowlands creatures did not go down without a savage fight. Your injuries were the most severe. The wound on your shoulder had opened, and you were covered with deep cuts. You had lost a lot of blood. Now that you are recovering, we will probably move on in the next day or two."

Tetsuko leaned back on the pillow as Jikkyo looked at her. "How did you come to be at a Scorpion village, so far from your patrol route?" he asked. "And where did you get a wound such as that?"

Briefly, Tetsuko recounted the capture of the bandits, their arrival at the village, and the duel with Gonshiro. She also told Jikkyo about the old samurai's Scorpion lies. When she had finished her tale, Jikkyo sat back.

"Whoever is stung by a Scorpion is changed. Some do not live to find out how."

"There were moments when I doubted I would," Tetsuko said, pushing the tray aside. "I thought about what you would do in such a situation, and that helped guide me."

Jikkyo smiled in thanks at the compliment. He changed the subject. "You were consumed with a fever," he said softly. "You were delirious and said many things that you keep hidden in your heart."

She closed her eyes wearily and sighed. "Tamura," she said simply.

"Yes, that and more," Jikkyo said. "I do not think that those who heard you understood everything you said as I did, but some of your secrets are out."

"Thank you, friend," she said. "I will remember."

"Sleep now, and I will return later," Jikkyo said. "Yasamura wants to see you, and I promised I would take you to him today." Tetsuko nodded as her friend rose and made for the tent flap.

"Jikkyo?" Tetsuko called. He paused at the tent door and turned.

"If we are to see the Unicorn commander . . ." she said.

"Yes?" he asked.

"Take a bath," she mumbled as sleep descended on her mind once again.

Jikkyo snorted, and then was gone.

▲▲▲▲▲▲▲▲

Later, a well-scrubbed Jikkyo returned to escort Tetsuko, also freshly bathed and dressed, to Yasamura's tent. Tetsuko had seen the young, brash Shinjo only once, and she was eager to see if he was anything like his reputation.

At the entrance to his large tent, the two paused while the guard announced their arrival.

"Good luck," Jikkyo said, bowing and grinning at the same time.

"You are not going in with me?" she asked, surprised.

"Ah, no," he replied with a smile. "This audience is for you alone. If you like, I will return to escort you back to your tent."

"Only if there is sake waiting for us. I think I shall need it," she replied.

With a flourish, Jikkyo bowed to his friend and nodded in agreement. "Certainly, Battle Maiden," he said as the guard returned. "You can count on it."

The guard held up the tent flap, and Tetsuko ducked inside. The interior of the tent was more luxurious than she had imagined a field tent would be. It was oval, cut through the center with a large silk screen painted with scenes of battle. On her side, a simple but elegant circular table was ringed with cushions. Boxes and travel chests were piled on one another in an attractive masculine display, as if an artist had arranged them rather than a battle commander. Rich mats covered the bare ground. Tetsuko was careful to wipe her boots on the grass at the edge of the tent as she entered. The musky scent of incense filled the tent.

"Just a moment, please," a light male voice called from the other side of screen when she entered.

Tetsuko stood, slightly uncomfortable and nervous, her arm beginning to throb.

Yasamura appeared. He was young, not more than twenty. His long hair was tied loosely with a leather thong. He wore a clean and carefully pressed black kimono patterned with the Shinjo mon, which was a black unicorn's head on an orange background, edged with fiery red. He gave Tetsuko a slightly crooked smile that was both endearing and mischievous.

Tetsuko found herself smiling at this outgoing young man. She bowed. "Greetings to you, Shinjo Yasamura," she murmured politely.

"Greetings, Utaku Tetsuko!" he replied. His pale eyes took in Tetsuko's short chestnut hair, her wide, beautiful eyes, and her trim form. "You are as beautiful as you were the day I saw you at my father's battle meeting. So you are the wild and reckless Battle Maiden who saved my skin in the village?"

"That was you?" Tetsuko gasped, remembering the lone horseman overwhelmed by the goblin swarm.

"Yes, curse my own thickheadedness," he replied, waving toward the cushions. "Sit, sit, and we shall talk." As Tetsuko sat, the young man rang a bell.

A young boy entered and bowed.

"Are you hungry? I am famished. Achi, see what can be found for two hungry soldiers," he said in a rush. "And please bring some mint tea immediately." The boy bowed and raced away as Yasamura flipped his kimono behind him and sat with a flourish.

Instantly his expression became serious. "I must apologize to you," he said sincerely, all traces of his exuberance gone.

"Me? Why?" Tetsuko stammered, taken aback at Yasamura's abrupt change of mood.

"I failed to save your warriors," he replied simply. "I arrived too late."

Tetsuko was stunned. She did not know what to say.

"I am deeply sorry. I was unable to come to the aid of the village in time, and because of my slowness, the village and your warriors were destroyed."

He raised his head and there was honest sorrow in his face. "When I realized my mistake, I flew here as fast as our mounts could carry us, but it was too late."

He leaned toward Tetsuko, and she flinched back slightly. He didn't notice her discomfort and continued, "Even in the destruction, I saw what you had done, how you had banded the people together to defend their village despite desperate odds. It takes a strong leader to convince doomed people that they have a chance, and I admire you."

"Did any villager at all survive?" she asked, shaken a bit by the young man's sincere appreciation.

"No," Yasamura replied. "We searched the debris of the village, but we found no one living."

Tetsuko looked away and blinked hard, trying not to shed the tears that threatened to spill onto her cheeks. She turned to Yasamura and said, "They were an honorable people, those forgotten Scorpions. I know few will mourn the deaths of a village full of traitors, but they showed us kindness. They faced death with as much honor and courage as any Unicorn samurai I have ever known."

Yasamura looked quizzically at Tetsuko as she spoke. "I have not heard the words *honor* and *courage* used to describe a Scorpion in a long time," he said, "but I will trust your word. Their memory will not be forgotten or besmirched as long as I am alive to tell the tale, I promise."

At that moment the servant returned with a covered basket and a tea tray. Soon cheeses, bread, and slabs of cold roast venison were laid in front of Tetsuko and Yasamura, and two sturdy ceramic cups were filled with steaming mint tea.

Yasamura broke off a chunk of bread and laid a piece of the meat on top of it, followed by a piece of creamy yellow cheese. Tetsuko did the same in typical Unicorn fashion.

As they ate, Tetsuko recounted everything that had happened since they had stumbled upon the thieves' hiding place almost two weeks before. Yasamura listened intently until her story was complete. Then he sat back, sipping his tea thoughtfully.

"I saw the blue-garbed leader during the battle, but I did not see his face," he said. He shook his head thoughtfully. "I do not understand how Hoturi could have been at the village. I have heard from my father that the Cranes seek an alliance with us."

"I had hoped the chaos of battle had played tricks on my mind," Tetsuko replied, "but I saw him lead the charge. I am sure of it."

"This is quite a puzzle," Yasamura mused, "one that we do not have enough pieces to solve." He drank the last of the tea, and then stared into the depths of the empty cup.

Tetsuko cleared her throat. "There is another puzzle I wish to solve," she said, "but you do have the pieces to this one."

Yasamura looked up with a bemused expression on his face.

"How did I escape death?" she asked. "When I looked

into Hoturi's eyes, I was certain they were to be the last things I saw in this life."

Yasamura smiled wanly. "You have an enraged ogre to thank for your life. I saw you fall to your knees, and I rushed to attack the blue-clad rider. At the same moment, the ogre smote you with one blow of his club, and then crashed on top of you. Before I had time to throw a blow, the rider turned and raced through the gate. I followed him, but he had vanished in the smoke and fog."

Yasamura put his cup down with a clatter. "Tetsuko, this is not an isolated incident. Shadowlands forces are on the move everywhere. They have been sighted far beyond their own lands. These are not random, small bands of disorganized creatures. They are large, well-equipped armies that seem to have specific destinations in mind."

"Do you have any idea where they might be heading?" Tetsuko asked, rolling her cup in her palms and watching the green liquid slosh against the sides.

"No, not yet, but that is not the worst of it," Yasamura said. "More are coming, many more. The other clans are too busy killing each other to realize that a bigger threat to Rokugan is rising in the south. I fear the Unicorns will be the only ones to stand against the most deadly enemy of all."

He leaned toward Tetsuko once again. This time, she did not shy away, knowing the nearness was simply his way. "You were at the meeting at Toshi No Aida Ni Kawa. You know my mission. The Crab will not ally with us, but perhaps the Dragon will. Ride with us to Mirumoto Castle. I am sure my father will forgive your abandoning your mission, under the circumstances."

The circumstances were that she had no more patrol to lead. Tetsuko was grateful he left those words unspoken.

She sighed, suddenly feeling empty and fatigued. "Yes, I will ride with you."

"Good," Yasamura said, rising to his feet. "Now, Battle Maiden, rest. We ride tomorrow. My father expects us to arrive in Dragon lands in two days' time. Do you think you can make it?"

"Of course," she replied, rising to her feet and bowing to her commander. "I will be fine."

"The Utaku are strong as well as beautiful," Yasamura said, returning the bow. "I look forward to having you in my army."

When she emerged, Tetsuko found Jikkyo leaning against a tree outside Yasamura's tent.

He saw her and said, "So? How was your first encounter with the dashing son of our daimyo?"

"Interesting," Tetsuko replied. "But I am in need of that sake, and then a nap."

Jikkyo laughed. "By all means, Battle Maiden," he said, holding out his arm. "Follow me."

14 TRUTH, BROKEN

Kachiko,

Dark forces are on the move. The army—more than ten thousand in number now—increases with each passing night, and they grow strong under the leadership of a powerful samurai. They have destroyed numerous smaller villages, a few farming towns, a temple, nothing significant. But it is only practice.

I bow to your intellect, Sister, and I beg forgiveness for arguing against sending Unicorn patrols beyond their borders. Unicorns have been seen defending small villages everywhere, and their unnatural loyalty to the dirt-nosed heimin of all clans has cost them many lives and much respect.

As for the "Master" of the Four Winds, he

sits astride his horse like a clown, trying to convince the world that barbarians are worthy of trust. But the Battle Maidens are deadly, and there are those who would swallow their distaste and join with the Ki-Rin for that advantage.

It is now clear that among the six clans, the Crab must march alone. No clan will join with the Bear in alliance. His son Hida Sukune still lives, and his Crab force of twenty thousands marches to Kyuden Kakita. It is virtually undefended, and Hoturi's pitiful Crane army plods slowly westward. Sukune steps with care, for the plague still ravages Crane lands. He will retreat at the first sign of sickness to keep his army strong while the enemy screams in the agony of pus-ridden death. If the plague can do the job better, why not let it?

Tsuko tries to roar, but the Lion has her tail between her legs in the face of the Phoenix. Her hatred of Tsukune and the sting of dishonor drives her, and her armies move with discord. We will watch and see.

Hametsu

Kachiko looked out the round Unicorn window as she slowly rerolled the scroll and touched it to her lips. She turned to the ebony-clad form who bowed at her feet and said, "Many thanks. I will send a reply. Wait until midnight."

With the briefest of nods, the messenger rose and disappeared. Immediately Aramoro appeared and bowed to his sister-in-law.

"The black army moves," she said, returning her gaze to the garden beyond the window. The grass was bathed in early afternoon sunlight. "It cuts all in its path."

"Good news," the handsome man said, rising to stand near Kachiko.

She glanced at him and noticed with detachment that today he had chosen a simple mask that framed his beautiful eyes. "We must be cautious," she replied, lowering her head slightly and looking at him from beneath her long, dark lashes. "Alone the Crab march and alone the Crane fall. Plague still lingers at Kyuden Kakita, and there are no guarantees that it will stay confined to its walls."

Aramoro looked away. Longing and pain flickered briefly on his face.

"Sukune's Phoenix attack was a surprise," Kachiko continued. "No one is sure what those shugenja will do next."

"And the Unicorns?" the man asked, lowering himself onto a cushion before the carved table and pouring two cups of sake. "What of the Battle Maidens?"

Kachiko sighed and sat across from her brother-in-law. She wore a loose kimono of deep scarlet, and her hair hung unbound, tumbling over her shoulders like an ebony waterfall. A lock of her hair had fallen forward as she sat, and she absently pushed it over her shoulder with a delicate, feminine movement. He handed her the cup.

"I am unsure about the Unicorns," she replied, nodding in thanks as she raised the sake cup to her lips. "They scattered many of their good soldiers into the countryside to defend the heimin, which was foolish."

Aramoro shook his head slowly. "I do not understand them, nor will I ever want to."

"But their cavalry cannot be ignored," Kachiko said, and Aramoro nodded in agreement. "A large Unicorn force rides north, to Dragon lands to seek an alliance."

"They are fools to think that the Dragons will join them," Aramoro replied with a snort.

"Perhaps," Kachiko said, taking another sip of sake. "It is hard to read the minds of the Unicorns. They are so unlike our own."

"What of Ide Tadaji?" Aramoro asked, putting down his cup and clasping his hands together on the table. "Do you know his mind?"

"Better than he thinks," she replied. "He is a smart man, but there is conflict in his mind. That will work to our advantage. I had not counted on his seeing Hoturi as he left the palace that night. Did the stable hand ever remember what he heard?"

"No, he was useless," the man responded. "Too deep in his cups to be of any help."

There was a pause. Then Kachiko said, "I do not believe there is a place at the palace for a useless stable hand."

Aramoro nodded in understanding. Before nightfall, there would be an accident in the stables.

She put the matter out of her mind and sighed. "Tadaji cannot be dismissed," she said at last. "Although his mind is breaking, his heart is still strong. It is unclear which way he will finally go."

Kachiko chewed her lower lip thoughtfully. She rose, pulling her scarlet robe tighter around her trim waist. "Where will Tadaji be today?" she asked, moving casually so that the robe slipped over one creamy shoulder.

Aramoro's expression did not change, but his eyes saw what she intended them to see.

"He usually walks in the south garden in the hour before the evening meal," the Bayushi samurai replied.

"Perhaps he would like company," the Scorpion Lady said with a light laugh.

▲ ▲ ▲ ▲ ▲ ▲ ▲ ▲

"I am honored you allow me to escort you this evening," Tadaji murmured as he and Kachiko strolled along the garden pathway. It was the time between daylight and twilight, when the sky deepened from azure to ebony. Amaterasu turned from yellow to red as she slid toward the horizon.

"Yes, the sky promises to hand us another beautiful sunset," she replied, looking out onto a pond. Two snow-white birds glided just above the surface, their wings moving in tandem. "Do you see the cranes, there?" she asked, her voice as excited as a child's.

Tadaji's eyes traveled to where she pointed. He smiled and said, "They are beautiful, aren't they?" He had no idea why Kachiko requested to see him, but he knew she must have a reason. He waited to see how and when this Scorpion would strike.

"One Crane that we both know has been found," Kachiko said steadily. "Hoturi."

"Really?" Tadaji said, acting surprised. He expected Kachiko to tell him Hoturi emerged with an army near Unicorn lands.

"Yes, the Crane now leads a Shadowlands army," she said, carefully watching him. She was caught off guard by his intense reaction.

Tadaji's face turned white, and he stopped dead in the middle of the pathway. "What?" he whispered. "What?" His mind reeled from this news. The pathway before them had filled with images of mutilated animals, Tamura, and blood. He swayed as if he had been struck.

"Tadaji, please, are you all right?" Kachiko said with concern. "Aramoro!" she called.

Immediately the man, who had been following behind, appeared at her elbow. Aramoro half-carried the stunned ambassador to a nearby stone bench and set him down carefully.

"Tadaji?" Kachiko said loudly.

He slowly turned to her, his eyes gradually focusing on her face. "How?" he asked, swallowing to wet his dry throat. "When?"

"It is hard to say," Kachiko replied, somewhat relieved the old ambassador had control of his senses once again. "Just today I received a report that Hoturi and the Cranes have allied with the Shadowlands."

"That is not possible," Tadaji said, shaking his head. "Simply not possible."

"Yes, it is," Kachiko replied impatiently, waving Aramoro away behind the ambassador's back. "He has been seen by many, though the Cranes continually insist that he's with his army. Even some of your Unicorn patrols have witnessed him leading the foul creatures."

Tadaji slumped on the bench. He felt as if all the life had drained from him. Of all the news Kachiko could have given him, this was the one report he would never have predicted. His mind replayed the scene in the stable, but the conclusion was the same: Kachiko was right. The Shadowlands, so close to the Crab lands, would be the perfect ally for a desperate Crane daimyo who had been refused help from the Imperial Palace.

As Tadaji's mind grappled with the news, Kachiko rose from the bench and went to the edge of the garden where irises grew. She touched the delicate violet and white petals and ran her fingers down the wide green leaves. "Tadaji, I know you and Hoturi are friends. It is clear you have a great deal of respect for one another. I am sorry to have brought this ugly news to you."

Tadaji raised his head and looked at the beautiful

woman. "Yes, Hoturi and I have our differences, but there is a bond of friendship between us." As he spoke, his mind filled with the sound and sight of Hoturi. Suddenly it became simple. He did not believe what she told him. It could not be true. This Scorpion was hiding something.

Tadaji bowed, still sitting on the bench. "I am honored you chose to tell me yourself," he continued, speaking slowly so that he could control the trembling in his voice. "This is indeed harsh news."

Kachiko reached into her obi and pulled out a pair of scissors. "Do you remember these?" she asked with a smile. Tadaji stared at the delicate metal scissors.

"Yes," he replied. He had presented her the Unicorn scissors when she had become empress, in a gesture of goodwill. He had always assumed she had thrown the "gaijin" things away. It was a shock to see them in her hands.

Kachiko knew exactly what effect she produced. With a single snip, she cut a flower. The Unicorn implement flashed in her fingers, killing a beautiful thing and making it her own. Kachiko came and sat by Tadaji once again. She lifted the scentless flower to her nose and said, "Unicorns are honorable soldiers and loyal friends. Whom does the Unicorn count among its friends now, in these troubled times?"

Tadaji's eyes fixed on the flower in Kachiko's hand. She was still trying to get information from him. Tadaji's trembling has subsided somewhat, and fear loosened its grip around his heart. He was entering familiar territory now, that of diplomacy. It calmed him. He knew he had to proceed with caution. Whatever was spoken between him and Kachiko in the next few minutes would have a tremendous impact on many lives.

"It is hard to say," he said at length. "I just received a

message from Shinjo Yokatsu late yesterday. He told me that many Unicorns have died on the patrols. I think his mind is on that, more so than on whom he can count on in a battle."

"I did not know that there had been so much loss of Unicorn life," she said, her eyes widening in surprise. "If I had known the assignment was so dangerous, I would never have agreed to it."

"It is not your fault, Empress," he said, shaking his head. "I grieve for each life lost, but the Unicorn patrols were defending those who were unable to defend themselves."

Kachiko seemed momentarily amused by the idea that anyone would risk his or her life for heimin. She too was a skillful diplomat, though. "Their sacrifice was a worthy one," she said demurely.

"But as to other friends, I don't know that we have any," Tadaji replied honestly.

"None?" Kachiko asked. "Not even the mysterious Dragons?"

Tadaji gave a quick, humorless laugh. "The Dragons are as mysterious to me as they are to you, Empress."

"Then why do the Unicorns move into their lands?" Kachiko asked calmly, as if it were an afterthought.

Tadaji sighed. He knew she would find out sooner or later where Yasamura's army was headed. He suspected she had known for awhile. He also strongly suspected she knew they were not on an invasion.

"No, attack is not on Yasamura's mind," Tadaji said wearily. "He travels there to seek an alliance with Togashi Yokuni."

"Ah, I see," Kachiko said, a small smile playing on her lips as she sat back. "Somewhat of a risk, don't you think?"

"Everything these days is a risk, Empress," Tadaji replied.

Kachiko was silent. She leaned forward and placed a small hand on Tadaji's knee, peering intently into his face.

The contact shamed him. Taken aback, Tadaji shrank from her.

"Tadaji, I know that a Crane army marches toward Shiro Shinjo, hoping to convince Yokatsu to help them in the war against the Crab," she said earnestly. "It is certain the Crane will fall. You must know that. They have been weakened by the plague and fractured by bad military judgment. Hoturi has allied many of their armies with the dark creatures, and it is only a matter of time before all who live in Crane lands are overcome with the Shadowlands taint.

"It is imperative that no other clan joins the Crane. Any who does would be destroyed beneath the blackness of Fu Leng. Tadaji, if the Unicorns ally themselves with the Crane now, you will be fighting alongside Rokugan's most deadly enemy. Keep the Unicorns from this evil alliance." Kachiko straightened and removed her hand.

Tadaji's breathing slowed down somewhat. "I cannot mold the minds of others," he said slowly, trying to take even breaths as he spoke. "I hope my daimyo would not be so foolish as to ally my clan with the Shadowlands, but it is possible he does not know of Hoturi's treachery. There are forces working in the land beyond our control."

A great weight of exhaustion suddenly descended on Tadaji, and he bowed his head in submission. "It seems we both have much to consider before we act," he said without looking up. He could feel Kachiko staring hard at him, but he did not look up into those beautiful eyes. Instead he closed his own eyes and waited.

He felt her rise from the bench. Without opening his eyes, he bowed low to the Lady Scorpion. When she was gone, he slowly opened his eyes.

The last moments of daylight were rushing toward the west along with the setting sun, which cast a crimson glow and colored the clouds pink.

On the ground in front of him lay the iris that Kachiko had cut. Its Unicorn-hued petals had already begun to wilt in the darkness of the coming night.

15 THE GATHERING

For two days, Yasamura pushed his Unicorn division toward Shiro Mirumoto as if the entire Shadowlands army were in hot pursuit. He had orders from his father, and he was determined to follow them to the letter. So the army rushed on.

On the morning of the second day, the army entered Dragon lands. At first, the area looked much like the rest of Rokugan. Rolling hills were dotted here and there with small peasant villages, and occasionally a heimin on some errand stepped off the road to watch their passing. It was well known that the meadows of the Mirumoto lands contained almost all of the clan's farms and centers of business, and that it was the most "normal" of the Dragon lands. Even so, there was an odd shimmer to the air that made it seem to Tetsuko as if she had stepped into a watercolor scroll.

As the day wore on, the landscape changed from pasture to rocky cliffs. The air grew cooler, and wisps of mist peeked out from behind the boulders that encroached on the pathway. These stones were unlike anything Tetsuko had ever seen. Some looked like the heads of giants or the bodies of great sea monsters. Others rose like the towers of a grand fortress built by a forgotten race. Some were spindly and fragile, like shriveled fingers reaching for the darkening sky above. Sparse vegetation hugged the rocks, clinging desperately to the rough, gray stone.

From somewhere far beyond the cliffs, Tetsuko heard the sound of roaring water. She well knew the stories of the mysterious Dragon rivers: the placid River of Gold and the ghostly Oboreshinu Boekisho Kawa, the Drowned Merchant River. There were even stories of hidden streams not on any maps, that wound through secret places. Tetsuko shivered.

Gradually the road narrowed. Soon the horses were flank to flank. Walls of stone rose on either side. Just as the sun began to set, they rounded a bend. Tetsuko reined in Cloud Dancer and stared at the scene in front of the army, her mouth agape with wonder.

The road rose perilously beyond them, spiraling upward into a narrow ravine with high stone walls streaked in red and gray. Before them stood Shiro Mirumoto. The castle seemed to grow out of the living rock. It rose from the mist like a vision and loomed over the army with such power that it took Tetsuko's breath. The castle was built entirely of white stone, which glowed as bright and luminous as a giant pearl. The bright red roof seemed to float atop it, and its gold edging sparkled like sunlight off moving water.

The sight struck the Unicorn army silent. Unicorns had been raised with tales of the Burning Sands. Legends of grand castles, wondrous sites, and weirdly beautiful lands were as familiar to Unicorn children as stories of Shinjo and the Ki-Rin. But nothing had prepared them to see a legend of their own time come true. For the first time in Tetsuko's life, she knew what her ancestors must have felt like to return to Rokugan—strangers in a strange place they now had to call home.

Yasamura approached Tetsuko's column. He smiled and nodded in greeting. Then he turned to address the soldiers. "We have traveled long and far to arrive here," he began in a loud voice that carried through the host. "I am honored you have stood by me on this journey. I thank each of you for your loyalty and honor."

Tetsuko was surprised that a man with such a light tone could sound so commanding on the field. Her respect for him went up a notch.

"As you have guessed, this is Shiro Mirumoto, the home of the Mirumoto family of the Dragon Clan, and our destination. We have been granted entry into the castle. The Dragons have agreed to provide food for us during our stay."

Yasamura surveyed his dusty troops. "The last stretch of this road is the most difficult, and it will take us the rest of the day to climb to the castle. Once we are inside the castle gates, you will make camp and await further orders."

The exhausted Unicorn army soon forgot their awe at Shiro Mirumoto as they fought their way upward. Above them, the castle seemed to appear and disappear behind the cliffs as the army followed the twists and turns of the tiny ravine pathway.

At last, the army struggled through the main gate of the

castle and found itself in a vast field ringed by trees. The red roof of the castle peeked from the tops of the trees.

Tetsuko was wondering where she would make camp when Jikkyo rode up to her. He was dusty and sweaty, but he still carried himself as if he had just returned from one of the most elegant baths in Rokugan.

"Tetsuko, Yasamura has requested our presence," he said breathlessly. "We are to meet him immediately."

"Why?" Tetsuko asked as she turned Cloud Dancer and fell in beside her friend. "Can we not even rest before he has a job for us?"

"Doubtful," Jikkyo replied.

The two cantered toward Yasamura. He stood at the head of the army, looking fresh and bright, and conferred with someone.

The man was tall and muscular, and his head was shaven. Tattoos completely covered his body. On his forehead he wore a sinister-looking dragon tattoo that seemed to breathe real fire. His rough face was covered with the scars of many battles. But the most amazing thing to Tetsuko was his clothing—or lack of it. All he wore were deep red leggings. Sandals made from the best Unicorn leather were strapped to his long, rough feet.

The two men turned at their approach. Tetsuko and Jikkyo dismounted and bowed to them in unison.

Yasamura's crooked grin welcomed them both. "Ah, Utaku Tetsuko and Ide Jikkyo, thank you for attending me with such speed. May I present Togashi Mitsu of the Dragon Clan?"

The two bowed again.

Mitsu, a friendly grin on his face, bowed in return. "I am honored to meet an Utaku Battle Maiden. The stories of your fearlessness are renowned," he said in a rich, mellow voice. "And the Ide family is very well respected by myself and many others in Rokugan," he said, nodding to Jikkyo.

"Mitsu has spent much time at my father's home," Yasamura said, "and we have shared many discussions and games of Go. He only recently returned to Mirumoto Castle himself, and he will be at the gathering tomorrow."

"Gathering?" Jikkyo said, straightening.

Tetsuko cast a sideways glance at the imposing Dragon before her. She was fascinated by his tattoos, which seemed to crawl upon his skin like living beings. She blinked, thinking that it was the fading light that played tricks on her eyes. He noticed her attention and smiled a devilish grin. Tetsuko could not help smiling in response. Perhaps her eyes were not as wrong as she thought.

"Yes," Yasamura responded to Jikkyo's question. "There is to be a gathering of all the forces who have arrived here. We are not the only clan to send representatives to the Dragon, it seems. Tomorrow is an important day for the Unicorns, and I want you both to be there."

He turned to Tetsuko and said, "You will represent the Battle Maidens. The rest of the Maidens are gathering at Shiro Utaku Shoju now, and Kamoko was unable to leave them to travel here for this meeting. She sent word that you are to act as her representative."

Stunned, Tetsuko bowed in thanks. Utaku Kamoko, the legendary leader of the Battle Maidens, was one of the most honored warriors in all of Rokugan. Every clan admired and feared her. Despite her youth, all the Battle Maidens looked to her for leadership and guidance. It was unheard of for such a great samurai-ko to be represented by a disgraced Battle Maiden.

Yasamura saw the incredulous look that swept across Tetsuko's face, and he understood. "Perhaps," he said, with a slight gleam in his eye, "she has received reports of your courage against the Shadowlands army."

Speechless, Tetsuko bowed again deeply.

Yasamura turned to Jikkyo and said, "As one of my commanders, it is your duty to be at the meeting. As honored guests and elite members of the Unicorn army, the two of you will be housed inside the castle. A servant will show you to your quarters."

"Hai, my lord," Jikkyo replied with a bow.

Yasamura smiled. "In the meantime, relax. This may be the last time for comfort for many days.

"Now I must attend to the troops," the young Unicorn commander said. "Togashi Mitsu, will you accompany me? I would like for the army to see the friendship between Dragon and Unicorn. And you might see a familiar face or two from your last visit to our lands."

"I would be honored," Mitsu replied, bowing. "Until tomorrow then, Utaku Tetsuko and Ide Jikkyo." With that, the tall, mysterious Dragon and the exuberant Unicorn walked in friendship toward the camp, already deep in discussion.

▲▲▲▲▲▲▲▲

Later, after hot baths and a good meal, Tetsuko and Jikkyo met in the Story Gardens of the castle. Tall, carefully clipped hedges created a mazelike walkway through the garden, and the two strolled along the pebbled pathway.

They eventually came upon a tiny fountain. A bamboo pipe stuck from a hedge, and clear water splashed onto a flat stone beneath it. Beside the fountain was a small wooden cup. Tetsuko took a drink. Jikkyo settled himself on a comfortable bamboo bench nearby.

"Congratulations on your promotion to commander," Tetsuko said, refilling the cup and handing it to her friend. "I am glad you have finally been noticed."

Jikkyo smiled as he took a deep drink of the clear water. "I am honored. I just hope I will not fail my clan when it is time for battle."

"Which will be soon, I expect," Tetsuko said. She seated herself beside Jikkyo and impatiently pushed the long, deep sleeves of her kimono up to her elbows. No matter how many times she donned her best dress kimono, with its deep violet silk and simple lavender Utaku mon on each shoulder, she always found it cumbersome. She was much more comfortable in armor or in her leather leggings and simple fighting kimono. "What do you think will happen tomorrow?"

Jikkyo leaned back and crossed his feet in front of him. "I do not think of tomorrow now," he said with a smile. "When it comes, I will think about it then."

For a while they were both quiet. Around them, guests enjoyed the garden, and an occasional laugh drifted over the hedges.

Finally Jikkyo broke their silence. "Do you remember the time you had me thrown from that horse?"

Tetsuko thought for a moment, and then laughed. "Yes, I do!" she said, shaking her head and flashing a rare smile. "You thought you could ride that spiteful beast. I couldn't wait to see you try."

"You could have told me that he had already thrown you three times!"

"I will never forget the look on your face when you realized you were in the dirt!" Tetsuko replied, still smiling.

"I deserved it. Tamura always told me my arrogance would get me into trouble, and he was right."

Tetsuko became quiet.

Jikkyo immediately regretted his words. "I am sorry, Tetsuko, I did not mean to open that wound," he said softly.

"No, it is fine," Tetsuko replied, with a sad, faraway look on her face. "The memory of him becomes easier to bear each day. Besides, he was your cousin. You should be able to speak of him."

"Did he ever tell his father about you?" Jikkyo asked carefully.

"I don't know," she replied, picking at a stray silken thread that fluttered on one sleeve of her kimono. "When Tadaji summoned him to the palace, Tamura promised to tell him. By then my belly was too big to continue my training, and I was sent away."

Jikkyo said, "I had no more news of you until I saw you again at the Battle Maiden school. I was shocked, for I did not think you would return."

Tetsuko sighed. "After the child died, I waited. Each day I prayed to Shinjo that I would see Tamura walking up the pathway to my house. But a messenger came instead, and blackness settled upon my heart."

Jikkyo had never asked Tetsuko what had happened when she left the Battle Maiden school, pregnant by a garrisoned soldier and expelled in disgrace from her training. Although Battle Maidens were allowed to marry and have children, it was dishonorable for a Maiden to be so distracted during her training.

"I blamed his father for sending him away," Tetsuko said, burying her head in her hands. "I do not think that I can ever forgive that old man for it."

"Tetsuko," Jikkyo said gently, "when he agreed to Tadaji's plan, Tamura chose the path of a son who honors his father. You know that."

She did know, but she did not want to understand it.

The pain and longing were still too close to her heart. It was not yet the time for forgiveness.

The silence between them lasted a long time. Finally Jikkyo said, "You never told me how you got back into the Battle Maiden school."

"For weeks I could not even rise from my futon each day," Tetsuko finally said with a sigh. "Mama-san was frightened, for she had never seen me so. Finally she sent me to Utaku Benjiro, who was a great Battle Maiden in her day, many years ago. She pushed me hard, forcing my body to heal and, in turn, forcing my mind to do so as well. I owe her a great debt."

Tetsuko paused. "I think she might have spoken to someone at the school. A few months later I was summoned back. I expected a formal disgrace, but instead I was told to return and complete my training.

"I was empty, Jikkyo, like a well in a drought. I realized I needed something to fill me again. So I returned."

"And that is where I saw you again," Jikkyo finished the story, "when I requested a Battle Maiden for my patrol."

Tetsuko nodded.

Jikkyo thought for a moment. A grin slowly spread across his face. "You know," he said, "if you had married me, as we'd pretended as children, we would be living comfortably with a dozen little Battle Maidens at our heels. Instead, we're a couple dusty soldiers at the cusp of a great war."

Tetsuko smiled and looked into the soft, strong eyes of her friend. "If our parents had allowed it, Jikkyo, you might be right. But I was to become a Battle Maiden, and you were to become a great Unicorn commander."

"And here we are, exactly as our parents hoped," Jikkyo proclaimed, throwing his arms wide. "And only Shinjo knows what is to become of us."

With a final tug, the silk thread that Tetsuko had been fidgeting with came loose. She threw it on the pebbled pathway. Rising, she said, "If I do not get some rest, I will snore through the meeting and become disgraced all over again," she said.

"Let us go, then," Jikkyo said, taking her hand as he had so often done when they were children. "The last thing the grand Unicorn cavalry needs on its hands tomorrow is a Battle Maiden out of sorts from lack of sleep!"

▲▲▲▲▲▲▲▲

The next morning, Tetsuko rose and carefully donned her Unicorn ceremonial armor, freshly cleaned and shining. She met Jikkyo. The two of them made their way to the area where the Unicorns had camped the night before.

The early morning sun shone brightly on the deep violet lacquered armor of the soldiers. A hand-picked group of fifty Unicorn samurai had lined up to accompany their leaders into the castle. They were an impressive sight, and Tetsuko's heart swelled with pride. Tetsuko and Jikkyo assumed their positions flanking Yasamura. They were to be his personal guards at the meeting.

Shinjo Yokatsu stood at the head of the group of Unicorn samurai, looking uncomfortable in his finery. He was attended by his own personal guard of six Unicorns, all dressed the same as Tetsuko and Jikkyo.

When Yasamura saw his father, he strode up to him and bowed so low that his forehead almost touched the ground.

"Honorable Father, I am glad to see you well," the young man said.

"And I, you, my son," Yokatsu replied, shifting from one

booted foot to the other. He glanced behind his son and recognized Tetsuko. "Ah, it is she of numb foot and fearless abandon," he said, making Tetsuko blush as she bowed to the great Unicorn daimyo.

"I hope you have learned how to fold your feet beneath you properly, Battle Maiden," he continued, his stern expression unchanging. "This will be a long meeting."

"Honorable Master of the Four Winds," Tetsuko said gravely as she reached into her armor, "I am prepared." She pulled out a pair of soft silk shoes, and then bowed deeply to the older man.

His laugh rang out across the dew-covered field. Yasamura winced in embarrassment at his father's lack of decorum. Tetsuko and Jikkyo smiled.

"Well done, Battle Maiden," Yokatsu said, chuckling.

Tetsuko bowed again, pleased that her small surprise met with such success.

Then Yokatsu became serious. With one look to his guards, he turned. The Unicorn soldiers fell in perfect ranks behind him. Yasamura took a position to his father's right, flanked by Tetsuko and Jikkyo. Then the Unicorn contingent marched proudly to the Great Clan Gathering.

The large Visiting Room of Shiro Mirumoto occupied most of the ground level of the castle. The vaulted ceiling rose and disappeared into the dim shadows far above, making it impossible to see how high the room really was. The tops of the columns in the room also seemed to vanish as they reached for the ceiling. A light mist swirled in the gray shadows high above their heads. There was a dais at one end of the room, filled with chairs for the clan leaders, and a great wooden door at the other. The door was sealed with a single bar of gold and silver, carved in strange swirling shapes and odd symbols. The door itself was more than thirty feet tall, and it too had been carved with mystic symbols.

The floor was made of the same cool white stone as the castle. Tetsuko's boots made a loud noise as she pushed through the crowds that had gathered. For once, however, she was not the only person in the room wearing hard leather boots.

The Unicorns marched into the room and assumed their position along one wall. They stopped in unison and bowed to the assembled crowd. The representatives of the Dragon and Phoenix clans were already there, and they bowed in reply. The room was filled with row upon row of soldiers—the violet-clad Unicorns, the deep green-and-gold armor of the Dragon, and the crimson and gold of the Phoenix.

The clan leaders took their seats upon the dais. One chair remained mysteriously empty.

The clear, metallic call of a gong rang through the hall. The noise of conversation and movement quieted. As one, all soldiers in the room lowered themselves onto cushions on the floor. Tetsuko did the same, careful to adjust her feet as she did so.

A tall, stern man wearing full Dragon battle armor rose to speak to the assembled crowd. "Greetings to all of you," he said. Everyone in the room bowed in return. "I am Mirumoto Sukune, brother of Mirumoto Shosan, uncle to his honorable children, Mirumoto Hitomi and her brother, Mirumoto Daini. I am the administrator of this castle, and I welcome you."

Sukune cleared his throat. The entire room was silent, waiting to hear what the Dragon would say.

"It is unusual for us to have so many Rokugani within these walls," he said, surveying the assembly. "In truth, were it another time I doubt such a gathering would have occurred at all. But these are unusual times, and you are here because you realize this. We must decide on a course of action."

With that Sukune took his seat. A small, unassuming man rose to speak. He said in a quiet voice, "Greetings, I am Shiba Ujimitsu, Phoenix Clan Champion."

Tetsuko's mouth dropped open. She had noticed Ujimitsu surrounded by Phoenix samurai, but he had seemed too demure to be a clan champion.

Yasamura noticed her surprise and whispered, "The Phoenix will always surprise, you, Battle Maiden."

Quickly, the Phoenix Clan Champion described the Phoenix battle with the Lion, Kitsu Koji, on Crane lands. He praised the Phoenix general, Shiba Tsukune, and briefly outlined her campaign. Then his face grew grave, and his eyes raked the assembled group.

"The plague continues to devastate the Crane, much more than the other clans," he said. "For some reason it lingers within the walls of Kyuden Kakita. The castle is vulnerable." Then he detailed the Crab movements within the Crane provinces, including their threat at Beiden Pass. It was clear that he was an intelligent, thorough man, and as Tetsuko listened, she was impressed by this Phoenix's ability to convey his thoughts simply and clearly, without pomp or arrogance.

When his report was complete, Yokatsu stepped up to the dais. Yokatsu took a deep breath and faced the crowd, his fingers drumming against his thigh.

"Three days ago, Hoturi's sensei, Toshimoko, arrived at the gates of Shiro Shinjo. He had been sent by Doji Hoturi to requested an alliance with the Unicorns against the Crab. He told me that Hoturi now leads a smaller Crane force that is now near Beiden Pass, and he showed me a message from his commander to verify this."

Yokatsu continued, "There have been rumors that Hoturi has allied the Cranes with the Shadowlands. I do not know if the honorable Doji has become so desperate as to resort to such an alliance, but Toshimoko came to us in good faith. He had no knowledge of his commander's apparent treachery and insisted that his errand was sincere. He is an honest man, and I believe him."

The short, dignified Unicorn cleared his throat again. "While it might be true that Hoturi has convinced other Cranes to follow him into treachery, it is clear that neither Toshimoko nor the army he commands are allied with the darkness. They were welcomed by my clan, but it was too late for them to make the trip to this meeting, so they wait for news."

Tetsuko was shocked. She leaned to Yasamura, who had a scowl on his face. "But we saw Hoturi, in the village," she whispered urgently. "He was leading the Shadowlands force himself."

"Yes, Yokatsu knows this, and he believes us," Yasamura whispered in reply. "But you and I are the only ones who witnessed Hoturi at the massacre in the village. My father must convince the others that Hoturi poses a darker threat, but for now his greater concern is this alliance."

Tetsuko nodded slowly as she began to understand Yokatsu's motive. The clans must first agree to unite. Once that occurred, they could face the enigma of Hoturi.

With that, Yokatsu left the dais. The assembly was buzzing with all the news, clearly confused and uncertain. If Hoturi had convinced the Cranes to ally with the Shadowlands, no clan would dare help them. But if Yokatsu were right. . . .

Mirumoto Sukune returned to the dais and motioned to someone in the back of the hall. Suddenly the huge double doors at the end of the room swung open. All heads turned. A rhythmic *thunk thunk* of marching soldiers began and grew louder. The crowd parted to let the newcomers through. Leading them was a man Tetsuko had never seen before.

He was very tall, almost six feet. His skin was so pale that Tetsuko wondered if it had ever seen sunlight. His stern, clear face reminded Tetsuko of the look of a small child who had been bullied but was determined to stand up to his tormentor. He was dressed in full battle armor, solid black, with no mon or clan insignia anywhere. He was followed by a dozen ronin, all fully armed.

"Who is that?" Tetsuko whispered as they passed.

Jikkyo leaned to Tetsuko and said, "You are looking at Toturi, disgraced ronin and onetime Lion Clan Champion."

Everyone in the room was stunned. Tetsuko felt a mix of surprise and anger in the air. She watched the legendary man stride forward.

Toturi was the greatest general—and failure—that Rokugan had ever seen. His prowess on the field and his honor and loyalty to his clan and his emperor were once unquestioned throughout the Emerald Empire. He had never failed in his duty to the throne or to his clan—until the disastrous events of the coup. Now he walked before the assembled crowd as an outcast, a ronin—a samurai without a master.

Looking straight ahead, seemingly oblivious to the heavy silence that filled the vast room, Toturi went to the dais and sprang upon the platform. Clasping his hands behind his back, he stood quietly beside Sukune. Toturi eyed the gathering with calm assurance that galled Tetsuko.

Beside her, Yokatsu drummed his fingers. His face was a stern mask as he watched Toturi.

"Toturi has agreed to lead the Dragon army," Sukune said simply. No one in the room moved or spoke at this stunning announcement, but the air crackled with astonishment. It was as if each person in the room had become a statue.

Toturi bowed to Sukune, and then he stepped forward.

"I will be brief," he began. "Rokugan is threatened with a danger far greater than plague or petty warfare between clans. We teeter at the edge of a great cliff. There is only eternal blackness and agony below. I know, for I have glimpsed it."

Toturi surveyed the assembly, his face betraying no emotion. "I see friends among you, and I see also those I once counted as enemies. No more. We now have a purpose that is greater than the squabbling of clans. That purpose comes from far to the south. For years it has lain dormant, but the darkness now is rising. No one clan can battle it alone. We must unite in battle and bloodshed. If we do not, I fear we all will fall.

"You do not trust me," he continued. "I am disgraced, ronin. I have no right to stand before you and ask for your support. But still, I am here. You are among the most powerful leaders in the Emerald Empire. You are here because you also see what I see—an uneasiness in the world, an open wound that cannot heal. We can defeat this threat, if we join forces to face it."

Toturi's voice became a cadence, steadily rising as he spoke. "There is no honor in my presence here. But I am here. There is no honor in the deaths of our families, who fell to a black disease that flew like the wind over the land. Yet they are dead. There is no honor in the twisted creatures that rise against our farmers, spilling their blood and leaving their homes in blackened waste. But the people still die, and the land still bleeds.

"We must regain the honor that Rokugan is losing!" Toturi's voice filled the silence of the room. "Each of us has a duty to protect our lives, our freedom, our honor, from the forces that try to wrench it from our grasp. Some of you may say I have no honor. I will live with dishonor if I must. I will live with your hatred and your contempt if I must. But can you live with the shame of defeat, when the Shadowlands army comes? There will be no honor in watching your families die."

The word "die" hung in the air. It slowly faded. Toturi spoke again, but now his voice was even.

"The fate of the Emerald Empire lies in our hands," he said. "I will fight alongside anyone who believes the same, anyone who will fight with me."

Then Toturi bowed and stepped back. No one breathed or moved. The great ronin stood quietly, his hands clasped behind his back. He gazed out at the sea of faces.

Slowly, in perfect unison, the twelve ronin who accompanied Toturi into the hall rose to their feet in silent support of their leader.

On the dais, Sukune turned to Toturi and bowed.

"You are the new leader of the Dragon forces," he said. "Our clan puts our faith and honor in you."

At his words, the Dragons in the assembly rose silently to their feet in agreement.

For a long moment no one spoke or moved. Then to Tetsuko's amazement, Phoenix Clan Champion Shiba Ujimitsu slowly rose to his feet. His steady gaze locked with his lieutenant's. He too rose, forcing those behind him to come to their feet. The only sound was the soft clanking of the armor of the Phoenix as, one by one, they stood and faced their leader.

Yokatsu had long ceased drumming his fingers. His

stern expression had not changed throughout Toturi's speech, but the usually fidgety Unicorn daimyo had become deathly still. Although no one looked in his direction, it felt as if every eye in the room was upon him. The air hissed with anticipation and uncertainty.

Slowly, without taking his eyes from the floor, Yokatsu too rose to his feet.

"For eight hundred years, we rode in the wilderness," he said softly. The cavernous room was so still that each word could be heard clearly. "We longed for the land of our ancestors beneath our feet. Now that we are home, we will defend it with our lives."

No other word was spoken. Tetsuko realized she was holding her breath. She let it out slowly.

She, Yasamura, and Jikkyo stood. Behind them the entire Unicorn force rose as well.

They all stood—ronin, Phoenix, Dragon, and Unicorn—side by side in the huge, silent room, united. Toturi's expression didn't change, but Tetsuko thought she saw something flicker behind his eyes.

There was pride, there, certainly. But there was something else too. Relief. As the young Battle Maiden stood tall and proud beside her leaders, she wondered if it was Toturi's relief she saw, or only her own reflected in his eyes.

▲▲▲▲▲▲▲▲

"The greatest threat we face is the Crab, who gather near Beiden Pass. It is imperative that the pass remained open. That much we all agree upon."

It was evening, and the Unicorn daimyo had invited Yasamura, Jikkyo, and Tetsuko to dine with him. Now they sat at an elegant low table in Yokatsu's quarters, feasting on grilled fish, rice, and sake. Earlier that afternoon, the leaders of each clan had met to discuss the strategy they would use in the weeks to come.

Yokatsu shook his head as he sipped his sake. "Toturi has always considered strategy to be more important than bloodshed," he said. "I do not quite know what to make of him, but he speaks with a strength born of both victory and defeat."

Yokatsu drained the sake cup and turned his attention to his meal. "Yasamura, it has been decided that you will lead the main force of the Unicorn cavalry toward Beiden Pass."

Yasamura bowed to his father in respectful silence. Tetsuko could see the excitement in his eyes at this great honor.

"Toturi is to take the Dragon army, along with the other samurai who have sworn loyalty to him, and join Shiba Tsukune in the Crane lands," Yokatsu continued. "We hope he will be able to defend Kyuden Kakita from the Crab threat. I will lead a small Unicorn unit and go with Toturi. Tetsuko will ride with me."

They continued the discussion far into the night. Afterward, Jikkyo returned to his quarters. Tetsuko was still wide awake, so she donned her loose leather leggings and a soft, light kimono and headed for the Story Gardens.

At this time of night they were deserted. Tetsuko found the small fountain and once again took a drink of the clear, icy water. After that, she sat on the bamboo bench, letting her nerves relax and her mind slow down from the day. The sound of the water splashing quietly on the rock calmed her, and she fell into a light meditative trance.

Someone approached nearby.

Tetsuko did not sense danger, so she allowed her mind

to lift slowly from inside itself before she turned to see who was there. It was Toturi, eyeing her with curiosity. The unexpected appearance of the ronin made her start. She rose to bow to him.

He returned her greeting, and then said, "Please, be comfortable. I did not realize there would be someone else at the fountain at this time of evening."

"You come here?" Tetsuko asked, a note of disbelief in her voice. Toturi's name had been part of the stories of Rokugan for as long as she could remember, and tales of his exploits during the coup had settled into legend and nightmare. To be in the presence of such a famous person, and to see that he was merely human, was a bit of a shock.

Toturi could see what she was thinking, and he smiled. "Yes, even disgraced samurai can enjoy the solitude of a quiet garden." He eyed the bench that Tetsuko was sitting on. "May I join you, Battle Maiden?" he asked.

"Why . . . yes, please," Tetsuko stammered, moving so that there would be room beside her. Her heart pounded in her chest from nervousness, and inwardly she cursed herself for being so childish.

He sat beside her and gazed at the fountain. His simple brown kimono fit him well, and his dark hair was pulled from his face in a simple knot. For a time they both sat in silence.

Finally Toturi spoke. "I have heard of you, Utaku Tetsuko. Yasamura speaks highly of you and your skills in battle."

Tetsuko turned to the older samurai in surprise. "Me?" she laughed shortly, shaking her head. "I am only a disgraced Battle Maiden, hoping to salvage a shred of honor."

"Then we have much in common, I think," Toturi said quietly. Behind his dark eyes Tetsuko saw a deep sorrow. She turned her head and was quiet, for all words had left her.

"What was it like for you, battling the Shadowlands creatures?" Toturi asked, honestly curious.

Tetsuko closed her eyes and for a long time did not speak. Finally she said, "At first it was like any other battle. My only task was to figure out how to defeat them, and then do it."

She was silent for a moment. "But it was not the same. Evil surrounds them. It cannot be touched or seen, but it is felt all the same. The chill of it froze my blood."

Toturi nodded as Tetsuko continued. "The zombies were the worst, for they had the faces of ones I loved. Although I knew that they were not the people I once knew, I almost could not strike them."

The young woman looked at Toturi and confessed, "My hesitation almost cost me the lives of myself and others, and I will never forget that lesson."

"See that you don't, Tetsuko, for that is how the darkness works," Toturi replied. "It comes in the disguise of friendship and honor, and it uses your emotions to weaken you." He looked at the young samurai-ko, whose face was twisted with memories. Of all people, he would know what lived in her head. She would have to make peace with those memories, or they would torment her for the rest of her life.

"You have a strong heart, Battle Maiden," he continued. "You faced an entire Shadowlands force and fought with fierceness. I have respect for you." To Tetsuko's astonishment, he bowed slightly, and she bowed back.

Then he unpinned a brooch from his kimono and showed it to Tetsuko. It was a simple gold disk with a deep violet stone embedded in the center. She looked at him quizzically.

"When I was a small boy, I was sent to live in a monastery

within Phoenix lands," Toturi began. "While I was there, one of the monks took a great liking to me, for I was bookish and serious. He told wonderful stories, and for some reason I especially enjoyed the dark tales of the Shadowlands. Years later, right before he died, he sent this to me, along with a note that read, 'Hold it close, little cub, so the dark will not get you.' His kindness to me has never been forgotten." Toturi had a faraway look in his eyes as he spoke.

Toturi roused himself from his memories and continued. "I have seen the dark, Battle Maiden, and I wish it upon no one else. I would like you to have this, so that the dark will not get you too."

Tetsuko's eyes flew wide open, and she bowed immediately. "Great Toturi, I could never accept such a gift. I am not worthy of this."

Toturi smiled, and Tetsuko was surprised by how much it softened his weary face. "You are Utaku, which means your heart beats strong and fierce in your chest. You have battled the demons of Fu Leng and you will do so again. This will help you in your fight."

Bowing again, Tetsuko replied, "Your skills and courage are legendary, and I am content merely to speak to you. Your words are gift enough for me, Toturi."

Toturi stood up and gave Tetsuko a final small bow. "I thank you for your kind words, Battle Maiden," he said. "But this gift will protect you far more than my clumsy words will ever do. Take it and wear it with the same pride I have in giving it to you."

Slowly Tetsuko took the pin from the meaty, war-worn hands of the man who stood before her. Its violet jewel was so dark that it seemed almost black, with flecks of deep purple and light lavender dancing in its depths. She pinned it to the shoulder of her kimono and bowed deeply.

"I am honored by your gift, and I am ashamed that I do not have something to offer you in return," she said, unable to look the ronin in the face.

"No matter, young Utaku," Toturi said. "I suspect that when the time comes, you will offer me something far greater in value than a jewel set in gold. In the meantime, wear the pin over your heart, and think of it when the breath of darkness whispers to you." With that, the great, sad ronin turned and disappeared in the maze of hedges, leaving Tetsuko to make her way thoughtfully back to her rooms alone.

16 DANCING IN A GARDEN OF DEATH

Most Honorable Sister,

I apologize for the strange way in which this letter comes to you, but I strongly suspect that my correspondence is being watched.

Things have become worse here at the palace. Since the death of the Lion ambassador, the air tingles with tension, and no one can be trusted. I have been followed at least twice that I know of, once while on my way to the baths and again returning to my rooms from a meeting. Although I have not been able to see who it is that watches me, I know he is there. I do not walk in the palace gardens alone at night, and now I no longer feel safe during the day.

I did not believe Kachiko when she told me that Hoturi has allied with evil. I know his love for his clan is so strong that he would do *desperate things, but not that, I am sure. I do suspect, however, that Kachiko refused to provide him the forces he needed against the Crab.*

Empress Kachiko is still to my mind the Scorpion Lady. She continues to nurse our emperor, and it is common for her to disappear for days at a time. When she appears, however, it is as if she has never been gone. She does not mention the emperor or seek to calm anyone's fears about his condition, but perhaps she puts on a good face. It is almost as if she forgets his existence when she leaves his chambers.

Natsumi knew something, I am certain, and it cost her her life. But I do not know if Kachiko had anything to do with it. The Crane ambassador, Umi, hated Natsumi, and she also knew that something was amiss with Kachiko. If Natsumi did stumble upon a plot to kill the emperor, then that knowledge would be worth a great deal to Hoturi, desperate for the military favor of the Imperial Palace. It would also be of some importance to the Scorpion Lady, who would crush the murderers with one stroke.

Many in the palace knew of my friendship with Natsumi. It does me no good to insist that I know nothing, for lies flow like water here now. I must be careful.

Beloved sister, I must close. If the situation at the palace does not improve, I may return home for a while. If so, I will send word to you before I leave.

Tadaji

Tadaji sighed and sat back, reading the words he had

written. He sprinkled rice powder over the pages to dry the elegant characters, and then gently blew it away. He carefully rolled the pages, sealed them with wax, and rang the small bell on the table.

The door slid open, and Eda entered, moving to Tadaji with practiced ease. She bowed low.

"Eda, please see to it that this message is sent, the same way as before," Tadaji instructed.

"I understand," she said, bowing.

"And please be careful that you are not watched or followed."

The older lady bowed again. She rose and cocked her head expectantly.

Tadaji noticed and said, "Yes, is there something else?"

"Yes, Ambassador," she said in a light voice that belied her years. "A message came for you, delivered by a woman I have never seen." Eda handed Tadaji a dirt-streaked sheet of rice paper, folded into a clever origami shape of a crane.

"What did she say?" Tadaji asked as he fingered the folded paper animal.

Eyes downcast, Eda replied, "She told me to deliver it to you before sundown and instructed me to wait for a reply."

"Thank you," Tadaji said. "Please wait."

The woman bowed and retreated to a corner.

Slowly Tadaji unfolded the origami and read the brief message.

The Lion knew. Meet me in the birch garden, alone, an hour past moonrise.

Daidoji Asira

Beneath the signature was the official stamp of the Crane Clan ambassador.

Fear washed over Tadaji. He stared at the hastily brushed words. He vaguely remembered Asira as one of Kakita Umi's secretaries, a tall, willowy man with the look of a librarian about him. He did not seem the type to be sneaking around a garden at night, caught up in palace intrigue. "If he is the one who sent this, of course," Tadaji said aloud.

He shook his head as he absently folded the note back into its origami shape. He could hear Tamura's voice deep in his mind, a constant presence since the horrible vision in the garden. His hands trembled, and the delicate crane's wings beat lightly at the movement, as if it were trying to fly from his grasp. Tadaji cried out, dropping the paper bird.

Eda was instantly at his feet.

"No, no," Tadaji replied, his voice catching in his throat. "Tell the messenger I will be near the waterfall in the birch garden an hour past moonrise. Then send Numo to me."

Eda looked keenly at her employer, whom she had served for years. He had always been a strong, steady presence in the palace, using his wit and intelligence to the greatest advantage in every situation. She had grown to respect and care for him over the years. Since the death of his son, however, he was distant and preoccupied. Something ate at him, something that made him cry out in his sleep and made him fear the dark.

She bowed and silently disappeared through the sliding rice-paper door.

Tadaji, feeling anxious and restless, puttered about his rooms until a soft knock came soon after.

"Come in," he said.

Numo entered. Occasionally, when the dreams got very

bad, Tadaji had hired this silent, honorable yojimbo to stand watch outside his chamber at night.

"I have need of your services tonight," Tadaji said.

▲▲▲▲▲▲▲▲

The evening was cool when Tadaji made his way to the birch garden. The waxing moon cast a white light on the smooth stone pathway Tadaji walked. He glanced to either side of him, trying to glimpse his guard. He didn't see Numo anywhere, but he was certain the yojimbo was somewhere nearby, ready to come to his aid.

Tadaji smiled a little as he felt the familiar bulk of his tanto carefully hidden within the folds of his obi. He was prepared.

Finally, Tadaji reached the delicate bamboo gate that led into the gardens. He lifted the latch and went inside.

Although this section of the palace grounds had escaped the ravages that had destroyed other areas, it was neglected and overgrown. Tadaji felt sorrow that such a lovely garden had been left unattended for so long. But in the silvery moonlight it was still beautiful.

Hundreds of tall birch trees stood in narrow rows, their white trunks rising like the marble columns of a forest temple. The sweet scent of honeysuckle filled the air and mixed with the musky scents of animals and plants. For a moment Tadaji forgot his danger as he breathed the heady aromas.

Tadaji made his way toward the sound of falling water. A small waterfall cascaded over a carefully crafted pile of rocks that had been placed in the stream centuries before. Soft moss and honeysuckle bushes grew alongside both banks of the stream.

As Tadaji made his way carefully through the birch garden, the moon went behind a cloud.

Tadaji was not alone. It was not a noise or a smell that alerted him, but a sudden sensation of unease in his gut.

He stopped in midstride. All his nerves tingled with the instinct to flee. He froze.

There was no sound in the garden save the waterfall and the light whisper of wind as it wound through the trees. The leaves far above moved with a gentle sigh.

"Numo?" Tadaji called softly.

A sturdy figure stepped from the brush on the other side of the stream. With one swift movement, the figure raised a bow to his shoulder and let an arrow fly. At almost the same instant, something whizzed past Tadaji's nose and hit a tree beside him with a solid *thwack!*

Tadaji stared at the thin arrow as it vibrated crazily in the tree, less than an inch from his head. He jumped off the path and into the undergrowth beyond the tree. He rolled on his shoulder and sprang up on his feet the best he could. With one quick motion, he pulled the tanto from the folds of his obi and stood in a crouch, breathing heavily from the exertion. From beyond the path, he heard a rustle.

The dark figure on the other side of the stream again drew his bow.

Tadaji sucked in his breath and dived for the ground. A second arrow whizzed above him. A muffled curse came from the figure.

"Numo!" Tadaji yelled as he dodged through the trees, his heart pounding. Behind him he could hear the sound of footsteps in pursuit. The cold fear of being hunted gripped the Unicorn's heart. He looked wildly about in the semi-darkness, confused and disoriented. He thought he was running toward the gate, but he wasn't sure.

The figure crossed the stream with a splash of footsteps.

Tadaji realized with a sick feeling that the man was between him and the gate. He halted and crouched beside a large bush, holding his hand to his mouth to muffle the loud gasps for air. He could no longer see the figure in the darkness, but he could hear him as he crept through the brush.

The man's silk-clad shoes made almost no sound on the soft, mossy forest floor. As the figure drew closer, the moon emerged from the clouds.

Tadaji's pursuer was only a few feet away, and the older man could see the glint of the moonlight in his eyes as he searched the garden.

Tadaji jumped from his crouch and fell upon the figure, taking him completely by surprise.

With a shout, the man dropped his bow and flung Tadaji to the ground.

Tadaji rose and fled toward the gate—somewhere ahead in the darkness.

From behind him Tadaji heard a yell, and then a crash. He stopped and turned around. The moon's pale light trembled in the trees, and in the shadows two figures struggled. Curses filled the woods as the men fell in a heap of pounding fists and kicking feet. He watched in fearful fascination. One managed to pin the other down, and in the half-light Tadaji saw him straddle the prone figure and raise something large and round above his head.

Then a sickening crunch echoed through the trees. The victor threw the rock away and sat for a moment, breathing heavily. He slowly rose from the body of his enemy and looked directly at Tadaji.

Relief flooded the ambassador. He was about to call to his bodyguard when the figure reached down and picked up the bow.

With a gasp Tadaji turned and ran for his life. It was only a matter of time before the assassin caught up to him. Terror chilled him as he stumbled through the forest, tripping over roots and rocks as he ran in the direction of the gate. The moon had disappeared behind a cloud again and an inky blackness covered the world.

Behind him, the assassin had ceased caring about making any noise and crashed through the brush as loudly as Tadaji did.

Suddenly Tadaji's lame foot caught on something soft on the ground. He fell headlong into the underbrush. He lay there, realizing he was surely a dead man.

His pursuer had stopped as well.

Tadaji thrust a wad of his kimono sleeve into his mouth to muffle his breathing and hoped that the loud hammering of his heart would not give him away.

For a long moment nothing moved. Then slowly Tadaji reached a trembling hand toward the thing that had tripped him. It was the body of a man. His chest did not rise and fall, but his skin was still warm.

The moon reappeared. A cold night breeze sent a shiver through Tadaji as he recognized the face of the man: Numo.

With a gasp of horror Tadaji jumped up. Instantly he felt a blaze of pain in his back, beneath his right shoulder bade. He stumbled backward, right into the large chest of a tall, sturdy figure.

"Ide Tadaji?" a voice said. It was Aramoro, holding a bow.

Tadaji's mind swirled. Thousands of colors burst in front of his eyes. Blinding pain streaked through his body.

"Help me," Tadaji whispered.

Another arrow cut the air and grazed Tadaji's scalp, hitting Kachiko's brother-in-law in the shoulder. With a gasp, the huge guard fell backward, taking Tadaji with him.

Tadaji crashed to the ground and lay still.

The dark figure, bow cocked and ready, loomed above him. Tadaji closed his eyes, strangely calm, and waited for death.

17 THE COMING STORM

Morning dawned bright over a ruined Kyuden Kakita. A fatal battle had just been fought here. Another such battle was about to begin.

Yokatsu and his Unicorn cavalry camped beside Toturi and his ronin. Dragon and Phoenix forces filled out the army. The allies gathered along this stretch of road to block the route from Kyuden Kakita back to Beiden Pass. They had sent scouts to spy on the Crab army that had destroyed Kyuden Kakita. The scouts reported that the Crab forces massed in a forest beyond the castle. They prepared for battle, intent on returning to Beiden Pass at all costs. The allied army intended to stop them.

Tetsuko looked up from Cloud Dancer, whom she brushed in preparation for the day's battle. She shaded her eyes against the early morning sun and gazed at the ruined castle.

Kyuden Kakita sat on a wide, round hill in the center of a vast plain. Although the structure itself was of moderate size, its strategic position atop the hill made it appear to be much larger. Many years ago, it had been well fortified with a moat, but the deep stone ditch that had once held water had long been filled in. In the past few days, the moat had been sorely needed. Rams had opened three separate breaches in the outer defenses. The castle walls, made of a blue-gray stone, were marked now by soot from the fires of the Crab conquerors. Roofs had burned away, and courtyards were filled with rubble. Even the great gates, which in peacetime had never closed, now could never close at all. They hung shattered on twisted hinges.

The castle was surrounded by a plain that rolled in all directions. In the morning breezes, the tall grasses seemed a golden sea, but their stalks hid an awful secret. Dark forms littered the ground, and flies buzzed in bloated swarms. Most of the dead were Crabs, but many—too many—were the Crane warriors that gave their lives in defense of Kyuden Kakita.

The Crab had not even wanted to hold the castle, only to take its food stores and destroy it.

"May Shinjo watch over me," Tetsuko whispered.

She continued grooming Cloud Dancer for the battle to come. The motion of the brush always soothed them both. Tetsuko remembered the hours she spent in the stables, brushing the magnificent animal until she shone like polished ebony. A brush-down had always felt good after she and Cloud Dancer had worked one another to exhaustion, training on the fields of the Utaku Battle Maiden School.

Tetsuko winced, remembering one horrifying time

when Cloud Dancer had stumbled over a jump and landed hard on the ground. She had lain still, her eyes wide in fear and pain. Tetsuko had not left her side, stroking her neck and singing the ancient songs until the shugenja had assured her that the leg was not broken. That incident had only strengthened their bond. Afterward, Tetsuko had spent hours astride Cloud Dancer's strong back, silent and still. She had opened her mind and learned to feel the thoughts of the animal. The horse had learned to sense her thoughts as well.

As the brush did its work, Cloud Dancer turned her head and gazed with huge, intelligent eyes at Tetsuko. The woman could feel power flow between the two of them. This was the secret of the Unicorn; the ability to become as one with the animals that bore them through battle and through life. It was a bond of such strength and spirit that no one spoke aloud of it. There was no word to describe that bond, but every Unicorn understood and respected it.

Tetsuko finished brushing Cloud Dancer. She wove dozens of tiny bells into the horse's thick, black mane, and threw the well-worn leather saddle onto the animal's back. Positioning her wakizashi short sword in its saddle sheath, she mounted.

All around her, the rest of the Unicorn army was preparing as well. Horses neighed, armor clanged, and the low buzz of conversation filled the air. Shouted commands from unit leaders rang out, and soon the mighty Unicorn cavalry began moving into battle formation. Violet battle standards rippled in the crisp morning breeze, and the golden Unicorn mon embroidered on them glinted in the sunlight.

Tetsuko fell into position within the ranks. She sat easily in the saddle as she adjusted her armor and weapons.

Before the army, Yokatsu sat astride his mount, surveying

the troops. He appeared relaxed, happy to be in the saddle once more. His armor shone, and his personal battle standard fluttered in the wind above him. Tetsuko marveled at the honor and strength that radiated from him. He gazed with pride at his clan's army.

Yokatsu rode to address his troops. "The strategy is simple," he said, his voice carrying easily over the sounds of the field. "The Crab cannot outrun us. They cannot skirt us. They must attack us if they want past. We will wait for them to attack here, on the open plain.

"The Crab had hoped to lure us to them, knowing that our cavalry is useless in the dense forests. They hoped in vain. The Crab knows nothing of patience. The latest messengers say that they are on the move."

No sooner had he finished than a sound like distant thunder tore the air.

Beyond Kyuden Kakita, the Crab army flowed out of the forest and spread across the golden fields. Although easily two miles away, they could be seen clearly, advancing toward the allied army like a flood. They moved slowly—infantry troops. Few Crab fought on horseback. That fact would work to the Unicorn's advantage on the huge, empty plain.

Yokatsu dug his heels into his mount's side. "They march! It is time!" he bellowed as his horse jumped forward.

Tetsuko sucked in her breath, feeling the familiar rush of fearful excitement that always flowed through her before a battle. With a yell, she raced to her position in the Unicorn cavalry column.

Yokatsu galloped back and forth along the front ranks, stopping to give orders to the commanders. "The army approaches! Hold your positions until the order is given to move."

The rumble of the Crab army grew louder.

Horses neighed and reared in impatience to be off. Their riders held them back. Behind the unit, a force of Unicorn archers made ready. Tetsuko could hear the distinctive sound of hundreds of bowstrings being drawn. Few of the arrows that flew from those bows would miss their marks. Smaller units of soldiers wielding slings were scattered through the ranks. Although slings were considered dishonorable weapons in the rest of Rokugani society, the Unicorns were of another mind. They were masters of these deadly weapons. The bullets they flung from their leather slings could kill a person from fifty yards.

The Crab army seemed almost to be upon them. The thunder of their march filled the air.

Tetsuko stood in the stirrups, impatience and fear pulling at her with a palpable force.

"Hold . . ." Yokatsu yelled, his katana brandished high.

Tetsuko pulled her golden katana from its sheath, and pressed her knees against Cloud Dancer's side. The army twitched and trembled as the Crab army charged. Dread and excitement mixed into unnatural grimaces on the Unicorns' faces as they forced themselves to remain still.

Less than a mile before them, wave after wave of Crab burst from the plain, waving their blades as they moved across the valley.

"Hold . . . !" Yokatsu stood on his stirrups, pulling his mount's reins so tightly that the horse reared. For a moment, the great warrior appeared to fly in front of them.

Horses stamped impatiently. Their eyes were white-rimmed at the sounds and smells rolling toward them.

Then the air seemed to change. For the briefest of moments the entire allied army held its breath. A great calm settled upon them. They trusted their leaders, they believed in their cause, and they were ready.

The Crab forces surged over a small rise in the land. They rushed straight toward the main allied force. When the first waves of Crab were so close that Tetsuko could see the silk cords that held their armor, Yokatsu silently sliced the air with his blade and kicked his mount forward.

The whole world exploded.

With a yell that rent the fabric of the air, the allied forces charged. They reached a full gallop before crashing into the oncoming Crab army. Armor and horseflesh tangled with katana and tetsubo. Archers let their arrows fly, and the air was filled with the sound of shafts whizzing overhead in a rain of death.

Smashing through the front lines, the cavalry divided and swung like a violet gate to either side of the Crab force. Crab charged through, only to be trapped within a wall of Dragon, Phoenix, ronin, and Unicorn.

With a yell, Tetsuko attacked the nearest Crab soldier. She leaned on Cloud Dancer's neck and delivered a strong slash to the man's chest, but the samurai was clearly accustomed to battling foes on horseback. He dodged the move with a fluid motion and swung at Tetsuko's leg. Cloud Dancer reared, saving Tetsuko's leg from certain amputation, and brought her powerful hooves down on the Crab infantryman. He yelled and doubled over. Tetsuko took his head in one clean motion.

Tetsuko felt a sharp pain in her thigh and wheeled her horse around.

A young Crab samurai-ko wielding a long, razor-sharp naginata polearm had managed to thrust its tip between the slats of Tetsuko's leg armor. The thick leather leggings that Tetsuko wore beneath her armor had kept it from stabbing completely through her leg.

Tetsuko stood in the saddle. In a fast one-two motion, she knocked the polearm away with the flat edge of her blade and dealt a blow to the woman's sword arm. The severed limb fell to the ground, still holding the naginata.

Tetsuko pulled Cloud Dancer's reins and turned as another volley of Unicorn arrows flew overhead. She watched as a row of Crab forces fell beneath the onslaught of the arrows. Immediately behind them came another wave of soldiers.

Tetsuko pressed her heels to Cloud Dancer's sides and drove toward the new threat.

▲▲▲▲▲▲▲▲

While warriors fought and died on the fields below Kyuden Kakita, six Phoenix shugenja calmly sat in a circle on the castle wall. Each person held a scroll. As they read the words inscribed on the scrolls, they aligned their energies as one. The shugenja chanted softly, their voices rising and falling as they cajoled the Fortunes. Then they dropped the scrolls and were silent as they focused to draw on the powers they had called.

The air around the six shugenja seemed to shift. With eyes closed, they lifted their faces to the sky. Immediately the breeze picked up and turned into a cold wind that whipped their kimonos. The sky grew darker. The plain was cast in a blue-gray light. The air trembled. Dark clouds rolled over the horizon and covered the valley, crackling with green and blue lightning.

In the air above the battle, the clouds began swirling. Winds started to howl.

The Crab forces paused.

The dark clouds swirled faster. They broke from the sky and sent a spiraling finger into the Crab armies.

Screams of terror and pain mixed with the shouts of battle. Dozens of Crab cavalry, horses, and weapons were sucked upward into the huge, twisting cloud.

On the ramparts, the six shugenja sat as still as jade statues, their faces upturned to the dark clouds above. Tiny beads of sweat covered their serene faces. Calling upon such powerful forces was dangerous and draining. The lives of all the shugenja depended on the strength that each possessed.

▲▲▲▲▲▲▲▲

Far below where the shugenja sat, the wind screamed. It tore up the very ground. The soil beneath the Crab army began to rumble and shake, as if it boiled just under the surface. Turf rolled in undulating waves, throwing hundreds of soldiers off balance and tossing them like corks in a sea. As the rumbling got louder, the ground tumbled upward in huge mounds, spitting out rocks and throwing them hundreds of feet in the air. They shot out and felled dozens of Crab before the soldiers realized what had hit them.

"Fall back along the road!" yelled Toturi. "Don't let the Crab past."

His commanders followed, urging their troops away from the wild wind and the erupting soil that it created.

In confusion, the Crab broke formation and retreated from the storm.

Suddenly a huge force of new Crab troops spilled onto the plain. The column circumvented the torn ground and the ravaging wind. They sought to slide past the whole battle.

Toturi ordered a charge. His Dragon forces rushed to engage this new foe. Blades sang in the air as they slashed and cut.

With calm ferocity, the Crab forces overran the Dragon troops. They cut a large hole through their ranks.

"They're breaking through!" Toturi shouted.

Yokatsu saw the threat. He ordered a cavalry charge.

Mounted warriors rushed toward the fray. Katanas glinted in the storm light as they attacked the Crab ranks.

Tetsuko rode in the forefront. She reached a Dragon samurai who struggled with four Crab infantry. Side by side on horseback, the allied soldiers fought, knowing their lives depended on every move they made.

The Crab were cool and calm, wielding their weapons with great skill.

Tetsuko exchanged quick blows with one soldier while another struggled to pull her from her horse. With a growl, she landed a blow to the sword arm of the second assailant.

The man yelled in pain and quickly switched his blade to his left hand. His right arm dangled uselessly at his side. Blood gushed from a huge gash.

Just then, the Dragon beside Tetsuko slumped. A Crab warrior dealt a lethal blow to the leg of the Dragon. A clean slash to the abdomen sent him quickly to the spirit world.

The remaining warriors turned on Tetsuko.

Cloud Dancer, her flanks crisscrossed with bloody gashes, frothed pink foam from her mouth. She jumped and pranced in all directions, moving so that the soldiers could not get a clean cut at her mistress.

Tetsuko saw the new threat and was prepared. She let go of Cloud Dancer's reins and clasped her knees tightly around the grand horse's sides. She reached to her saddle and whipped out her wakizashi, the short sword that was the companion to her golden katana. She attacked both Crab at once, taking them by surprise. One soldier fell immediately, the recipient of a clean blow that cut her waist in two. Tetsuko turned both blades onto the last Crab. The swords converged. He never knew which wound sent him to his grave.

Breathing heavily, Tetsuko slid her wakizashi back into its sheath. She tried to ignore the blinding pain from the old wound in her shoulder. For a moment the battle around her slowed. The ground was littered with dead from all sides. She could smell the sickly-sweet fetor in the midmorning air. The main action of the battle seemed to be moving westward. Tetsuko was about to ride toward it when another, larger wave of Crab appeared.

They swarmed the Dragon forces, who were exhausted and unprepared for the new onslaught. The Crab soldiers who were already engaged in battle saw the reinforcements. They turned and attacked with renewed fury. The Crab converged on the Dragon.

With shock, Tetsuko saw the allied forces crumble. Dragon units on the palace road wavered, and then broke. With a hoarse yell, the front line of Crabs marched through the tatters of the allied force.

"They've broken through!" Toturi shouted.

Tetsuko couldn't win free. She flung a stinging blow at the Crab opponent who battled her.

He deflected her blow, which should have taken his arm, and swung a well-placed stroke to her leg. This time Cloud Dancer was not fast enough, and the blade opened a gash.

Focusing on her opponent, Tetsuko slashed his neck, severing an artery.

The man fell facedown onto the bloody ground and was still.

Tetsuko heard her name and wheeled Cloud Dancer around. One of the Unicorn unit leaders, Moto Xiu, pounded toward her.

"We must ride like the wind," he yelled. "The Crab are driving through to Beiden Pass. Yasamura is in danger. He will be joined there by a small force of Phoenix shugenja, but they cannot hope to hold the pass alone. They will be destroyed if we do not get there in time. Ride!"

Tetsuko's cheeks burned with the shame of defeat and retreat, but she followed her commander without question. Soon the Unicorn force was away from the main battle. They thundered across the plain.

Unperturbed, the huge Crab army marched behind them. There would be no hope of defeating such a large force.

▲▲▲▲▲▲▲▲

It was late afternoon a week later when an exhausted and embittered allied force reached Beiden Pass. There had been few Unicorn casualties during the earlier battle, but it was clear that the soldiers had fought fiercely for their lives. Most of Yokatsu's warriors were covered with blood, and a few of them were bandaged. They arrived to an even graver situation. They had outrun the main Crab force only to find that another contingent of Crab already held the pass.

Yokatsu and his Unicorn cavalry spread out on the plain, approaching the cavalry forces led by his son, Yasamura. In flashing armor, Yasamura rode back and forth, bellowing curse after curse. To attack the Crab now would be suicide, and every soldier knew it.

Stern-faced and angry-eyed, the Master of the Four

Winds reined in his steed before Yasamura.

The young man jumped from his mount and bowed low to his father. The ancestral armor of the Unicorn shone on his back. "Father," he said, "I was not able to secure the pass. I am not worthy of command. I have failed you."

"What happened?" Yokatsu asked. His voice was calm and even.

"Crab reinforcements came from the south," Yasamura said. "They appeared from the eastern edge of the forest just as the main force pushed toward Kyuden Kakita. We were overwhelmed. I decided it would be foolish to force my small army into certain death, with no hope of victory, so we retreated."

"And the Phoenix shugenja force that was already at the pass?" Yokatsu asked, but he already knew the answer.

Yasamura did not reply, but lowered himself deeper in his bow of shame. "I am not worthy to wear our ancestral armor."

The daimyo glared at his son. "That is for me to decide," he said as he surveyed the Crab force that now bottled up the pass. "You have brought dishonor to us by failing in your task. Your mistake caused many deaths. But you were wise not to attack a superior force. You chose the path of a wise commander rather than a reckless one.

"However," the great Unicorn commander continued, "you should not have been caught off guard so completely, especially with such an important mission. See that you do not fail again."

"I will not."

Then Yokatsu turned to the cavalry. "Toturi rides to us with the remainder of the allied army," he said. "We will make camp here and wait."

He looked toward the north. Tetsuko followed his gaze.

The allied army was moving slowly toward them. Their defeat was plain from the way they slogged slowly toward the Unicorn force. Once they arrived, they would face the combined might of the Crab.

"There has been much failure this day," Yokatsu said to himself. "Tomorrow, there can be none."

18 TRUTH, REPAIRED

From deep in his mind, Tadaji heard someone call his name. The sound bumped and echoed in his skull, a shout inside a narrow ravine. His body felt like a stone cast into deep water. He sank into darkness. Tadaji opened his mouth to breathe, but a great weight pressed on his chest. A comfortable warmth enveloped him.

Suddenly, liquid fire spilled into his dry mouth. It burned a path down his throat into his belly. All at once the pressure on his chest lifted, and he gasped. His stomach lurched. Fiery nausea rose in his throat.

"Try to keep it down," the voice said.

Without thinking Tadaji clamped his teeth together and fought the nausea until it passed. A cold breeze ruffled Tadaji's kimono. He shivered. The fire in his belly had begun to send tingling fingers to the deep, throbbing ache that came from his back. Tadaji moaned and tried to move, but could only open his eyes.

He was lying on the ground in the birch garden. Tall silver trees towered crazily above him. The moon was still out, but it had passed its zenith and now hung low in the sky. Tadaji blinked, trying to focus in the feeble blue light. The form of a man squatted beside him, his face hidden behind a dark mask.

"Tadaji?" the man said, relieved. He leaned forward and peered into Tadaji's face.

"Who are you?" Tadaji replied thickly.

The man gently raised him to a sitting position so he could breathe easier.

"Try to relax your muscles and let your lungs work normally," he said, rubbing the older man's chest to ease his breathing. "The arrow struck you in the lung. It will take some time before you will be able to breathe comfortably."

The man picked Tadaji up and folded him over his shoulder as gently as he could. Tadaji was as limp as a dead animal. The man adjusted the weight as he said, "I will explain everything, but we must get out of the garden quickly."

He made his way quickly and quietly out of the garden, stepping carefully through the shadowy trees and underbrush. The man dodged branches and brambles so skillfully that no one would have been able to tell which way he had gone.

"It is not safe to return to your chambers," the man whispered. "Where can we go?"

Tadaji felt groggy and dizzy. He had trouble creating a clear thought. Images of Tamura and the flames rose instead. Tadaji moaned in familiar dread at the dream that tormented him. The man picked up speed as Tadaji fell into unconsciousness once again, crying out his son's name.

Outside the gate, the man paused and adjusted the weight on his shoulders. "Tadaji," he said, shaking him gently.

Tadaji cried out again and opened his eyes into slits.

"Is there somewhere that will be safe for us? Someone you can trust?"

"Eda," Tadaji whispered. "Eda will help." The last thing he remembered was the smell of jasmine and humus as he bounced on the shoulders of this mysterious samurai, out of the garden and toward the palace.

The servants' district was dark and quiet. The man carried the unconscious Tadaji from door to door, checking the small banners that identified each inhabitant by the master he or she served. He finally found the Ide mon hanging limply in front of a small, tidy house at the end of a narrow path. Saying a quick prayer that this was the right place, he slid open the rice-paper door and stepped inside.

A single lantern burned in the center of the room, illuminating the form of a thick woman. She snored softly on her well-worn futon. Years of serving in the palace had made her a light sleeper, however. At the sound of the opening door, she sat upright, her eyes wide with fear.

"Eda?" the man asked.

The older woman shrank back, clutching the thin sheets about her. Then she recognized the limp body folded over the man's shoulders.

"Is he dead?" she gasped. She rose from the futon and went to Tadaji's form, feeling his head and his cheek for signs of life.

The man shrugged her aside. He deposited Tadaji on the bed as gently as he could. "No," he replied, dropping to his knees and reaching into the folds of his dark kimono. "But it will take time for the antidote to work." As he moved in the lantern light, Eda noticed that he wore a kimono of deep violet.

He drew out a small glass vial half-filled with a glowing blue liquid and removed its stopper with a quiet pop. Then he carefully raised Tadaji's head and poured a few drops into his mouth. The old man's body went rigid. He coughed, sucking air into his damaged lungs with raspy gasps.

"Will he live?" Eda asked in a low voice.

Tadaji moaned, the antidote burning through his body once again.

"I hope so," the man replied, replacing the stopper and tucking the bottle back into his obi. He pressed his gloved hand against Tadaji's cheek, wiping away the beads of sweat that made his skin slick. "If the cure doesn't kill him, that is."

Eda disappeared into a shadowy corner of the room and soon returned with a small basin filled with cool water. She bathed Tadaji's face, and he seemed to relax a bit.

"What cure?" she asked softly as she wiped the sweat from his forehead.

"Spider's kiss," the man answered, leaning back on his heels and sighing. "It comes from the roots of a plant that grows only in the Shinomen Forest. Some shugenja use it to ease the pain of wounds, for a tiny drop can make the body forget its hurts. But too much can kill."

"How did he come to be shot by an arrow?" Eda said, no longer afraid of the stranger.

He shrank a bit under her gaze and mumbled something she couldn't hear.

Just as Eda was about to press the man further, Tadaji moaned loudly and opened his eyes. His breathing had become more regular, and his skin had lost its deathly pallor. The man leaned over Tadaji and said, "Tadaji, can you hear me?"

Tadaji blinked his eyes and squinted up at the wide, friendly face that hovered above his.

"Jikkyo?" he said thickly. His face relaxed in recognition. The barest hint of a smile played around his dry, cracked lips. "Nephew."

"Old man, you are very hard to kill, and I thank Shinjo for that," Jikkyo said softly, smiling.

Tadaji whispered, "How? Why?"

"First, you are safe," Jikkyo replied, smoothing the old man's damp, gray hair from his face. "Foolish man, you walked into a trap in the garden. You must have known you were in great danger."

"Numo?" Tadaji replied, still squinting to see clearly in the dim light of Eda's room. "He was supposed to protect me."

Jikkyo sighed. "He did, with his life."

Tadaji closed his eyes and shook his head. "I do not understand," he said. "Numo is dead, you are here. What happened, and who shot me?"

Jikkyo shook his head. "Rest now, we have a few hours before dawn."

"No," Tadaji replied as he struggled to sit up. "You must tell me what happened."

Jikkyo looked hard at his uncle. Tadaji was trembling, and he wheezed with each breath, but his eyes were bright and clear. They flashed with a hint of anger and impatience that Jikkyo knew well.

"Very well," Jikkyo said. "But tell me first, why did you walk into the trap?"

Tadaji swallowed hard. He had told no one about his conversation with the Lion or the things he had overheard Kachiko say. He had also told no one about his visions. He was afraid that the statue would be ripped from him before he could give it to Hoturi, to save him from death. And to save his son from eternal damnation.

"I received a note from the Crane ambassador's secretary," he said finally. "He claimed to have information I needed, and I felt it was worth the risk."

"Was this Crane very tall, and did he smell of rice paper and ink?" Jikkyo asked quietly.

Tadaji looked at his nephew quizzically, and then realization dawned on his face. "The note wasn't a trap," he breathed. "Daidoji Asira intended to meet me."

"I do not know what the Crane had in mind," Jikkyo said. "Whatever it was, it died with him."

"Died?" Tadaji choked.

Jikkyo sighed. "Let me start at the beginning," he said. "This afternoon I arrived at the palace to deliver a message to you from Yokatsu, but the guards made me wait for hours. By the time they granted me entry, it was already dark."

Jikkyo paused, and then said, "Your chambers had been ransacked. All your belongings were scattered and destroyed. Your futon was slashed into rags. Someone was searching for something, and they made sure to leave nothing untouched."

A look of alarm spread over Tadaji's face, and he clutched his obi. He sighed, feeling the familiar square shape of the wooden box still secure. Then he thought of his beautiful cane, gone forever, and sorrow gripped his heart.

Jikkyo continued. "A servant told me she had seen you near the gate to the birch garden, so I went there, hoping I was not too late. I caught the flash of robes in the moonlight, and knew it was you, but just as I was about to call your name, someone rose in the shadows before you and let an arrow fly."

Tadaji looked up and stared at Jikkyo. "The arrow struck the tree near my face," he said.

"Yes, and your reflexes are still good, Uncle. You hit the ground so quickly that a Battle Maiden sensei would be proud," Jikkyo said, smiling a little. "I backed into the shadows, watching, for I wanted to take your attacker by surprise and I assumed he would give chase. But instead he fought with another in the garden, your Crane secretary. Did you see that?"

Tadaji nodded slowly, remembering the sound of the hard stone on the innocent man's skull. He closed his eyes.

Jikkyo said, "When you stumbled, your pursuer disappeared into the shadows. I did not see him again until you stood up, and he rose like a ghost behind you."

"Aramoro." Tadaji said in a dead voice. "And I thought he was there to save me."

Jikkyo let out a short, humorless laugh. Then he looked sadly at Tadaji and bowed his head. "I only wish my first shot had been true. I am deeply sorry, Uncle, for it was I who shot you, as I aimed for your killer."

Tadaji said nothing but continued to shake his head slowly, remembering the events in the garden. "He must have killed Numo, for it was his body I stumbled over as I tried to flee."

Jikkyo nodded. "I found him when I found you. I am sorry, he was an honorable man and a devoted servant."

"Is Aramoro dead as well?" Tadaji asked.

Jikkyo's face twisted in anger. "I do not know, and I do not care," he said. "My second arrow struck him in the shoulder. I did not pause to check him before I carried you away."

For a long time the two men sat in silence, both absorbing the events of the night. Eda quietly brought them steaming cups of tea, and then melted back into the shadows as they sipped absently.

Finally Jikkyo looked up from his cup and said, "Uncle, we must leave the palace as fast as possible. Do you think you can travel?"

"I will have to, it seems," Tadaji replied, coughing softly. "What message did you bring me from Yokatsu?"

Jikkyo put down his cup and looked squarely at his once-strong uncle, now frail and trembling. Quickly the young samurai told Tadaji of the great gathering and of the appearance of Toturi as leader of the Dragon army. Throughout his tale, Tadaji's face did not change expression. He sipped his tea, his eyes staring blankly at the wall as Jikkyo related the news.

"Now the allied forces march to Kyuden Kakita, hoping to stop the Crab from their onslaught against the Crane and to secure Beiden Pass," Jikkyo finished. "Yokatsu ordered me to bring you with me when I returned. He suspected you might be in danger here after word came of the Unicorn's march with Toturi and the Dragons."

"It seems he was right," Tadaji said. Then he turned toward the shadowy corners of the room and said, "Eda?"

The woman appeared at Tadaji's side and bowed. The ambassador rose stiffly from the futon.

"I will be leaving the palace tonight," he said. "When I am gone, you are officially released from my service, for I doubt that I will be returning." Eda nodded, still crouched on the floor in her bow. Tadaji reached out and gently took Eda's hand and pulled her up. "You have been loyal and honorable for many years, and I thank you," he said as she cast her eyes downward.

He looked at Jikkyo, who rose and stood beside his uncle, supporting the older man gently with a hand beneath his elbow. "It will not be safe for you to return to your rooms, Uncle," he said. "We must leave immediately."

Tadaji nodded. Jikkyo helped toward the door.

Eda watched the two Unicorns disappear in the direction of the stables. There was no emotion on her lined, life-worn face as she watched them go.

Soon after, Eda made her way quickly down the path that she had traveled each day for more than thirty years. She carried a small basket on her back, a bundle slung over one shoulder, and a lantern in her hand. Silently she entered the rooms where her master had lived.

Eda raised her lantern to see better in the darkened room. She was dismayed at the scene before her—clothing and bedding torn and scattered, boxes broken and their contents spilled, even the beautiful rice-paper walls slashed beyond repair.

For a moment she surveyed the damage. Then her eyes lit upon something that lay in the center of the room, apart from the destruction that surrounded it. It was Tadaji's magnificent violet and gold silk ambassador kimono, cast aside by whoever destroyed his rooms. She gently placed the lantern on the floor and picked up the garment. Its rich golden embroidery shone in the lantern light. The silk glowed beneath her fingers as she felt the smooth surface of her master's possession.

She thought of the man she had loved for thirty years. Then she tucked the kimono into her basket and gently tipped over the lantern. The flames caught the edge of the rice paper wall and burst into sparks of red and orange.

Eda turned, feeling the warmth of the fire against her back. She disappeared as the fire cast a red glow of false dawn over the gray shadows of the palace.

19 THE QUIET DARKNESS

From the battle journal of Shinjo Yokatsu:

Near Beiden Pass. The weather has been chilly, but the troops shiver from something more than the cold. Although they fought valiantly at Kyuden Kakita, our defeat left them fearful and uncertain. Their hearts have grown cold to fighting. The sight of such a larger force has sapped their resolve.

My son Yasamura astonished me. The shame of being unable to secure Beiden Pass against the Crabs awakened something inside him that I have never seen. Without rest or food, he rode through our ranks, speaking to the soldiers and reassuring them. His words calmed and invigorated the troops. My heart filled with pride.

We are camped near the northern end of Beiden Pass, within sight of the Crab, who have seized the opening and now hold it. After the first battle, Yakamo's forces joined Sukune's army. It now appears that our forces more evenly match that of the Crab army. Our scouts report that the Crab are strong, but their leaders disagree about a course of action.

I have heard darker whispers, that a great black host is coming. I do not know whether to take these reports seriously. It seems inconceivable that Kisada would ally his Crabs with a Shadowlands army. Once it was said that Hoturi had allied with evil, but such rumors have since been disproved.

Hoturi himself arrived at Beiden Pass after the destruction of his family's palace, leading his Crane forces. When he saw the devastation, his anger knew no end. It was all I could do to keep him from tearing into the Crab forces with his own hands. I convinced him his day for vengeance would come. His Cranes now camp with us, adding ten thousand strong and honorable warriors to our allied army.

But I fear something is amiss with the Crane daimyo. My warrior's mind knows what lengths a leader will go to to save his people, perhaps even to bow in friendship with evil. Once I would have said Hoturi was incapable of such an act, but now I do not know.

Yesterday Yasamura led a small force to the ridge above the pass and was immediately attacked by a force of Crabs stationed there. We now know that the ridge is vital for the capture of the pass. It commands a clear view of the northern section of the pass and is an easily defensible spot.

Other than that, all has been quiet. Both sides are readying for the battle that we all know is coming. Neither side is eager to press the advantage. When it begins, it cannot be stopped until one side falls. So we wait and prepare.

Jikkyo arrived with his uncle, Ide Tadaji, late last night. Jikkyo told me of a fight in the palace garden. A Phoenix shugenja tended Tadaji's wound, but something else eats away at the ambassador's heart. His eyes constantly dart about, and he clutches a small carved box at all times. I have always known our ambassador to be a man of strength and honor. Now I fear his mind has left him. I have assigned a guard to him. He laughs and assures me he has no need of a keeper, but he has already tried to slip past his guard once. I no longer trust him. But what will he do? My instincts caution me to be very careful.

Dawn will soon be upon us. I have not slept this night, from excitement and, yes, fear. My armor has not left my body. It is good to be in the saddle commanding an army, instead of wrapped in politics like a silk worm in its cocoon. Although Toturi commands the entire allied army, I lead the Unicorn cavalry, which includes our Battle Maidens, who arrived two thousand strong from Shiro Utaku Shojo early yesterday morning.

What will the day bring? If battle comes, it will bring death to some, honor to others, and disgrace to a few. The Unicorns are ready and their hearts are filled with resolve. I know they will prove themselves worthy in battle. There will be no disgrace for us if we fight with courage and honor.

I hear someone calling my name. The time for reflection is over. May Shinjo watch over us all.

▲▲▲▲▲▲▲▲

"Shinjo Yokatsu?"

The servant spoke his master's name and bowed. "Utaku Tetsuko has arrived."

Yokatsu nodded. "Allow her to enter." He replaced his quill pen in its carved box, corked the glass ink bottle, and quickly added the new pages to his journal. He rolled the sheaf of paper into a tight cylinder, tied it with a length of well-used leather thong, and shoved the scroll into his leather travel bag.

The flap of his tent flipped open. Tetsuko entered and bowed low.

"Honorable Shinjo Yokatsu," she murmured. "You sent for me?"

"Yes, Battle Maiden, thank you for attending me," Yokatsu replied formally, nodding in return. "Please, be seated."

Tetsuko sat, expertly tucking her leather-clad feet beneath her. The servant placed a tray of tea and rice before them and left.

"There is something I must ask you," Yokatsu began as he picked up his tea cup from the tray. "It is about the battle at the Scorpion village."

"Hoturi," Tetsuko replied, not taking her eyes from the cup in his hand.

"I do not doubt your word, Battle Maiden. You have proven yourself in battle, and you have shown great honor both to your clan and to those you protected while on patrol. But I must be sure."

Tetsuko took her mind back to that horrible day. "I will be honest with you: There is much about the day that is lost to me, but I do remember the blue-robed samurai who led the

Shadowlands charge. He wore a Crane mon. It was Hoturi."

Yokatsu sighed. "And you were the only one to see him?"

"Yes. Yasamura did not see his face."

"Do you know that Hoturi has arrived and joined his Crane forces with the allied army?"

"Yes. I cannot explain it," Tetsuko said, her voice flat. As the days had passed, her memory of the battle has become weaker. Once she was sure it had been the Crane daimyo who had almost struck her down. Now, however . . .

"I believe you, Tetsuko," Yokatsu said softly, seeing the troubled expression on the young samurai-ko's face. "But there may be other explanations for what you saw. For now, we must trust that his heart is true."

The two were silent for a moment.

Tetsuko said, "My lord, may I ask you a question?"

The daimyo peered at her over his teacup, then said, "Yes, what is it?"

"You speak of trust and a true heart. I do not know Toturi, but I have heard the stories. Can we trust . . ." she stopped, self-recrimination ending her question. If Yokatsu trusted him, she would obey. But her encounter with Toturi in the Story Garden had left many unanswered questions in her mind.

Yokatsu drummed his fingers on the table, thinking. "Can we trust him? I think we can. Toturi is a superior warrior, and he commands with skill. His presence can cause an entire army to fall silent, so great is his personality and his power."

"But there is always a slight disrespect that radiates from all who are near him," Tetsuko said.

This samurai-ko is perceptive, Yokatsu thought. Aloud he said, "Some say that no ronin deserves respect. But he fights for the same thing we do—the freedom of the Emerald Empire."

The servant entered the tent again. Tetsuko gulped tea while Yokatsu exchanged words with him. When the servant left, the Unicorn daimyo nodded to her and said, "Domo arigato, Utaku Tetsuko."

Tetsuko bowed low and replied, "I am honored by your trust, my lord."

As she left the tent, Tetsuko was surprised to see Utaku Kamoko and Toturi sitting astride their horses. Tetsuko bowed to her commander and to the ronin, and then she quickly mounted Cloud Dancer.

A servant had already saddled Yokatsu's mount and stood holding the reins, his head bowed in respect.

Yokatsu emerged from the tent and mounted his steed. The three commanders rode into the gray fog of predawn.

Tetsuko watched them disappear into the mists. She turned and made her way thoughtfully back to the Battle Maiden camp. Everyone around the fire was already suited up in their violet armor. Battle was coming, and soon.

Dismounting, Tetsuko nodded a greeting to the other Maidens at the fire. She fetched her bowl, filled it with sweetened rice from a pot on the campfire, and silently ate her breakfast.

Tetsuko had joined the Battle Maiden force as soon as they had arrived. Friends had welcomed her into their ranks. Beneath the polite conversations and warm greetings, though, Tetsuko had felt the familiar undercurrent of suspicion and mistrust that she had known when she returned to complete her training. Not even her Utaku blood had convinced them that her heart was true.

It would be only in battle that she could prove her worthiness. Tetsuko was determined to remove the taint on her name once and for all.

After breakfast, Tetsuko was adjusting Cloud Dancer's

saddle when Kamoko galloped into camp.

Instantly every Battle Maiden stood at the ready before her. Tetsuko was one of the first to spring to attention. She stood in the front ranks, in full view of the legendary Battle Maiden commander.

Kamoko surveyed the elite group and smiled with approval.

Tetsuko watched Kamoko with awe and some envy, amazed that one so young could be so fearless and strong.

"Maidens!" she cried. Her soprano voice projected power. "Battle is near, so I will be brief. The Crabs who defile Beiden Pass are on the march, moving toward our army with speed. It seems their leader, Sukune—" she punctuated the name with a snort of derision "—is convinced that news of Toturi's presence is a trick. His disbelief will be his downfall. We will show Sukune the 'Unbelieving' that the only trick his mind plays is the vision of his own success!"

Murmured agreements met this proclamation. Tetsuko found herself being carried away by the mounting excitement. Pride rippled through the Unicorn ranks.

"Even now, Sukune leads an army away from the pass, toward our position," Kamoko continued. "Our orders are clear: join the main Unicorn cavalry force to cut off his retreat back to the pass. We will ride around his army and attack his back. Once Sukune discovers his mistake, he will have the Battle Maidens of the Unicorn Clan to deal with!"

A shout went up from the women. Tetsuko's voice joined the rest. Her face was stern, but her eyes shone. A thrill sang in her blood as she quickly mounted Cloud Dancer, who pranced and shook her head in excitement along with the other steeds. The bells braided into her mane rang frantically.

Throughout the camp, the allied clan army jumped to

the ready. Soldiers shouted as they mounted their steeds. Sunlight gleamed from purple lacquer. Hooves sent dust clouds up on the wind. The air was thick with the smells of smoke and sweat and metal.

Quickly Kamoko gave orders, calling various Battle Maidens and giving them specific instructions. Then she looked around her and shouted, "Utaku Tetsuko!"

Tetsuko rode up to her leader and bowed in the saddle. "Yes, Kamoko-sama."

"You will command a force of fifty Maidens that will defend the rear of the Unicorn force."

Tetsuko was so surprised that she almost disgracefully whooped in joy. She managed to merely nod and say, "I am at your command." Her heart burst with pride. Kamoko trusted her. Tetsuko would not fail her.

Kamoko gave further assignments and then shouted the order to move.

Tetsuko's heart beat wildly. The mighty Battle Maidens roared a unison war cry. Their voices filled the air. Their steeds sprang forward as one, neighing in a battle call of their own.

Soon the Maidens joined Yasamura's cavalry, who waited for them. Together they rode toward Toturi's main Dragon force, which was mustering in a rocky area below Beiden Pass. They made a grand scene, their proud Unicorn steeds snorting and thundering across the plain, each warrior clad in deep violet armor that shone like amethyst. Standards snapped in the wind as they rode, displaying the Utaku mon and the Unicorn emblem.

As the cavalry and the Maidens approached, the allied army let out a yell of joy at the scene, cheering and waving their weapons. The famous Unicorn cavalry wheeled in unison, and then halted.

Tetsuko's heart sang. Her clan was welcomed by the others as allies and comrades. She sat tall in her saddle, proud of the fact that she was a Battle Maiden, an Utaku, and above all, a Unicorn.

Kamoko broke from the Battle Maidens and rode to Yasamura. Tetsuko watched as the two Unicorn leaders rode to Daimyo Yokatsu, who sat his mount at the head of the entire Unicorn army. Kamoko conferred with the daimyo for a moment, and then quickly rode back to the Battle Maiden ranks.

"All is as planned," she yelled across the air. "Sukune rides to his doom! Take your positions, you know your orders." She stood in the stirrups. Although she was a youth of barely twenty, she commanded such a presence that she seemed a giant.

"To battle! May Shinjo smile on you all!" she cried.

A yell rose from the Maidens, so clear and strong that in the distance, Sukune paused, trembling at its power. Kamoko pulled the reins. Her mount reeled. With a jump, she was gone, a large force of Maidens following her.

Tetsuko wheeled Cloud Dancer and rode with her force to the rear of the allied army.

She flew past Toturi. Their eyes met. Tetsuko slowed for a brief second, bowing in the saddle as she passed. Her hand clasped the precious gift he had given her. Toturi's face did not change, but he gave her a short nod in response. Then he turned his own mount and disappeared into the chaos of the coming battle.

Tetsuko glanced over her shoulder as she rounded the right flank of the allied army. The Crab army was almost upon them.

Toturi, relying on the fact that Sukune was inexperienced, had chosen to meet the Crab head on, knowing that

Sukune's anger and confusion would make him heedless of his danger. With the shadow of Beiden Pass to the south and the ruins of Kyuden Kakita far to the north, he was ready.

Tetsuko reached her position and drew her katana.

At that moment, the Crab attacked. Sukune's warriors shouted as they rushed upon Toturi's troops. The armies met with a sickening crash of steel and flesh.

It was full morning, but the clammy fog that had greeted the day still hung in the air. Heavy, wet air obscured the fighting. The sounds and smells of battle filled Tetsuko's senses and told her everything she needed to know. Warriors died. They died by the thousands. For the moment, all Tetsuko could do was wait at the rear of the allied army as the battle in front of her tore the air and the fog swirled in clouds of green and gray.

"Form up!" Tetsuko shouted.

The other Maidens in her squad tightened their formation and readied themselves for orders.

Suddenly to their left, a troop of Crab cavalry burst from the fog, bent over their mounts and riding like the wind. They thundered to a stop, clearly surprised that a squad of Battle Maidens had been placed so far to the rear of the army.

Tetsuko was equally amazed to see a Crab force on horseback. Their cavalry were rare. For a split second no one moved.

"Attack!" Tetsuko shouted. She led the charge. Her Maidens leapt to join her.

Tetsuko chose the nearest target, a tall Crab on a sturdy horse. Her katana zinged above her head like something alive. The horses bumped and bit at each other in the fog. The two traded quick blows. With a powerful thrust, Tetsuko tore into the Crab's chest and shoved her blade upward. His face was still twitching in surprise as he fell.

A blow struck Tetsuko in the thigh. She turned, pulling Cloud Dancer into a quick rear.

The Crab who attacked her threw a second blow. It missed Tetsuko but opened a nasty gash in the Cloud Dancer's flank. Cloud Dancer screamed and reared with the pain.

As the horse came back down on all fours, Tetsuko used the momentum to deal a stinging blow to the Crab's left arm. The blade struck home. It sliced cleanly through the cords that held the armor together and bit deep into flesh beneath.

The Crab yelled in pain and grabbed her arm. She wavered in the saddle as her mount jumped back. The woman's legs went slack. She slid from the horse's back and hit the ground with a thud.

Tetsuko drove deeper into the battle. She chose a target at random and attacked with a vengeance. Her next enemy, a stocky Crab, wielded his blade with skill. He managed to cut Tetsuko in several painful places before she dispatched him with a decapitating slice.

Around her, the sound of battle changed. Yells of attack turned into screams of fear. The ear-splitting sound of clashing weapons became louder. The small Battle Maiden force found themselves suddenly overwhelmed as wave after wave of Crab infantry appeared. They looked like wild ghosts rushing through the murky fog toward them.

Taken completely by surprise, the Unicorns' fighting turned from fierce offense to desperate defense. The air grew thick with the smell of blood and fear. The Battle Maidens realized that they were outnumbered and alone.

"Maidens!" Tetsuko screamed at the top of her voice, "Do not despair! We are Unicorn, we ride the wind! Fight on!" Ragged shouts followed Tetsuko's call. The Maidens turned to their work with determined energy.

Tetsuko fought madly, slashing and deflecting blows

with no thought to finesse or strategy. Her mind was empty, and her body moved with the automatic skill of a true warrior. She cut down opponent after opponent. Cloud Dancer and Tetsuko fought as one body. The great steed carried her through the raging battle, stepping over the dead that crowded the bloodied ground. Cloud Dancer knew Tetsuko's mind. Her mistress attacked again and again.

Tetsuko had just decapitated her last foe with one heavy slash to the man's helm when Kamoko appeared through the fog.

The commander galloped madly toward the Battle Maiden force. Behind her, a fresh group of Maidens rode. With a "Banzai!" they launched into attack. In no time they had killed the remaining Crabs, cutting them down with a speed that astonished Tetsuko.

She sat in the saddle, her breath coming in quick gasps. Cloud Dancer's coat was covered in foam. The great horse also gasped for air, exhausted to the point of collapse. Her mane was matted with blood, and the cheerful bells had long since been torn away.

The sounds of battle quieted. The fighting was ending.

"Tetsuko!" Kamoko cried as she rode to Tetsuko's side, brandishing her katana with flair. Though Kamoko had fought long and hard that day, she looked as if she had just risen from her futon on a bright and lazy morning. Her armor sparkled, and she had a wild, happy gleam in her eye as she grinned at her fellow Battle Maiden. "The Crabs retreat!" she exclaimed. "Your force was hit hard because the enemy was falling back. We tried to reinforce your troops sooner, but we had our hands full with a retreating squad of Crabs. Sukune trembled when he saw that Toturi was not a trick. He could not flee fast enough, but we hadn't expected him to do it so soon."

Kamoko grabbed the silver horn that hung across her shoulder. She blew a long blast that echoed through the air. "Battle Maidens!" she called.

The women emerged from the remains of the battle. They gathered around her, their armor smeared with blood and their mounts frothing from exertion.

"Today's battle is over. The Crabs have fled back to the pass," Kamoko exclaimed. "In their arrogance, they have lost many warriors. The force that remains in the pass will soon be crushed beneath the hooves of the Unicorn! Tomorrow, we take the battle to them! "

"Banzai!" The shout from the Maidens rose above the distant sounds of battle. An answering call came from the faraway Unicorn cavalry.

The sound sent a thrill through Tetsuko, and she allowed a smile to cross her weary face.

Kamoko looked at Tetsuko and said, "How did you fare? Was anyone cut down as the Crabs fell upon you?"

Tetsuko's eyes searched the familiar faces of the Maidens under her command. She turned to Kamoko and replied, "It seems that almost all of us still walk among the living of Rokugan."

"By Shinjo!" Kamoko exclaimed. "That is good news! The allied forces suffered few casualties as well. It seems we have won the day. Tomorrow, we will win the pass. We must ride to the head of the Unicorn cavalry. Yokatsu has ordered us to lead the troops."

Kamoko stood in the saddle. "Form up!" She motioned for Tetsuko to join her at the front.

Tetsuko's eyes widened slightly at the great honor. A nervous exhilaration gripped her heart. Without realizing it, her chin rose. Pride squared her shoulders. She guided Cloud Dancer to a place along with the other troop commanders.

Kamoko's favor was not lost on the other Battle Maidens. They looked on the disgraced Tetsuko with a glimmer of respect.

With another blast of the great silver horn, Kamoko gave the order to move. The mighty Battle Maiden force galloped toward the head of the allied troops. The sun had begun to burn the heavy fog away. Through the wisps, Tetsuko saw the carnage of the battlefield all around them. Hundreds of dead Crabs littered the ground. Among them lay the familiar purple armor of the Unicorns.

Far in the distance, the ragged remains of the Crab force struggled back into Beiden Pass. Their lines were broken. The troops marched in full retreat.

Beyond them, along the horizon, a shadow passed over the sun, and then was gone.

20 BLOOD ON A DOVE'S WING

The sun had long since set. The room was enveloped in darkness. It was a large, elegant space, furnished with exquisite lacquered furniture decorated with the imperial symbol. Elaborate arrangements of fresh flowers left a sweet scent in the air. The room was large enough to accommodate dozens of people comfortably, which it had done on many occasions. Now, however, the room was empty and silent.

The few ambassadors who remained at the palace huddled in their private chambers, fearful of the plague, or the war, or any number of real and imagined horrors that haunted the shadows beyond their rice-paper doors. Servants and guards had been sent away. The imperial wing of the palace was empty of people, save two. One lay dying on a silk-wrapped futon in the center of the room. The other sat at his side, watching.

A single lantern sat on the low table beside the emperor's futon. Golden light glowed across the young man's feverish face. It lit also the face of the beautiful woman beside him.

Empress Kachiko sat silently, a warm blue kimono wrapped tightly around her willowy form. Her hair was braided in a single plait down her back. The soft ends brushed the floor each time she moved her head. Wayward strands of hair framed her face. Her deep eyes gazed intently at the form moaning softly beneath the white silk sheets. A small glass box rested in her lap.

Outside the paper walls, the wind blew mournfully. Inside, the room was silent except for the labored breathing of the emperor. He struggled to hang onto life.

The expression on Kachiko's face was unreadable; neither her eyes nor her face gave her emotions away. Years of hiding behind her masks had made honest expressions impossible. Even alone and in the dark, she did not dare show her true feelings.

Kachiko reached out one delicate, white hand and smoothed the emperor's damp hair. He murmured and turned his head away from her touch as if it burned his skin. She paused, pursing her lip thoughtfully, and then dropped her hand back into her lap.

"Husband," she murmured, knowing full well he could not hear. "I have news. Ide Tadaji lives and has fled the palace. His rooms have been destroyed by fire. No one knows who aided him. His servant also is gone. Your loyal servant, Aramoro, lies nearby, an arrow wound in his shoulder."

She looked down at the box in her lap. It was small and feminine, a Unicorn trinket made of stained glass in strange, abstract patterns that were oddly pleasing to the eye. It had been her first jewel box, given to her by her mother on her seventh birthday. She caressed the cool glass with the tips of her fingers, and then slowly opened the lid.

Inside were three tight rows of small glass vials, all stopped with tiny corks. They rattled slightly against one another with a light tinkling sound. Kachiko grasped one with her thumb and index finger and gently pulled it out. It contained a strange brown liquid that swirled and sparkled of its own accord. Kachiko held it up for a moment to watch the play of light as it moved. She closed the box and reached for a pair of fine waxed silk gloves that sat on the table beside the bed. She always wore these gloves when tending the emperor, she had explained, so that his sores and sickness would not contaminate her hands.

She carefully opened the vial and poured three drops of the brown liquid into a large wooden bowl of cool water at her feet. She gently swirled a sponge in the water and began bathing the emperor's feverish face. Occasionally she filled the sponge with water and squeezed a trickle onto his dry, cracked lips. He swallowed it greedily, moaning in delirium as the cool liquid slid down his throat. She continued this daily ritual until the bowl was empty.

The emperor's face turned ash gray. The moaning was replaced by a low gurgle deep in his throat. Kachiko smiled down at her husband and returned the tiny vial to its place beside its companions in the box. She carefully removed the gloves and hid the box once again in the vast folds of her heavy silk kimono.

The emperor's body had become rigid and stiff—one of the classic symptoms of the dreaded plague.

"Forces gather at Beiden Pass, Husband," Kachiko said softly, careful not to touch his skin until the water had been completely absorbed. "The Crabs have destroyed Kyuden Kakita. Sukune is thirsty for blood. Your 'friend,' Toturi, commands the forces that stand against the Crabs. I am sure you are pleased to know that!" She chuckled, but the sound was not pleasant. "The ronin thinks he still can roar. The Great Bear Kisada has different ideas. We shall see, won't we?"

She gazed lovingly at her husband, who now lay unmoving beneath the silk sheets. His breath came in shallow gasps. She rose to her feet and pulled her kimono tight about her milky shoulders.

"We shall see."

21   SWEET SCENT OF DEATH

It was completely dark on the plain near Beiden Pass. The air was heavy with the dread of the battle that both sides knew would come with the dawn.

Pinpoints of firelight dotted the darkness across the vast plain. To the south, a force of Crabs squatted beneath the towering walls of Beiden Pass. Their campfires were so close together, they made an even, orange glow against the rocky cliffs.

The ring of hammers against anvils mingled with the sounds of restless horses. Soldiers murmured. Commanders plotted. Shugenja chanted. No one slept, including Tadaji.

He sat in his tent and stared at the single lantern that burned beside his futon. His

wide, haunted eyes were ringed with dark circles. He was ter-
rified of sleep now.

Each night, as soon as his eyes closed, dreams tormented
him. During the day, he managed to maintain his honor and
dignity by calling on his powers of diplomacy. But there
were times—as he dined with the daimyo or watched soldiers prepare for battle—when Tadaji saw his son, faceless
and laughing.

Suddenly, the tent walls seemed to close in on Tadaji.
Anxiety clutched his heart. He had to get out, but a guard
was posted outside his tent. Tadaji resented the daimyo's
lack of trust, but he had no recourse.

Tadaji rose and put out the lantern. He pulled the silk
sheets across the futon, making sure the guard heard the familiar rustling of the fabric. Then, silently, Tadaji went to
the rear of the tent. The day before, he had loosened the
ropes that tied the tent walls down from the outside. With
one look toward the shadow of the guard who stood at the
doorway, Tadaji lifted the tent wall and slipped out.

The air was cooler than Tadaji had expected, and he
wrapped his sleeping kimono tightly around his thin
shoulders. Tadaji wandered through the camp. Everyone
was so intent on preparing for the coming battle, they did
not notice the lone ambassador gliding through the camp
like a ghost.

He followed a makeshift path through the middle of the
camp, passing tents filled with soldiers.

Soon Tadaji found himself at the edge of the camp. The
sounds of preparation faded behind him. Before him was
the vast plain, so dark it looked like an enormous black hole
gouged into the land. He looked up. Clouds covered the sky.
There was neither moon nor stars to light his way. Tadaji
could not tell where the sky ended and the world began.

For the moment, Tadaji's mind was calm. He was grateful for the respite from his torment and allowed himself to relax and breathe in the clean night air. The evening breeze ruffled his kimono, but Tadaji no longer felt the cold.

Hoturi was somewhere in the camp behind him. It was only a matter of time, now, he knew. Soon Hoturi would be safe, and Tamura would be satisfied, and Tadaji at last could rest.

He stood for a long time, allowing the cool air to cleanse his mind and spirit. Then he turned to make his way back to his tent. He had taken only one step when he heard the metallic hiss of a katana being drawn from its sheath.

"Who goes there?" a strong female voice said softly.

Tadaji peered into the inky darkness, but he could see no one. He sighed and said, "It is Ide Tadaji. Who are you?"

"Tadaji?" the voice repeated. It seemed to tremble slightly with confusion.

"If you are going to kill me, make it quick," Tadaji said impatiently. "Chances are good that we won't survive the day, anyway."

The woman did not respond at first. Instead, she returned her blade to its sheath. "It is Utaku Tetsuko, Ambassador," she said, stepping close enough so that Tadaji could see her. She was dressed in a soft, white battle kimono and a pair of leather leggings.

"What are you doing, Battle Maiden?" Tadaji asked. "Shouldn't you be preparing for the battle to come?"

Tetsuko didn't answer immediately. Finally she said, "There are some preparations that are best made alone."

Tadaji understood. "Well, then, Utaku Tetsuko, I will leave you to them." He started to walk past her. Her hand grasped his sleeve. He recoiled slightly at the touch, but paused.

"Ambassador," she said, and he was surprised to hear her voice trembling, "perhaps we could speak for a moment?"

The tone of her voice made Tadaji uneasy. Mustering his diplomatic skills, he bowed and said, "I am at your service. What is it you wish to discuss?"

"Your son," she said.

Tadaji was so shocked, he took a step back. "What is it you wish to discuss about Tamura?" he said, and he heard Tamura laughing in the wind.

"I . . . I knew him," she replied. "He was an honorable man. I, um, was saddened when I heard of his death."

Tadaji blinked, uncomprehending. He said simply, "Hai."

"Did he ever speak to you of . . . me?"

Drawing a deep breath, Tadaji said, "Tamura had great regard for the Utaku line. He admired the formidable fighting skills of the Battle Maidens."

As he spoke, a shadow passed over Tetsuko's face and settled there. "Not a day goes by that he is not greatly missed."

"Thank you, Battle Maiden," Tadaji replied, shaking at the sound of laughter only he could hear. "I must return to my quarters now."

He pushed past Tetsuko and made his way quickly back along the path to the camp, his head down. As he neared his tent, he stopped abruptly and his head snapped up.

"Her!" he breathed.

Tamura's laughter burst into his mind.

Tadaji sank to his knees on the twisted grass. He saw the flames, the drums, and his faceless son cackling with glee. The young man screamed as he held a burning bundle in his hands.

▲▲▲▲▲▲▲▲

Jikkyo sat before a small campfire and silently prepared for the battle to come. Around him, other Unicorns worked in grim silence.

Tetsuko appeared at the edge of the firelight. Without a word she sat beside her friend. She unsheathed her blade, unpacked her sharpening kit, picked up the whetstone, and set to work.

The only sounds were the crackle of the fire and the methodical hiss of stone against steel as Tetsuko honed her golden blade to killing sharpness. Beside her, Jikkyo scraped the last of the dirt and gore from his helm and began polishing it.

When Tetsuko was finished with her work, she raised her blade to the dying firelight and stared at it.

Jikkyo glanced up. "It looks ready to slice the necks of many Crabs," he said. "Are you?"

Tetsuko did not reply. Jikkyo wisely let the comment drop and returned to his own work. One by one, the other soldiers at the fire murmured their good evenings and left, seeking whatever rest or redemption they needed before the battle to come. Finally just Jikkyo and Tetsuko remained.

Without a word, Tetsuko rose and sheathed her blade. She wandered toward the area where the great Battle Maiden steeds were tethered. Soon she found Cloud Dancer calmly grazing in the darkness. The horse raised her head and neighed softly at Tetsuko's approach. Tetsuko stroked her massive head and neck. The horse nuzzled the woman's shoulder.

Jikkyo followed her quietly. He reached out a hand and petted the horse's nose, velvety and warm.

"Tetsuko, I . . ." Jikkyo began.

"Stop," her voice came through the darkness. "We will survive the day. I trust Shinjo to bring us victory. Anything you wish to tell me you can say when the battle is done."

Jikkyo sighed. "We have been through much, you and I," he said. "My love for you goes far beyond that of a man for a woman. I trust and respect you as no other."

Tetsuko tried to swallow, but there was a lump in her throat. "You have stood by me as no one but Benjiro ever has," she said, "and there is a place in my heart for you that will belong to no one else."

Jikkyo reached out and found Tetsuko's battle-roughened hand. "I know your heart still bleeds for Tamura," he murmured, "but it is healing; I can see it. No matter what happens tomorrow, I will always be with you."

A rush of fear and longing washed over Tetsuko. She took a step back, pulling her hand out of Jikkyo's grasp. "Of course you will," she replied awkwardly. "We will tell the stories of the Unicorn victory at Beiden Pass to our grandchildren one day."

"We shall see. But will you promise me something?"

"What is it?" Tetsuko said.

"Talk to Tadaji," Jikkyo replied. "He too bleeds for Tamura, but his wound is far more serious than yours."

Tetsuko sucked in her breath. She was about to tell Jikkyo of her encounter with Tadaji, but the words caught in her throat.

"I do not need him," Tetsuko said finally, her voice breaking.

Far to the east, a thin line of deep gray stretched across the horizon, just slightly lighter than the darkness above and below it. Jikkyo paused and looked at the coming dawn, and then replied in a voice so low that Tetsuko barely heard it. "But perhaps, Battle Maiden, he needs you." Then he turned and was gone.

▲▲▲▲▲▲▲▲

For a long time Tetsuko stood there, her head resting on the horse's side and her fingers twining in and out of Cloud Dancer's silky mane. The new bells tinkled softly as they moved. A single tear slid down her cheek. She wiped it away with her sleeve. Then, glancing at the growing line of gray in the east, she left her beloved steed.

The line of dawn grew, spilling out over the plain and washing the flat land in a dull, chilly gray. Fires were extinguished one by one. Both armies roused themselves and prepared for the coming day.

Tetsuko donned her armor and emptied her mind of all things.

Long before the sun peeked out from beneath the horizon, the Battle Maidens had broken camp. They now mingled with the large Unicorn cavalry that mustered along the southern flank of the allied force.

Tetsuko took her new place with the other Battle Maiden commanders who rode behind Kamoko. Together they galloped toward Yasamura and Yokatsu, who sat side by side at the head of the Unicorn force. The father was calm and proud, the son fidgety and excited. Jikkyo was with Yasamura, and his eyes met Tetsuko's. Slowly they both smiled at one another.

In the distance, the Crab forces began to move into position.

Yokatsu dug his heels into his horse and rode among the cavalry, shouting orders that were instantly obeyed. Soon the force was ready. The grand Unicorn leader returned to the small knot of commanders.

"Unicorns!" Yokatsu bellowed. His rugged face was poised and his eyes clear and bright. The topknot on his head was tightly bound, and his armor looked newly made.

Tetsuko's heart swelled with pride that she was commanded by such a warrior.

"This day is vital for the survival of the allied army and of Rokugan itself," he began. "Our mission is simple: remove the Crab scourge from Beiden Pass and open it for good. At this moment, a large force of Crab hold the pass. Toturi has commanded the Unicorn cavalry to break their hold."

The commanders looked at one another in astonishment

Yokatsu continued. "The Battle Maidens have the most dangerous mission. A ridge at the top of the pass is vital to our purpose. It commands a clear view of the pass from end to end, and it is defended by a troop of Crabs who have been commanded to hold it at all costs. You must take the ridge."

Tetsuko looked up. Far above them, on the edge of the pass, a large rocky outcropping jutted out beyond the mouth of the ravine. She could see figures standing there, and one lone person stood apart from the group.

"You will have help, of course," Yokatsu said, motioning behind her.

A small group of Phoenix shugenja approached, led by a tall, bald Dragon covered with tattoos.

Tetsuko's eyes widened in recognition as she took in his red leggings and leather sandals. She grinned.

Togashi Mitsu caught her eye and smiled back, and then bowed to Kamoko.

Kamoko bowed to the Dragon. She turned then to Yokatsu and said, "Your orders are clear. We are Unicorn, and this is our moment to show the Emerald Empire that we are truly Rokugani!"

Every Unicorn raised a katana in silent salute. The

blades flashed and danced above them. Tetsuko lifted her blade in the air and joined in. Battle cries moved among the Unicorns and beyond, rippling through the allied army. The shouts and sounds of horns grew louder, chasing away all fear that still lingered within her.

"To your positions!" Yokatsu shouted imperiously.

As the soldiers took their position, the battle cries died away. Even the clomp of hooves grew quiet. For a moment all Tetsuko could hear was the ringing in her ears. She looked around in confusion. Why had the army paused? Anticipation crackled in the air. One by one, all heads turned toward the front ranks. A murmur echoed through the crowd. Tetsuko craned her neck to see.

The plain stretched to a series of small hills, and over one of them the enemy surged. Like a black flood, they flowed toward the allied army.

The Unicorns looked to Yokatsu. He was ready. He stood majestically in the saddle. In the last seconds before the armies collided, his katana rose. He sliced the air with his blade and jumped forward.

"Unicorns," Yokatsu yelled, "to the attack!"

Before them, the air filled with the thunder of hooves and charging feet. Then came the crash of weapons. The Crab army fell upon their foes.

"Battle Maidens!" shouted Kamoko, "follow me!"

Tetsuko turned Cloud Dancer and raced with the Unicorns toward the pass.

Immediately the cavalry was surrounded by a Crab force. The Battle Maidens pressed into the Crabs, creating a wall of horse and rider. Row after row of Crab fell to the onslaught

Tetsuko faced a determined warrior who fell upon her, striking her helm with a glancing stroke of his blade.

Tetsuko replied with a heavy slash of her own. The two fought furiously, their katanas slashing the air.

The Crab pressed his attack with a vengeance. A well-placed strike knocked Tetsuko halfway out of her saddle. It numbed her arm and opened the almost-healed duel wound on her shoulder.

With a yelp, Tetsuko jerked back in the saddle, the Crab's next blow barely missing her head. Cloud Dancer pranced away, kicking the Crab with her powerful foreleg. The man screamed as his leg snapped. He fell. Tetsuko quickly dispatched him with a single stroke to his throat. The tip of the katana emerged from his flesh before his blood had time to wash it with red.

Kamoko raced past her, with the Battle Maidens following closely behind. Tetsuko fell in with them, and they pounded toward the path that led to the ridge.

A line of Crab guarded the edge of the pass. Behind them, a wide, rocky path wound up through scrubby pines and disappeared around a huge boulder.

Kamoko stood in the stirrups and let out a yell that could be heard above the battle. "Banzai!" A chill went through Tetsuko as she gripped the hilt of her katana.

The Crabs that defended the pathway were formidable. They stood in the trail like an impenetrable wall.

The Battle Maidens rushed toward that wall. Turning their horses in unison, they divided themselves into four units. Each one pressed into a section of the Crab defense and attacked with controlled fury.

Divided and distracted, the powerful Crabs could be defeated.

Suddenly the air was filled with a rain of arrows. A piercing heat burned Tetsuko's thigh. She grabbed the arrow shaft that had embedded itself point-deep into her flesh and with a jerk pulled it. The wood snapped, leaving the tip of the arrow in her leg. Blood gushed freely over her armor and down her leg, making Cloud Dancer's side slick.

With a yell, she tossed the broken arrow away and pressed her hand on the wound to stanch the bleeding. She reached inside her armor and ripped a piece of her kimono from her body.

Before she had time to stanch her wound, a Crab attacked. He swung at Tetsuko's leg where the arrow was still embedded. His blade sliced through, but his angle was awkward. The blade hit the arrowhead deep inside her flesh and stopped with a sickening crunch.

She screamed and dealt a powerful blow to the Crab. His head flew off his neck and disappeared into the fray. Tetsuko held the reins with one hand and stuffed the cloth into the wound with the other. Clenching her teeth against the pain, she thanked Shinjo for the arrowhead that saved her leg and her life.

Around her, Battle Maidens fell from their mounts as other arrows found more deadly marks.

Tetsuko wrapped her arms around Cloud Dancer's muscled neck to make less of a target and glanced up at the ridge. A line of archers stood at the edge, shooting volley after volley down onto the battle below. Tetsuko was shocked to see how few archers it took to wreak such havoc on the allied forces. She realized for the first time just how vital it was that they secure the ridge.

Tetsuko's mind settled into the familiar place where no sights, smells, or sounds distracted her focus. Only the battle existed. She whirled and attacked with an easy skill. The Crabs who engaged her were skilled as well, and some of their blades found their marks. But no Crab who fought Tetsuko survived the day.

▲▲▲▲▲▲▲▲

The tide of the battle ebbed and flowed. Neither side could gain the advantage. One Crab fell, and then a Maiden, and then two more, and then two Crab.

By late afternoon, the entrance to the pass was littered with Crab dead. Lying among them were many Maidens; some cut down by enemy blades, others killed by the arrows and rocks that had been flung from the ridge. What remained of the Crab force that protected the ridge had fled up the path. They had barely enough samurai to hold the entrance to the ridge, but still they fought on.

Kamoko, Tetsuko, and the rest of the Maidens had gathered at the end of the clearing, away from the pass entrance. The women were bloody and disheveled. Some lay in pain on the ground. Others gamely used whatever they could find to bind and dress their wounds. Tetsuko's leg had gone completely numb, although the deep, jagged wound had long since stopped bleeding. She feared that if she tried to dismount, her leg would give way, so she stayed in the saddle.

"This has been a black day," Kamoko said, surveying the carnage around her. "The allied army has fared no better, although they crushed the left flank of the Crab forces."

As she spoke, a small boy rode up to Kamoko on an overlarge steed. He bowed, handed her a scrap of paper, bowed again, and rode away. She read it quickly.

"Our orders are to fall back for the night," she called to her Maidens. "Yasamura and the cavalry broke the Crab forces at the southern end of the pass, but they did not take it. A large Crab army still holds the northern end. Yasamura will soon arrive here with reinforcements, so that the Crabs do not think of sending more troops to hold the ridge against us. The Crabs are almost crushed, Yokatsu and Yasamura still live, and Toturi and the ronin army smashed a hole in Sukune's defenses."

Kamoko surveyed the women, who, despite their injuries and exhaustion, smiled with satisfaction. "We did our jobs well today, but the battle is not yet over. Tomorrow will see the end of Sukune and victory for the allied army! Now, set up camp."

By now, the sun had sunk beyond the walls of Beiden Pass, casting purple shadows onto the rocky cliffs.

Gingerly, Tetsuko climbed from Cloud Dancer's back. Her injured leg gave way, and she stumbled to the ground. Immediately two Maidens were by her side and helped her to the ground.

Kamoko, who had seen Tetsuko's struggle to dismount, dispatched a message to Yasamura. Before the sun disappeared behind the western horizon, Togashi Mitsu appeared.

Going to where Tetsuko lay, he gently removed the filthy cloth she had shoved inside her armor to stanch the blood. His face twisted in a grimace. "Is this how a Battle Maiden spends her time, running around a battle with a dirty wound?"

Tetsuko smiled weakly at him.

He carefully extracted the arrowhead and tossed it away. Then he bathed the wound and deftly bound it in clean silk cloths. "Do not walk on this leg tonight," he instructed.

Tetsuko nodded, too feverish to argue.

Mitsu closed his eyes, placed both hands on her leg, and began to chant softly. His hands were strong and muscular, with long, gentle fingers that carefully probed her wound. His fingernails were filed to a sharp points and painted green.

Tetsuko jumped as a jolt of hot lightning cut into her leg.

"Steady," he murmured.

She relaxed, and soon a soothing warmth spread through her leg.

After a moment Mitsu rose and looked down at the groggy Maiden. "Sleep now, Tetsuko," he said with a smile, "Your real battles will come with the new day."

Then he turned and went to find Kamoko, leaving Tetsuko to sleep on the edge of a battlefield, all too near the stiff, cold bodies of the dead.

22 FROM DARKNESS, NO ESCAPE

It was late, and the nighttime sky stretched tightly over the plain. A weak moon cast a feeble light, and a scattering of clouds stained the fabric of the darkness. The air was heavy with shadows and dread. Few on the plain far below dared to light even the smallest campfire.

Tetsuko was awake, sitting still and silent beside the cold ashes of a fire. Her leg throbbed. Each time she tried to move, a searing pain shot through her. Togashi Mitsu had returned to her sometime after dark, giving her a foul-smelling liquid to drink. She was grateful for his attention. Her wound would have been infected by now if it weren't for him.

Tetsuko sighed and leaned back, wrapping the edges of her heavy wool blanket around her against the slight chill of the night. All was silent except for the mournful sound of the wind. If Tetsuko closed her eyes, she could almost imagine that the plain was empty and deserted, it was so quiet.

But the plain was not empty. All around her, the dead lay where they fell, their broken and bloody bodies in unnatural angles on the hard, cold ground. Her warrior's mind ignored them. They were the slain enemy. But once in a while her eye rested on an unmoving shadow on the ground, and she shivered. Ghosts were all around her. She said a prayer to Shinjo that they would pass her by on their way out of this world into the next.

The Battle Maidens rested nearby, but none slept. They stood watch in groups of ten, sitting silently in their saddles, still clad in their battle-filthy armor. No Crab would get past them this night.

From the north, the wind picked up. Tetsuko clutched the blanket closer. Breezes blew her short chestnut hair wildly and caught the edge of her blanket. It rose to let a gust of cold air sneak under it. Shivering, Tetsuko reached down and tucked the edges of the cloth beneath her legs. She winced in pain as she moved. The wind continued to blow. It became harder, colder, and louder. It whistled through the camp, growing more vicious as the seconds went by.

The camp was roused by this strange wind. A few Maidens wandered about, speaking in low voices and shivering beneath heavy kimonos and blankets.

Without warning, the air turned frigid, and a bone-chilling wind screeched out of the pass. Everyone on the plain awakened to a hard, cold fear that gripped their hearts. Many jumped to their feet, crying out against this unseen terror in the dark. Even the horses felt it, neighing and rearing and screaming. They pulled against their tethers in a mad frenzy to escape. Beneath the howl of the wind came another sound that sent fingers of fear tickling up Tetsuko's spine.

It was the low moaning of the voices of the Damned as they marched toward the Crab camp.

▲▲▲▲▲▲▲▲

Far from the allied army camp, deep within the fastness of the pass, Sukune sat alone amid piles of stone. The wind whistled through the chinks in the rocks, swirling dust all about Sukune as it went.

He too had heard the wind as it howled, but he knew what it meant. Although he held his chin up with pride, his hands trembled. Sukune shivered. He wiped the sweat from his forehead with the edge of his kimono sleeve.

A form stepped out of the shadows. Sukune jumped.

"Who is there?" he called in a strong tone that belied his fear.

Silence.

"Kuni Yori, is that you?"

"You have failed," the form said.

Sukune clasped his hands together to stop their shaking, but it didn't work. "No," he replied, trying desperately to keep his voice strong and even. "I merely have not yet succeeded. One more day, and Toturi will be crushed. The pass will be ours."

"Your Father, Hida Kisada does not think so," Yori replied, stepping closer to Sukune. Sukune could not see the shugenja's face beneath his black velvet robes. All that he could see were two eyes, glowing softly in the shadows of his hood.

Sukune licked his dry lips and said nothing.

"I have a message from your father," Yori continued.

"For me?" Sukune asked hopefully.

The eyes glowed brighter. "No," Yori said. "For me."

"Ah," Sukune choked, his throat constricting in cold fear. He tried to swallow, but his mouth was dry, and his tongue felt thick. "And what does the Great Bear have to say?"

Yori said nothing. Instead, he took another step toward Sukune and cocked his head slightly, listening.

From below, a mighty host stirred. The sounds seemed faraway and dim, as if they waved through a dream. Moans and wails carried on the wind and reached Sukune's ears.

Yori was so close that Sukune could see his long mustache trembling on either side of his mouth as he spoke. "Many things," he said, and Sukune thought he saw the ageless shugenja smile. "He has given me very explicit instructions, which I must obey."

Sukune let out his breath, which he had not realized he had been holding. For the first time since he had climbed into the ghastly ruins of the palace, he let himself relax. He had never trusted this sinister-looking shugenja, but his father had the highest regard for him. He knew his father was displeased with him, and he resented the fact that the Bear had seen fit to send a Kuni to assist him. But Sukune knew his mission, and he was glad to have another ally. Surely they would decimate the allied forces now.

"Good, good," Sukune replied. "I too have explicit instructions from Kisada, which are to hold the pass. Now that your army has arrived, I think we can do it."

"I know we can," Yori replied, standing very still. "I know it."

Sukune looked hard at the shugenja. "I would like to see the message he gave you."

Yori stared at Sukune for a long moment, and then slowly reached into his black cloak and pulled out a small scroll tied with a red silk ribbon. The shugenja fondled the scroll in his fingers, touching the rice paper as if it were the skin of a beautiful geisha.

A movement behind him caught Sukune's eye, and he glanced over Yori's shoulder. A group of samurai were stiffly climbing the embankment behind the shugenja. The breeze turned icy cold and whipped Sukune's loosely tied hair across his face. A low moan began to rise.

Yori handed Sukune the scroll.

He snatched it in his cold fingers and began to read. Even in the weak moonlight, Kisada's strong, dark brush strokes could be clearly read. Sukune stared at the paper, reading the characters but not comprehending them completely. Slowly he raised his head and looked at Yori.

"So, young Crab," Yori said, "what do you read in that paper that turns your skin the color of porcelain?" He was smiling.

The samurai had reached Yori and now stood in a silent wall behind him. Sukune strained to see familiar faces behind the helms, but all he could see were shadows beneath the armor. Yori raised one finger. In unison the samurai drew their katanas. With a gasp, Sukune saw that there were no bodies encased in the armor. These were Shadow Samurai!

He dropped the paper. It fluttered to the ground and lay still.

"Yori," he said, backing up slowly as the shugenja advanced. The disembodied armor clanked softly behind him at each step. "Give me more time!"

"There is no more time," he replied as he stepped aside.

The troops lurched forward. Sukune's head disappeared within the crowd of armor that enveloped him.

A single scream rose from the ruins and was lifted on the cold wind. The paper blew upward, caught in a chilly gust and was thrown over the edge of the cliff. It floated on the breeze, and then landed face up, far beyond the field of battle.

"Toturi must die," the characters read. "If my son fails to keep the pass, Sukune belongs to you."

23   DARKNESS BY DAYLIGHT

"No. Your injury is too severe. You cannot fight today."

Tetsuko bowed to her commander again. "Honorable Utaku Kamoko, I beg to disagree. I can fight."

The two women stood near the Battle Maiden steeds, which had been saddled and prepared for the battle to come. Tetsuko had risen that morning, stiff and sore from her injury and from a sleepless night on the hard ground, but able to walk. Kamoko, responsible for the lives of her Maidens, was equally determined she would not fight.

"You can barely move!" the young commander exclaimed. "You could be a detriment to the force. This battle has been dangerous enough without another worry."

Tetsuko raised her chin in defiance. "I

understand your concerns, Kamoko-sama. I respect your superior battle skills. But the Dragon heals completely, and I can ride."

Kamoko looked hard at Tetsuko, and then sighed. "I heard of your legendary stubbornness at the Battle Maiden school," she said. "Very well, ride to your death. But do not expect any special help if your wound opens and your leg joins the limbs of the Crabs that will litter the field."

Tetsuko bowed to Kamoko, who snorted with anger as she nodded in return. There was a gleam in the commander's eye, and Tetsuko knew Kamoko respected her behind the anger.

Without another word Kamoko turned on her heel and walked away, leaving Tetsuko to struggle onto the back of Cloud Dancer. When she was astride the horse, she looked around her.

Dawn had broken over the eastern horizon with the promise of a gorgeous day. The early morning sky, filled with fog and clouds the day before, was now clear and blue.

"It is a good day to live, or to die," she said aloud.

Quickly, she tied her hair in a short tail and slid her helm on her head. All around her, the Battle Maidens and the Unicorn cavalry were mounting their steeds, and the sounds of clanking armor filled the air.

The mood in camp was grim as the forces mustered for battle. Tetsuko guided Cloud Dancer toward her position among the Maidens. Yesterday the battle had begun just before dawn. Both sides were deep into their deadly work almost before the sky lightened. Today was different. It was as if neither side wanted to begin.

In the distance, a few divisions were on the move. Dragon troops marched. Their feet rumbled on the otherwise quiet battlefield. A single horn trumpeted far ahead of them. They broke into a run. Battle cries filled their throats. Their foes appeared on a nearby ridge and with shouts of their own, rushed down toward them. There came a loud crash as the Dragon and Crab attacked.

"It's our turn," Kamoko said. Her eyes were fiery above the tossing mane of her steed. "Battle Maidens, we ride!"

Tetsuko, her golden katana in hand, followed her commander. She ignored the fire that burned in her thigh as her leg bounced in the saddle. She was eager for Crab blood, and she knew that the samurai force that still held the ridge was small but fierce. It would be a good day.

With a yell Kamoko and the Maidens raced up the pathway, expecting the Crabs to attack at each rocky bend. No attack came. Unhindered, they wound their way up the path that had been so completely defended the day before.

Fearing a trap, Kamoko called a halt. No sound came from the ridge above them.

"By Shinjo," she asked aloud. "What is going on?"

Kamoko peered up the pathway. They had almost reached the top. Still no Crabs moved to meet them. No bow fire came from the ridge.

The Battle Maidens looked at each other, just as confused as their leader. The horses, sensing the confusion, stamped and neighed impatiently.

From this vantage point, there was a clear view of the southern end of Beiden Pass. The armies below seemed tiny figures moving about a game board. Tetsuko watched, fascinated, as the Unicorn cavalry fought the Crab forces that held the pass. Like an enormous violet katana, the cavalry cut a swath through the Crabs.

Behind the cavalry came Toturi's allied force. They slowly pushed a huge Crab army back in retreat. Dragons and ronin fought side by side in the front lines. It looked as if the Crab lines before them simply melted away.

On either side of the grand allied force, the mon of the Crane Clan flashed in the morning sun. They held against the Crab onslaught. Before them, the Crabs seemed oddly distracted. Their ranks raced about in confusion, as if they fought without plan. It seemed their will to fight was gone.

"Brilliant," Kamoko breathed as she saw what Toturi had planned. "Pin the Crabs into the pass, with the Dragons on one side and the cavalry on the other. The pass will be ours by nightfall!"

She stood in the stirrups and whipped her katana around her head. "Maidens, trap or no, we must take the ridge. Watch your backs!"

With a yell the Maidens thundered forward. Their bewilderment and fear were forgotten as Toturi pressed his victory below.

After a final bend in the path, Kamoko and the Maidens burst onto the ridge. Their blades swung at the ready, and their hearts flooded with lust for battle. The ridge was a huge, flat rock, almost the size of a castle, ringed on all sides by large boulders. The rock jutted out from the rim of the pass, commanding a spectacular view of both the north and south entrances. The sounds of battle drifted up from below, filling the air with the din of screams and crashes.

Kamoko galloped onto the rock, followed closely by Tetsuko and the rest of the Maidens. She skidded to a halt, pulling her mount's reins so hard that the beast reared in pain and confusion, neighing loudly.

It was all Tetsuko could do to stop Cloud Dancer as well. She pulled hard on the reins and gaped at the scene before them.

All the Crabs were dead. Their bodies lay broken and twisted along the rock. Their bows lay intact beside them. Piles of untouched arrows lined the edge of the ridge. A good-sized catapult sat on one side, with a large stock of stones beside it. Two bodies were draped over the machine, and their blood had stained parts of the wood dark brown.

The women stared at the scene, not comprehending what had happened. Kamoko cocked her head, listening. A look of alarm spread over her face.

"Do you hear it?" she cried, her eyes wide.

At first Tetsuko didn't know what she meant. All was quiet. She heard the wind whistle across the ridge, but when it dropped away, all was silent.

The sounds of the battle below had stopped.

An eerie stillness filled the air. Each person in the pass stood frozen, some with weapons still held high.

A gust of wind screamed through the pass, and a shadow slid over the bright morning sun. The shadow dropped lower, filling the pass with a sickly green dimness. Slowly, every creature in the pass looked to what approached. A wild roar split the air.

The plain suddenly teemed with an enormous black army. Soldiers rushed toward the pass, screaming as they ran. Their weapons flashed like teeth in the mouth of a great beast. Behind them, rank after rank of warriors advanced like a great undulating wave of darkness that swallowed the land.

"A Shadowlands army," Tetsuko whispered in realization.

In the midst of the unholy army was a single rider on a silver horse. He wore no armor. Instead, he was wrapped in a heavy black cloak that billowed behind him as he rode. A dark hood covered his face. Beside him, a crowd of warriors held aloft a stout pole that bore the Terrible Standard of Fu Leng. Its deadly colors waved on the fabric as he rode. Nailed to the standard, splayed for all to see, was the body of Hida Sukune.

Kamoko let out a screech and wheeled her mount around. "Stand ready!"

As Tetsuko turned Cloud Dancer, the horse screamed and reared so high that Tetsuko had to struggle to stay in the saddle.

The ridge was no longer empty. The dead Crabs, their wounds still oozing, had begun to rise. From around the huge boulders came a swarm of zombies, their faces covered in porcelain masks. They were moving faster than Tetsuko had ever seen. They spilled over the rocks and dropped clumsily to their feet, waving their weapons and yelling in hoarse, inhuman gurgles as they advanced. More poured from the pathway that the Maidens had just come from, blocking their only exit.

Horrible memories flooded Tetsuko at the sight of the zombies. When Cloud Dancer's front legs hit the ground, the impact sent a blaze of blinding pain through Tetsuko's leg. She was thrown from the horse's back and landed on the hard rock with a scream of agony.

Tetsuko pulled herself up, gasping and clutching her leg. She shook her head and cursed her disgraceful blunder.

The first wave of zombies were upon them.

Tetsuko slashed her katana through the one nearest her.

The zombie, once a woman but now a hideous hag, screamed at the touch of Tetsuko's blade and recoiled back as if the blow had burned it. With a low growl, it attacked, raising its blade and bringing it down in a powerful stroke.

Tetsuko turned to deflect the blow, but she was an

instant too slow. She felt the blade hit her armor. It should have sliced through to skin and bone. She looked down to see the gush of blood that would mean her death. But there was no blood. Instead, the blow had deflected. Astonished, Tetsuko felt the place where the zombie's blow had struck. Her armor was intact.

On her breast, the simple brooch that Toturi had given her snapped and sparkled with a violet light.

Tetsuko looked from the brooch to the zombie that stood before her. Its arm rose to deliver a second blow. Tetsuko stepped back and, with a mighty swing, cleaved the zombie in half. The upper half of the corpse toppled slowly to the ground. Its weapon fell onto the hard rock with a clatter.

All around, the shrill neighs of horses mingled with the yells of the Maidens. They desperately attacked the advancing Shadowlands force.

Fighting her way back to Cloud Dancer, Tetsuko looked around as if in a dream. She could see every face, every slice and parry as the Maidens battled for their lives. Many of her comrades had already fallen beneath the unholy attacks of the zombies. The ground was littered with corpses.

Screams rose from below, echoed on the ridge by the yells of the Maidens. Along the edge of the ridge, the recently dead Crab force had picked up their bows once again and were shooting sheets of arrows down upon the allied army.

Kamoko tore into the Crab zombie archers. With one stroke, she took the head of the Crab nearest her. It bounced on the rock and flew over the edge, the body following close behind. The next Crab soon followed his comrade to the bottom of the pass. More Crab zombies converged on the Battle Maiden leader. Two dropped bows and picked up katanas. Two others turned from the battle below and aimed their deadly arrows directly at Kamoko.

Reaching Cloud Dancer, Tetsuko mounted. The pain in her leg forgotten, she shouted to Kamoko. With lightning speed, Tetsuko whipped out a small leather sling and let two bullets fly. One struck a Crab archer between the eyes. It stumbled against its partner. Their arrows whizzed harmlessly past Kamoko.

The commander dispatched the next Crab zombie in the archery line. She had heard Tetsuko's warning and wheeled her mount in circles, becoming a moving target as she slashed fiercely at the enemy.

Tetsuko flung more bullets in quick succession. She drew her katana and drove Cloud Dancer toward the zombie archers. Although the small stones did not fell their undead targets, they did distract them. The zombies that were hit by the bullets turned from Kamoko and focused their attention on Tetsuko.

She reached the first Crab just as it had nocked another arrow. The first blow took its arm from its shoulder, also splintering the bow. The second blow removed its head from its neck. It bounced down the rocky outcropping.

As Tetsuko turned to the next zombie archer, Kamoko appeared at her side. With a mighty swing, she severed the bow in the zombie's hands. Her next blow sent the creature crashing to the ground, its legs sliced away.

By now the remaining zombies dropped their bows and attacked with katanas and naginata, polearms with large blades.

Kamoko and Tetsuko fought shoulder to shoulder in opposite directions. Their mounts pressed together, rearing and prancing in a circle to protect their riders. A ring of Crab zombies closed in around them.

One zombie wielded a sodegarami, a polearm with wicked-looking teeth. The undead creature raked its weapon over Tetsuko's sword arm and tried to pull her from Cloud Dancer. She reached forward, grabbed the shaft below the barbs, and pushed with all her might. With a wail, the zombie fell backward and tumbled over the edge of the ravine.

Another zombie managed to hack away part of Kamoko's armor with the edge of a dull katana. She sent its head flying over the edge of the ridge to join the rest.

A third zombie lost both arms with a one-two strike from Tetsuko's blade.

The zombies pressed inward. Tetsuko and Kamoko fought fiercely. One by one, they felled the zombies until the entire unit of undead arches lay in pieces all around. When the edge of the ridge was secure, Kamoko and Tetsuko turned to the fray behind them.

It was not going well. As soon as one wave of zombies were killed, another took its place. The first zombie troops had been seasoned warriors, clad in armor and wielding strong weapons. They fell beneath the Maiden's superior skills and were replaced by lesser zombies, creatures recently made and ill-equipped for war.

Breathing heavily from exertion and covered in blood and grime, Tetsuko kicked Cloud Dancer forward.

"There are too many!" Kamoko yelled as another troop of zombies appeared over the rocks. "They have inferior weapons but their grip can snap bones!" She rode beside Tetsuko as they raced toward the new threat.

As Tetsuko approached, she squinted her eyes and peered at the zombies with puzzlement. Something about them looked different. Recognition hit her like a blow to the stomach. She stopped dead, pulling Cloud Dancer's reins so hard that the animal reared.

They were the Scorpion villagers, tattered and broken, their zombie eyes unfocused and dead. They still carried the same weapons they had used so valiantly against the undead that had attacked them: pitchforks, clubs, and well-worn katanas. Some had been badly burned. The glint of bone showed through charred skin. They all still wore their Scorpion masks. Tetsuko recognized them all.

The worst shock was yet to come. At the front of the hideous undead army was her old patrol: Eri, Kaori, Umio, and Hakuro. Tetsuko could barely see the glint of violet beneath the dried blood and dirt of their broken and filthy armor. Kaori's broken arm hung limp and twisted at her side. They all shuffled forward deliberately, their blood-caked blades raised and ready to kill. Beside them walked Tokiko, her mask dangling in tatters where a goblin had ripped her face with its razor-sharp claws.

Memories of the plague village and her first horrible encounter with zombies filled Tetsuko's mind.

Tokiko opened her mouth. An inhuman laugh burst from it, sending a cold wind shivering through Tetsuko. With that terrible sound, horror was replaced by cold hatred—hatred of the despicable power that would do such things to honorable people. Destroying them would not be shameful. It would be honorable mercy.

Tetsuko's mind grew quiet. She focused on what she must do. She moved to attack Tokiko.

The zombie's laughter still rang above the sound of battle. The undead creature was especially strong. It caught Tetsuko's wrist in its vice grip before she was able to throw the first blow. The zombie pulled her from Cloud Dancer's back.

As Tetsuko fell, she threw her entire weight backward, pulling the zombie off balance. As she hit the ground,

Tetsuko did a backward roll, just as Benjiro had taught her. She flipped the zombie over and flung it a few feet beyond.

Tetsuko jumped to her feet, still favoring her injured leg. She cut Tokiko's neck with a quick motion. Without pause, Tetsuko grabbed Cloud Dancer's reins and mounted.

Before she had time to turn to the next zombie, the sound of hoofbeats thundered behind. Jikkyo appeared at the ridge, followed by a unit of Unicorns. He shouted orders to his cavalry, which laid in with dancing steel. Jikkyo meanwhile fought his way toward Tetsuko.

His eyes widened as he reached her and saw the familiar faces among the undead, and then they narrowed in grim determination. Side by side, the two friends slew their former comrades.

Kaori was the next to fall. Tetsuko cut her broken arm from her body with one quick blow and took her head with another. Eri swung a sloppy strike at Tetsuko's leg. Grimly, Tetsuko deflected the zombie's attack and cut her in two.

Beside her, Jikkyo exchanged powerful blows with the zombie Umio. The creature managed to open a large gash on the Unicorn's arm before Jikkyo struck him down. Hakuro, a onetime shugenja with no armor or weapon, was quickly dispatched by Jikkyo with a blazing strike to his head.

The battle became a frenzy. The fresh Unicorn soldiers cut like a fiery blade through the zombies. The reinforcements invigorated the Maidens. They attacked with a renewed strength.

Soon the flood of zombies had stopped. The undead creatures that still walked were quickly destroyed.

In the reeling aftermath, Tetsuko and Jikkyo rode to Kamoko. She gathered the remaining Battle Maidens together.

They had lost many in the battle, and the survivors were wounded and exhausted.

"Ide Jikkyo," Kamoko said, nodding quickly. "Thank you for your help. Your honor and bravery saved us from certain death."

Jikkyo bowed in response. "When the Shadowlands forces attacked, I feared you would be overwhelmed here. Yasamura agreed that my unit should assist you."

The sounds of battle below changed. A high-pitched wail filled the air.

En masse, the Unicorns rode to the ridge to see what had happened. Tetsuko gasped at what she saw.

Below, the allied army fought for its life against a boiling sea of Shadowlands creatures. The main Dragon force had caught the full brunt of the Shadowlands attack. They battled desperately. The Unicorn cavalry meanwhile engaged the Crab forces that held the northern end of the pass. Most of the samurai who made up the army before them were undead.

Yasamura fought at the head of his troops, yelling orders and urging them on. His courage seemed to invigorate the army. They pressed down upon the unholy force, losing warriors but gaining ground.

Seeing the desperate situation, Kamoko said, "Return to the main battle with your force, Ide Jikkyo. Tetsuko, take a small unit of Maidens and ride with him. We will maintain the ridge."

The two quickly bowed to Kamoko. They then raced down the pathway, their units thundering behind.

⋏⋏⋏⋏⋏⋏⋏⋏

Near the northern edge of the pass, Yasamura had his hands full. The Unicorns had pushed through the last of the Crab forces that held the opening, but it was a hollow victory. Behind him Toturi and the allied army still fought for their lives against the Shadowlands troops.

Yokatsu and his cavalry had struck down the last of the Crabs when Yasamura rode to him, followed by the rest of the Unicorn cavalry force.

"My father, Toturi needs us on the right flank. The battle is not going well. Many of the troops fall in fear before the Shadowlands. Can you hold the northern end while we fight elsewhere?"

"Go!" Yokatsu bellowed, "We shall hold it." He looked around quickly, and then said, "Where are Kamoko and the Battle Maidens?"

A shout rose far above their heads. They looked up to see a line of forms along the ridge, bows at the ready.

"They were sent to secure the ridge, Father. Ide Jikkyo's unit was also sent to reinforce them," Yasamura said dully. "But they have been defeated."

"Defeated? The Maidens have not been defeated!" Yokatsu said with a laugh.

Yasamura turned to see Tetsuko's small but mighty band of Battle Maidens approach, followed by Jikkyo and the unit of cavalry that Yasamura had dispatched to the ridge.

Above them, the line of archers lifted their bows. With a signal, they let their arrows fly. The rain of shafts poured down on the heads of Crab and Shadowlands forces. Another volley of arrows whizzed after the first one. Soon the air hissed with wave after wave of them. Yells of joy turned to screams of death. Hundreds of Crabs fell alongside their dark comrades.

The Maidens had given the allied army a chance, and

Yokatsu seized it. With hurried shouts, he called to his weary, defeated units and pointed upward.

They saw, and the sight filled their hearts with renewed hope. Yasamura regrouped the cavalry and prepared them to ride to Toturi's aid. Jikkyo and Tetsuko rode beside him.

All exhaustion and pain had left Tetsuko. There was nothing before her but the enemy and the job she must do. She glanced at Jikkyo as they drove toward the fray, ready for whatever the Shadowlands threw at them.

Then she saw Hoturi.

He was in the midst of the battle, surrounded by his Crane forces. He rode in circles, giving orders to his samurai, beset on all sides by zombies. Hoturi himself did not seem to be touched by the Shadowlands creatures that swarmed his troops. He rode to join one of his Crane commanders, who was battling a small group of goblins. As he approached the Crane from behind, he took the man's head with one quick slice. The body fell from its horse. The goblins looked at Hoturi but did not attack him. Instead, they moved away and charged a troop of Dragons that fought nearby.

"Traitor!" Tetsuko screamed. She dug her heels into Cloud Dancer's side.

Jikkyo saw her sprint away and soon caught sight of her destination. "Follow Yasamura," he commanded the Maidens. With a curse, he turned his mount and followed Tetsuko into the thickest part of the battle.

"Doji Hoturi!" Tetsuko screamed as she galloped toward him. She pulled Cloud Dancer to a stop before him, her katana ready. Her armor was smeared with blood, and her features were twisted with anger. "Why, Lord Hoturi?" she asked in a cold voice.

Hoturi laughed but did not reply.

Jikkyo appeared by Tetsuko's side, a look of calm on his face. Hoturi's eyes widened slightly, facing two skilled Unicorns instead of one. For a long moment, they glared at one another as the Shadowlands forces continued their onslaught around them. Then Hoturi lunged forward.

His katana fell like a hammer. Tetsuko could barely deflect it. Cloud Dancer neighed and skipped aside. The power of Hoturi's attack left Tetsuko breathless. He turned his blade on Jikkyo, who struggled against Hoturi's blows. The Crane's blade sang as he cut and slashed with fury. He fought both samurai at once. Gashes opened in Tetsuko's arm and leg. The side of Jikkyo's helm disappeared in an instant. Blood drenched them both, but they fought on. The Unicorn's blades found its mark many times as well, and Hoturi was soon covered with cuts.

Abruptly Hoturi halted his attack. He sat on his mount, his chest heaving as he watched his two opponents. Inexplicably, a slow grin spread across his face, as his eye caught something behind Tetsuko's back. Fearing an old trick, the Battle Maiden kept her eye on Hoturi.

Jikkyo exclaimed, "Tadaji!"

The ambassador was on horseback. His once-grand robes were bloody and torn. His obi was half-untied, and it hung limply from his waist. His tangled hair moved wildly around his face, which was pinched and drawn as if he had not slept for days. Tadaji's eyes were mad, filled with equal measures of horror and hope. He stared at his friend and savior. He did not seem to notice Tetsuko and Jikkyo.

"Hoturi," he said. His voice could barely be heard above the chaos of battle around them. "You must live."

Hoturi's face softened. "Friend Tadaji!" he exclaimed. "Yes, I will live. Come to me and I will save you from the madness of battle."

Tadaji smiled at his friend and moved toward him. Suddenly Jikkyo was before him, his mount blocking Tadaji's way.

"Tadaji!" Jikkyo yelled. "What are you doing here! You must flee the battle or be killed!"

Tadaji broke his gaze from Hoturi and looked at Jikkyo as if he were a stranger. The ambassador's eyes narrowed menacingly as he said, "Be gone. This does not concern you."

Keeping her eye on Hoturi, Tetsuko glanced at Tadaji. "Ambassador," she said urgently. "Leave this place. For Tamura's sake, leave!"

The ambassador reeled as if struck. He fixed Tetsuko with mad eyes. Peering into them, she suddenly saw his torment.

▲▲▲▲▲▲▲▲

Stunned, Tadaji looked from Jikkyo to Tetsuko. For a moment he did not recognize her. Then the vision of Tamura and the bundle burst upon his mind. The sounds of battle around ceased. The sound of drums pounded in his ears. Flames and laughter rang above it.

Tadaji knew what he must do.

With a yell, he kicked his horse and pushed past Tetsuko and Jikkyo. The drumbeats continued to throb in his head. It seemed as if flames danced behind the great Crane daimyo.

Joy flooded the old man. This was his friend Hoturi, whom he knew and trusted.

Tadaji fumbled awkwardly inside his kimono. He pulled out the box, removed the horse statue, and reached out his hand to Hoturi.

With a grin, the Crane grabbed the statue from Tadaji's

grasp. For a brief second, they touched skin to skin.

A thousand lights burst inside Tadaji's mind. He saw Hoturi, sweating and trembling inside a cage of blades that glinted in the torch light. A black form, lithe and graceful, danced all about the cage. Musical laughter came from that figure, laughter dripping with poison. Scorpions crawled everywhere.

And in the fiery corner behind the cage, Tamura screamed and would not stop.

Tadaji clutched his heart, his eyes wide and wild. "Save me, Hoturi! Save me!" He slid from his horse and sank to his knees in the mud and blood of the field.

▲▲▲▲▲▲▲▲

"Hoturi, what have you done!" roared Jikkyo. Hoping to drive the traitor away from his beloved uncle, Jikkyo rode forward to slam his mount into Hoturi's steed.

The lord of the Crane did not fall back. In one swift movement he thrust his katana deep into the Unicorn's belly. Hoturi's blade emerged, dripping with Jikkyo's blood. Jikkyo fell from his mount.

Tetsuko shouted. She rode toward Jikkyo. His eyes were wide as he stared at the growing red stain on his armor.

Hoturi meanwhile turned his attention on Tadaji. "Save you, dear friend? I will save you. Your life is full of nightmares. Your death shall be full of sweet dreams!"

Hoturi raised his dripping katana above Tadaji's bowed head. Behind the samurai, hooves suddenly pounded like drums.

Hoturi whirled his mount just in time to deflect a numbing blow from Tetsuko.

Her eyes were fire, and her katana whipped the air as she attacked the Crane. She threw a second strike, and a third.

Hoturi labored beneath the power of her blows. He saw the stain of blood on her leg armor. With a quick cut, he re-opened the wound she had received the day before.

As he pulled back from the blow, Tetsuko slashed into his side. Her golden blade bit deep into his flesh.

Hoturi bellowed as he pulled back, sliding off her blade. "Finish her," he growled, seemingly to no one.

Before Tetsuko could deliver another blow, a group of three goblins swarmed up to attack her. Their long claws raked Cloud Dancer's flesh. She jumped and screamed. Tetsuko struggled to control her mount and drive off the beasts.

Hoturi meanwhile turned and disappeared into the thick of battle. As he left, his mount gently stepped over Tadaji, who was curled into a ball in the mud. The old man did not move as the battle went on around him.

Tetsuko's body and mind were numb as she defended herself against the goblins. The first one fell from a mighty slash to his neck. Black blood spurted in gouts as it fell. A second goblin managed to climb astride Cloud Dancer's rear and grab Tetsuko by the head. Tetsuko reached behind her, grasped the goblin's arm, and twisted. A satisfying crunch of breaking bone was followed by a screech as the goblin dropped its weapon. Tetsuko flipped her katana and caught it by the hilt, blade facing backward. One hard thrust behind her skewered the goblin. It fell screaming. The third goblin was already dead on the ground. A deep U-shaped indentation in its forehead showed that her beloved mount had been hard at work as well.

Tetsuko looked around wildly for Jikkyo and Tadaji. They were gone. Perhaps Jikkyo had taken the old man to safety. That's what Tetsuko told herself. This was not the time to mourn; the battle was not yet won. Perhaps Jikkyo and Tadaji were somewhere safe. If not, the best way to honor her friend and the father of her love would be to fight in their stead.

With a last glance at the field where Jikkyo had fallen, Tetsuko turned and raced for the Unicorn line.

The Shadowlands army dwindled. They fought desperately. The allied forces sensed their confusion and pushed hard against them. Slowly, the stubborn defense of Toturi and Yasamura gave way to a growing offense. Hope rippled through the Crane, Dragon, Phoenix, and Unicorn samurai of the allied army.

Tetsuko rejoined the Unicorn cavalry near the rear flank of the allied army. They regrouped for their final push into the battle. Finding Yasamura, Tetsuko rode with him to the front of the violet army.

▲▲▲▲▲▲▲▲

A low thundering sound rose from the rear of the allied army. Fear ripped through the ranks as they imagined another Shadowlands force attacking from behind.

At the front of the battle, Toturi said a quick prayer that Yokatsu and Yasamura could hold back the dark forces long enough for his troops to secure the northern end of the pass.

The thunder grew louder. The sound was mixed with shouts. The ronin commander paused and craned his neck to see what terrible force came from behind. Joy filled his heart.

It was the Unicorn cavalry, their violet armor glinting in

the shadowy light. Before them rode Yokatsu and Yasamura, flanked by a line of samurai. To Yasamura's left was Tetsuko.

With a yell that echoed off the walls of the pass, Toturi turned and gave the order to advance. The cavalry joined them in the attack. With a mighty crash, the allied force smashed into the Shadowlands army and kept moving. They cut straight through the front ranks and into the heart of Yori's evil force.

The cavalry pressed forward. Every creature in their path fell with screams of terror. The Shadowlands troops fell back and began to retreat.

Her eyes blazing, Tetsuko rammed Cloud Dancer into a line of goblins. Her blade hummed as she charged the first one, taking its head. Half a breath later she attacked the next.

Beside her, Yasamura cleaved a goblin in two with one swing. Its face was still twisted in a snarl as it fell. All around them, the stamping of horses mixed with the roar of the Crabs and the shrieks of Shadowlands troops. They shrank before the fury of the of the Unicorn onslaught.

The mighty Crab force was divided. Their ranks broke in confusion.

▲▲▲▲▲▲▲▲

Mounted in the midst of his beleaguered host, Yori saw the grand attack. His troops were doomed. He raised his eyes to the ridge. The hated Unicorn Battle Maidens still fired arrows into his army. Creatures were running in terror, screaming and falling in their attempt to get away. The Crab lines were completely broken. Hope for victory was gone.

With a last look at his once-great force, Yori cursed and shouted to his commanders to retreat. Then he turned his mount and galloped toward the plain.

24   TRUTH, REVEALED

When she had learned that Jikkyo indeed was dead, a searing pain broke Tetsuko's heart.

Eta retrieved the body of her friend from the field. Tetsuko went to him and sat by his side, unmoving for hours. Many other Unicorns looked at her with distaste, even revulsion, as she held his dead hand and sang the ancient songs to him. She ignored them. For her, the rest of the world had ceased to exist.

Yokatsu understood. He posted a guard to make sure she was left alone.

Yasamura, disturbed by the way Tetsuko had come undone, waited for her vigil to be done. When her tears were spent and there were no more songs to sing, he guided her to her tent.

For days after that, Tetsuko slept constantly, rarely emerging. In time, she could sleep no more.

Tetsuko rose and went in search of Yasamura. She found him in his tent. He appeared the instant the servant announced her arrival.

"Come, come, Tetsuko," he said kindly as he ushered her inside. His tent was as she had remembered it: masculine and disheveled, with boxes and cushions scattered about in disorganized artistry.

Without a word Tetsuko sat. A servant brought sake. Yasamura dismissed him, and then poured Tetsuko a large cupful. She took it and drank deeply, her eyes blank with sorrow and memory.

Finally Yasamura spoke. "Tetsuko, I do not know what to say to comfort you. I did not realize that you loved Jikkyo so."

Tetsuko raised her eyes slowly to meet his. "I did not, either," was all she said.

Yasamura leaned back, watching the woman who sat before him. In any other circumstances he would flirt outrageously with her, for she was beautiful in her deep purple kimono. But he had found something softer, more honorable, in his heart lately, and he wanted only to make her pain disappear.

"Tetsuko, you are strong," he said. "You will survive this. Call on Jikkyo's strength and yours to get you through. He will be with you always."

"First Tamura, and then Jikkyo," she said, and her eyes filled with tears. "My heart cannot stand it."

"Yes, it can," Yasamura said, stern but not unkind. "It can survive this and much more, for it will have to."

He leaned closer to Tetsuko and said, "My father is a wise man, and he once told me, 'The pain will make you strong, and it will make you compassionate, if you do not allow it to consume you.' I have never forgotten his advice, and now I give it to you. Never forget the feelings of your heart, good or bad, for you will have need of them in the future."

Tetsuko heaved a deep sigh and wiped her eyes with the back of her sleeve. The tears made dark streaks on the fabric, but she didn't care.

"There will be a celebration at Toshi No Aida Ni Kawa," Yasamura said cautiously. "Already, most of our forces have set out on the journey."

"Must I attend?" Tetsuko asked sadly. "I do not think I can do it."

"You can, and you must," Yasamura replied, and the tone of a commander crept into his words. "You are a hero, one of the great Battle Maidens who saved the allied army. It is a great honor to be there, and you must go. I will be with you."

Tetsuko nodded and looked up. There was something behind her eyes, something behind the sorrow. It was a hardness that Yasamura had not seen before. He smiled at her, and his face was filled with kind concern.

She gave him a small smile in return and rose, bowing deeply in respect. "Domo arigato, Yasamura-sama," she said simply.

"Do itashimashite, Battle Maiden," he replied with a nod as she slipped out quietly.

▲ ▲ ▲ ▲ ▲ ▲ ▲ ▲

Tetsuko sat alone in the center of the floor of the Golden Walk. Late-afternoon sun spilled through the glass and made a thousand prisms of light dance on the polished

wooden floor. All afternoon, preparations had been under-
way for the great celebration that was to begin that evening—
the one-month anniversary of the allied forces' victory at
Beiden Pass. The clan commanders had chosen Toshi No
Aida Ni Kawa as the site for the gathering for it was the
grandest of the Unicorn castles. For days, representatives of
the allied clans had arrived at the castle. The air buzzed with
joy and excitement.

It was a great moment for the Unicorns, but Tetsuko felt
only sorrow. The hallway was deserted. Tetsuko buried her
head in her hands. She felt like a small child hiding her hurt
from her parents.

Yasamura's words echoed in her mind, "I did not realize
that you loved Jikkyo so." And her words echoed back, "I did
not, either."

She had come to this spot hoping the sunlight and solitude would balm her soul. They did not. Nothing could.

Tetsuko rose. She meant to go back to her rooms, but instead found herself wandering through the empty hallways
of the palace's guest wing. She knew only one person who
had rooms in this section of the keep. Slowly she made her
way down the hallway to his door.

The room was set apart from the rest of the guest suites,
allowing its occupant plenty of rest and quiet. The guard
outside recognized her and nodded. Slowly Tetsuko opened
the door and entered.

The chamber beyond was large and comfortable, but
sparsely furnished. A simple futon lay in one corner. The
sheets were rumpled and unkempt. The only other furniture in the room was a small table, which was laden with a
tray of food. The tea was cold and the food sat untouched.

A movement in the shadows caught Tetsuko's eye. Tadaji
appeared. His kimono was wrinkled, and his hair hung

limply about his shoulders. He still moved like the graceful ambassador he had been, however, and he approached Tetsuko with only a hint of a limp.

"Ah, a visitor, welcome," he said, bowing formally and gesturing to the table.

Tetsuko bowed and took a step forward.

Tadaji jumped back, his eyes wide and fearful. He jerked suddenly, as if he had just been struck by a powerful blow to the head. For a moment his eyes were dull and unfocused. Then he clutched his head and doubled over, swaying unsteadily.

"Tadaji, what is wrong?" Tetsuko asked. Her fingers brushed his kimono, preparing to catch him if he fell.

With a gasp, Tadaji shrank away from her. Slowly he backed up, his eyes wide with terror.

"Forgive me," Tetsuko said as she moved toward the door. "We should have spoken that night. Now it is too late, forever."

Slowly she backed through the doorway and closed the heavy wooden door behind her. From behind it came a low moan, followed by a laugh. The moan started again, and then rose to a high-pitched scream. The scream went on and on, echoing down the hallway. Then it faded into silence, and all was quiet.

Tetsuko pressed her cheek to the door and stood there, waiting. The silence remained.

She whispered to herself, "Now it is too late, forever."

She turned, her silk-clad feet making no sound on the polished floors as she withdrew.

There was one other place she could go to feel better. There was one place that would soothe the ache in her heart.

▲▲▲▲▲▲▲▲

In another part of the keep, Yokatsu and Toturi met in Yokatsu's private rooms. The two men were enjoying a rare moment of quiet before the festivities were to begin. Yokatsu had donned the clothing he felt most comfortable in—his armor. It was repaired and polished to a high shine. The ronin, though, was dressed in traveling clothes rather than grand ceremonial robes.

"Must you leave so soon?" the Unicorn asked. "The celebration promises to be a lively one. The Dragon shugenja have guaranteed a fireworks show that will rival any ever seen."

Toturi smiled. "I do not think it is my place to be here. There are still those who see me as a disgrace."

Yokatsu stared into his cup, unwilling to agree with Toturi but knowing he was right.

"The Naga are stirring," Toturi said, breaking off a chunk of bread that sat in a basket on the table. "At least, that's what the rumors are. I have commanded a young Dragon, Mirumoto Daini, to find out if the rumors are true. He has asked me to ride to him, and I have agreed."

Yokatsu chewed on a slice of bread and then washed it down with a mouthful of water. "There are moments when I cannot believe what happened at Beiden Pass," he said with a note of wonder in his voice.

Toturi smiled. "The Unicorns have proven their honor above the expectations of all Rokugani. You have the respect of every leader of the allied forces, including me. And your Battle Maidens are respected above all others."

"I am honored by your words," Yokatsu replied. "The Battle Maidens are the pride of the Unicorn Clan, and they have shown great honor in battle."

"What of Ide Tadaji?" Toturi asked. "I had heard that he was found alive on the battlefield."

Yokatsu shook his head in sorrow. "Yes, our ambassador lives. He sits alone in his room, unmoving and unspeaking during the day. At night, the halls ring with his screams. The shugenja have tried everything. No one knows what torments him, and no one can help him."

"Do you think it has anything to do with the death of the Lion ambassador at the palace?"

"I do not know," Yokatsu replied. Then he said, "The Cranes insist that they had no part in the murder. There is a suspicion that Kachiko was involved, for it was revealed that a palace guard killed the woman. Perhaps Tadaji knew something, but we cannot ask him now. His mind is rarely clear these days, even when he is calm. He speaks only of Hoturi, but his words are a mystery."

For a long time the two man sat, each lost in his own thoughts. Then finally Toturi rose and bowed to his host. "Thank you, Shinjo Yokatsu, for your friendship and hospitality. I hope to share both with you again for many years to come."

Yokatsu bowed to the ronin. "My hope as well," he replied gravely. "Safe travels."

Toturi left and quickly gathered his belongings. He slipped quietly out of the castle, careful not to be seen by anyone. He went to the grand Unicorn stables and saddled his mount. As he guided the steed out of the stables, he saw a lone rider pounding furiously across the field beyond the barns.

It was Tetsuko. She rode Cloud Dancer hard, and they moved as one. She wore her leather leggings and a loose shirt, which was plastered against her body by the wind as she rode. Her hair whipped about her face as she bent forward, leaning close to the mighty horse's ear. The beast neighed and picked up speed.

Toturi paused. A strange feeling of pride grew in his chest as he watched the beautiful, proud Battle Maiden come to terms with her sorrow. His heart bled for her, for he understood what she was feeling, perhaps better than any other.

Tetsuko glanced in his direction as she rounded the green field. She immediately pulled Cloud Dancer to a stop and gazed at him. The late-afternoon sun shone on the young woman, casting her in a golden-red light. She sat tall and proud in the saddle as she faced him.

Toturi's breath caught in his throat at the sight.

Tetsuko bowed low over Cloud Dancer's head in respect and thanks. Toturi did the same. They looked at one another for a long moment, both knowing that it would be many years before their paths crossed again. Then the ronin turned toward the main road and left this world behind.

Tetsuko watched him go. She understood. She pressed her heels into Cloud Dancer's sides and thought of the great, sad Toturi. No matter what he achieved in his life from this moment on, his heart would never be light again. As he disappeared down the road, she also knew that some-day, somewhere, they would meet again.

She emptied her mind of all things and urged Cloud Dancer forward. Together they moved across the field and Tetsuko began her own journey—to heal, and to survive.

Enter the magical land of the Flanaess, world of adventure!

GREYHAWK is the setting of the role-playing game
DUNGEONS & DRAGONS. Each of these novels is based on a classic
D&D adventure module.

Against the Giants
Ru Emerson

A village burns while its attackers flee into the night. Enraged, the king
of Keoland orders an aging warrior to lead a band of adventurers on a
retaliatory strike. As they prepare to enter the heart of the monsters'
lair, each knows only the bravest will survive.

White Plume Mountain
Paul Kidd

A ranger, a faerie, and a sentient hell hound pelt with a penchant for
pyromania. These three companions must enter the most trap-laden,
monster-infested place this side of Acererak's tomb: White Plume
Mountain.

Descent into the Depths of the Earth
Paul Kidd

Fresh from their encounter with White Plume Mountain, the Justicar
and Escalla depart for the town of Hommlet. But life around a faerie is
never exactly . . . stable. Before he knows it, to save her life the Justicar
is on his way into the depths of the earth to fight hobgoblins, drow,
and the queen of the demonweb pits.

Ice Age Cycle

The Gathering Dark
Book I

From Jeff Grubb, best-selling author of *The Brothers' War*, comes the story of Dominaria in the age of darkness, when wizards and priests struggled for supremacy

The Eternal Ice
Book II

Available May 2000

Ice has covered the world of Dominaria. Now Lim Dûl, a necromancer with a taste for power, seeks to awaken a deeper evil.

The Shattered Alliance
Book III

The Ice Age has come to an abrupt end, but the world's troubles have not left with the receding glaciers.

Available
December 2000

Read the book that started it all.

The Brothers' War
Artifacts Cycle • Book I
Jeff Grubb

Dominarian legends speak of a mighty conflict, obscured by the mists of time. Of a conflict between the brothers Urza and Mishra for supremacy. Of titanic engines that scarred and twisted the very planet. The saga of the Brothers' War.